District Nurs
Anthony Wes

West to tell her it was no accident. Someone tried to kill him. Mary is skeptical at first, but when West dies, she's determined to investigate the matter. More blood is spilled, and Mary becomes embroiled in a tangled web of intrigue and murder as she joins forces with exiled Jewish German detective Franz Shaefer. And on top of everything else, Mary finds herself dangerously attracted to Anthony's beautiful and unattainable sister Harriet.

THE ILLHENNY MURDERS

Winnie Frolik

A NineStar Press Publication

www.ninestarpress.com

The Illhenny Murders

This is a work of fiction. Names, characters, places, and incidents are either the product of the author's imagination or are used fictitiously. Any resemblance to actual persons living or dead, business establishments, events, or locales is entirely coincidental.

Printed in the USA

ISBN: 978-1-64890-314-4

First Edition, June, 2021

Also available in eBook, ISBN: 978-1-64890-313-7

WARNING:

This book contains sexual content, which may only be

suitable for mature readers. Depictions of violence, murder, death of a prominent character, homophobic slurs, antisemitic slurs, ethnic slurs.

To everyone who like Mary Grey grew up thinking there was something wrong with them and/or they'd been assigned the wrong body.

Chapter One

October 1936, Illhenny, England

It was no longer night in Illhenny, but not quite morning. Those weird in-between hours, when the darkness began to retreat but the sun had not quite shown its face. Although at this time of year, the best Illhenny could hope for was some feeble rays of light peeking out from behind the fierce clouds dominating its sea line. Still, sunny or not, people had begun to stir. Fishermen went off in their boats to cast their nets and haggle with the sea. Tradesmen set out to open for the day. Farm folk had cows to milk and livestock to feed. Mothers began coaxing surly children from their beds to have breakfast before making their way to school. And the district nurse set off on her rounds.

District Nurse Mary Grey had known she would be quite busy that day. In preparation, she had eaten a solid, manly breakfast, and packed a ham sandwich for later. She wore an oversized knitted gray-green sweater, gifted to her by her sister, over her uniform to face the weather. She rode her BSA motorbike. Some uncharitable souls might have noted the bike was over a decade old, and hardly ideal for inclement weather. And in the UK, of course, inclement weather tends to be the norm. No matter. Mary loved the motorbike from the moment it had been issued to her by the Rural Nurses Association. She loved how the wind whipped in her face when she rode it full throttle. She loved the sense of power between her legs. She loved how speedily it could get her to her appointments. She loved occasionally beeping to people she met on the ride. Most of all, she loved the freedom and independence her motorbike represented. She even enjoyed cleaning it and keeping it fueled and oiled. Mary had never ridden a horse, let alone owned one, but she imagined her love for her motorbike was akin to what a rider might feel toward their faithful steed.

Mary rode her bike past the bakery, post office, the vicarage, and the forge. Her first task of the day was to check in on Mrs. Simpson, who'd recently had surgery in London. She was a widow of some sixty years of age, living on a small pension after her husband's death.

"You need not have come, my dear," Mrs. Simpson told her. "As you can see, I've made a full recovery." To punctuate her point, Mrs. Simpson did an elegant little curtsey. She was surprisingly limber for a woman her age.

"You certainly are looking better. You don't seem to have any trouble moving at all now," Mary noted.

"No. In fact, I took a long walk around the village yesterday and will take another today."

"You didn't mind the cold?"

"Oh no! I found it quite refreshing," Mrs. Simpson proclaimed. "There's nothing like fresh sea air and exercise for one's health, is there?"

"No argument there," Mary agreed. "Will you be going to tomorrow's meeting of the Illhenny Women's Society?" Mrs. Simpson was known for her needlework and her keen interest in village affairs.

"Wild horses couldn't keep me away. We are going to start decorating the church for Christmas. I picked up some new items in London to show everyone! There's no place like London for shopping."

"There certainly isn't. In fact, I'm taking the train down tomorrow to stay with an old friend of mine for a couple of nights while her husband's away."

"Wait, is that your friend Phyllis?" Mrs. Simpson asked. "You've visited her before, haven't you?"

"Well, her husband travels regularly, and she likes the company," Mary explained, not making direct eye contact with Mrs. Simpson.

"Oh, well, that's very kind of you then," Mrs. Simpson remarked. "How exactly do you and Phyllis know each other?"

"I met her when I was studying at the Queen's Institute for Nurses in London." This time Mary was on solid ground. "And we've stayed in touch. You know, I really have to get on to my other appointments."

"Of course, dear, of course."

Mrs. Simpson waved a cheerful goodbye and Mary rode off.

Mary next called on rheumatic old Caleb Barnaby. Caleb was a grizzled fisherman with several teeth missing, but one molar long and sharp as a harpoon. He'd been a big man once but in the last year or so had begun to lose weight and his clothes now hung on him rather alarmingly. He lived quite alone with only a large ginger cat, Ahab, for company. His rooms were shabby and dark, with only a single window, but they did have one charm—handcrafted shelves filled with little birds, fish, seashells, deer, and other creatures, all beautifully carved out of wood by none other than Caleb himself. Caleb's whittling and carpentry were famous in Illhenny. After coming in, Mary, as usual, opened the window to air the room a little, while Caleb groused.

"Just kill me all the faster, the chill air will."

"No, it won't."

"Will too!" Caleb retorted. "Cold gets worse every year for me old bones." He gave a melodramatic sigh. "This will be my last winter, it will. Ought to start planning my funeral."

"What would you have them write on your headstone?" Mary asked, amused.

"Don't want a headstone," Caleb pronounced. "Waste of time and stone if you ask me. Don't want to be left in a box in the ground to rot either. I'd rather be taken by the wind or the sea. That way, at least I'd get to travel a b—"

There was a loud crashing sound and a startled Mary turned just in time to see a pile of wooden carvings on the floor while an orange blur raced around a corner and out of sight.

"Go ahead and run, you coward! You cur!" Caleb shouted. "If I ever get my hands on you, I'll turn you into slippers!"

Mary had heard similar threats from Caleb before regarding Ahab's crimes, and knew them to be empty. She instead set out about picking up the wooden figures and returning them to their rightful place. As she did so, she spotted an envelope hidden in a cleft among the shelves and, on an impulse, took a peek at its contents.

Much to her amusement, it was filled with cheap little pictures of women in various stages of undress. Pornography and smut were illegal in England, but that didn't seem to diminish its popularity one jot. Most of the women were simply posing, but some of them were more active. In fact, several of the photos included men as well, engaging in all sorts of calisthenics with the women. Mary hurriedly put the envelope away.

"What you doing now?" Caleb asked.

"Nothing! Just examining your workmanship. How about I put on the kettle?"

"Tea? What good is tea? Now whiskey, aye, that's proper medicine. I'll have me a shot now."

"But it isn't even noon," Mary pointed out.

"Exactly. I need breakfast!" Caleb drained the shot with satisfaction. "Come you, nurse, join me in a tipple. It'll put some color in your cheeks, do you a load of good."

"Sorry, but I'm not allowed to drink on duty. Those are the rules."

"Too many damned rules," Caleb grumbled. "That's what's wrong with the world these days."

"I don't know that the problem is the number of rules themselves," Mary said thoughtfully, "so much as who makes them."

"Hmph. Speaking of people who make the rules, Lord Pool's called a town meeting tonight at the dance hall."

"A meeting? About what?"

"Don't know. Didn't say anything. But his friend from next door is going to be there as well."

"I heard The Laurels had just been rented out to some young man from London," Mary mused. "I wondered what that was about. We don't get many visitors from London here. In fact, we usually don't get any."

Caleb scowled. "No good will come of this. I can smell it. You mark my words!"

Mary did not respond to this premonition but kept to her schedule. As she rode past Mr. Legge's tobacco shop, she saw pretty, young Mrs. Legge assisting Mr. Winthrop, the vicar. Mr. Legge, who was quite a bit older than his wife, stood directly outside the shop, engaged in an argument with Dick Townley, Lord Pool's gamekeeper.

"No more credit for you, you wastrel! You ever darken my door without the money you owe me, and it'll be my boot up your arse!"

"I'd like to see you try." Townley spat on the ground, but he left the shop empty handed.

Mary passed Constable Evans as well. He was still a young man with plump cheeks, red as apples.

"Hello, Nurse Grey." He tipped his hat to her. "Busy day, is it?"

"It's always busy. What about you?"

"Getting a cat out of a tree has been the highlight of my morning. Had some more excitement yesterday though. Another one of those tramps came around and I had to clear him off. There seem to be more of them every week." He frowned.

"The slump perhaps," Mary suggested. "Too many

poor souls out of work with nowhere to go."

"Maybe, but they can't come here," Evans retorted. "I have my orders to keep them out. Well, I'll leave you to your caseload."

The saddest part of Mary's day was visiting poor Annie Capman with her consumption. Annie was from an industrial town in the north but, because of her health, she'd moved to Illhenny in hopes the fresh sea air would revive her. Sadly, while Annie did enjoy a respite from breathing in black smoke and soot, it soon became clear her days were numbered no matter where she lived. The other villagers in Illhenny kept their distance from the little cottage Annie lodged in, fearing contagion. Annie's coal and groceries were always delivered and left outside. Mary entered the cottage directly with a key left underneath a stone in the yard to see Annie's skeletal figure in bed, swallowed up by comforters and sheets.

"Mary." Annie's hollowed pale face shone at the sight of the nurse. "It's so good to see you."

"How are you feeling today, Annie?" Mary asked.

"Tired," Annie replied. "I know you say it does me good to walk outside, but today I'm afraid I haven't the energy for it."

"That's all right, Annie," Mary reassured her. "Let me open the windows at least and get some fresh air in for you. I've got another bottle of that tonic you like."

Mary dosed Annie, helped her bathe in the wash basin, and combed her hair before tucking her into her newly changed bed with tea and biscuits.

"Rest now," Mary told her as Annie shut her eyes and drifted off to sleep.

Mary's final appointment of the day was at the Martins' farm to check on Mrs. Martin and weigh the newborn twin boys who Mary had delivered herself just fourteen days before. This visit in particular gave Mary cause for worry. Not so much the twins themselves—they were both putting on weight nicely and had hearty lungs they kept in good order with constant roaring. No, the rest of the family concerned Nurse Grey. The birth of the twins had brought the total number of children at the farm to nine, all crowded together on top of one another. From the moment she entered the home, Mary was met with the smell of dirty nappies and unwashed dishes. Without electricity, plumbing, or running water, it was difficult to maintain even the most basic level of sanitation in the home. Mrs. Martin had dark circles around her eyes, like someone had smeared coal there, and a dull, blank stare. Her hair was tangled as a bird's nest and she had a nasty cough as well. She was uncommunicative and answered questions with just a "yes" or "no."

Finally, Nurse Grey had directed her questions to the eldest girl, Libby. Libby informed Mary that her mother hadn't slept for days thanks to the twins' constant bawling, and she had seemed off her food as well. Thirteen-year-old Libby had more or less taken charge of the household and the care of her younger siblings. Mr. Martin had not been present during the interview, and Eliza volunteered that her father had been spending less time than ever at home since the twins were born. His hours minding the farm had always been long, but now it seemed he didn't come home most nights at all. Rather he went to The Mud Crab or slept in the barn, finding it more comfortable than the Martin household at present. Looking at the dirt and grime around her, as the twins began to bawl once more, Nurse Grey understood why. Still, the absence of a father and husband in the home was only making things worse.

"Is there anyone who could come and help your mum? A neighbor perhaps? Or family?"

Libby thought a moment. "Aunt Amy," she said. "She's Mum's sister and she works as a housekeeper in Anchester." Anchester was a market town some six miles distant.

"Would we have to send a message in person, or does she have a phone?" Nurse Grey asked.

"The house she works at has a phone," Libby replied.

"Good! Do you know the number?"

Libby shook her head.

"That's all right. Directory can probably find you the number as long as you know who and where her employer is."

"I know that," Libby stated firmly.

"Then run down to the call box by the post office. Here are some coins for the phone. Tell your aunt to come here as quickly as possible, assuming she can get the time off."

Libby turned to go, and Mary called after her, "Remember to wear your mittens!"

Nurse Grey spent the next few hours doing her best to clean up around the household, having one of the children draw her water from outside, and delegating tasks of sweeping, mopping, and laundry. A hearty new fire was built to warm the place up a bit. The twins were fed, bathed, and changed. Meanwhile, Mrs. Martin was given hot tea and put to bed for some much-needed sleep. As Mary started making porridge for supper, Libby returned.

"I spoke to Aunt Amy and she spoke to her employer. She'll be here tomorrow."

"That's wonderful news! But we will have to keep an eye on your mum's cough too," Mary told Libby. "If it gets any worse or lasts much longer, she may need to see a doctor."

Libby nodded, though she did not look happy. "Doctors are expensive, ma'am."

Nurse Grey sympathized. "I know. Hopefully, though, once your mum gets some rest, she will start to get better on her own. Make sure she rests by the fire and drinks lots of hot tea."

By the time Mary left the Martins', it was nearly time for the public meeting. And while Mary Grey was no native to Illhenny, a district nurse should always try to stay appraised of matters within the local community. She rushed to attend and managed to get in the doors of the local dance hall just before the meeting began. It seemed half of Illhenny was crammed into the room, seated in rickety folding chairs, and Mary despaired of finding a seat.

"Hey, Nurse Grey, come you here!" Caleb Barnaby gestured to Mary to join him on a bench and somehow managed to squeeze in room for her.

"Thank you, Caleb."

"I may need you before the night is out," Caleb told her. Mary looked around. The walls of the hall were still decorated with the cheap paper and tinsel from the last dance. The wooden floor was scuffed from constant use over the years, and the air permeated with the smells of resin, varnish, and dried sweat.

At the far end of the hall, at a makeshift podium, stood Lord Pool, darkly handsome in a Savile Row suit. Next to him stood a remarkably fair young man wearing cream colored linen slacks, with white-blond hair that he'd grown out to a shocking degree. There was also a large free-standing presentation desk; recognizable from the form, but with a curtain drawn hiding the main display.

"That must be Lord Pool's friend," Mary noted.

Caleb gave a rude snort. "Looks like a poofter to me," he grumbled. "London's full of nancy boys and perverts."

Mary ignored this and waved to Mrs. Simpson across the room. At last, as the conversations in the seats built in a crescendo of curiosity, Lord Pool stood up to a microphone and, after a few staticky attempts, was able to make himself heard throughout the hall.

"I imagine," he began, "you're all wondering why I've called this meeting. Well, the reason is because I have decided to partake in an investment opportunity. And the opportunity in question directly involves all of you. As most of you well know, my family has been here for centuries. We consider ourselves deeply rooted within this community, and that its fortunes and ours are intertwined." Lord Pool paused and looked around the room meaningfully. Not a whisper was to be heard. "Which is why it truly grieves me to say that Illhenny has for some years been in a state of decline." Voices rose in a sudden murmur throughout the room. "Oh, it's no one's fault," he continued, "but neither the fishing or agriculture around here are what they once were, and mining's long gone. To survive, Illhenny must adapt with the times, which is why it is my great pleasure to introduce you to my old and dear friend, Anthony West, who happens to be one of England's most promising young architects. Anthony?"

The blond man was passed the microphone and Lord Pool stepped aside, and then, to Mary's surprise, left the podium altogether. It was almost as if he was fleeing the scene. Anthony West stared at a crowd full of strangers, eyeing him suspiciously, without quailing.

"As Edgar—I mean Lord Pool—just told you, I'm an architect," Anthony began, "and I'm proud to announce that my next project will be—" He put his hands on the display case and drew away the curtain. "—a grand, new seaside resort, right here in your community!" Now visible were schematics for a very modern looking hotel in the Art Deco style, all windows and curved white walls, with a huge veranda positioned right along the beach.

There was a moment of stunned silence, and then the whole hall exploded.

"What about noise?" someone shouted.

"What about all the new traffic?" Mrs. Simpson fretted.

"We'll be overrun with tourists," Mr. Wilberforce lamented, and there came a chorus of agreement.

"You bastard!" Caleb Barnaby had risen to his feet, his face as red as a tomato, and screamed at Anthony West. "I knew something was up. I knew you were no good just looking at you! And I was right! You're going to ruin this town!"

"Ruin it?" Anthony West was indignant. "I'm saving it!"

Mary noticed that Lord Pool was nowhere in sight.

"Bollocks! You'd turn this place into nothing more than a watering hole for rich fops like yourself!" The assertion on Caleb's part prompted a resounding "aye" across the room.

"Yes, well, better your town had a few more fops like me than drunken oafs like yourself," Anthony retorted frostily.

Caleb started striding to the podium.

"Wait a minute. What's he doing?" Anthony wondered aloud.

"I'll teach you a good lesson," Caleb snarled, and young Mr. West looked alarmed. Fortunately, at that moment, Constable Evans intervened and manually escorted Caleb away. The meeting broke up in a general disorder.

*

"I must say, Edgar, you really landed me in it this time!" Anthony addressed his old friend with heat once they had returned to The Laurels.

"Well, I did warn you," Edgar pointed out reasonably, "that the people around here can be set in their ways and don't like change."

"Well, you didn't warn me hard enough!" Anthony objected. "And I don't appreciate the way you left me alone up there to take the flailing!"

"I thought you could explain things better," Lord Pool rationalized. "You've always been more convincing than me when it comes to public speaking."

"Hmph." Anthony scowled.

"Well, you're the one who'll be designing the whole thing anyway! I don't know rot about building things myself." At the sight of Anthony's face, Lord Pool let out a sigh. "Sorry, old chap. That wasn't sporting of me. In my defense, I didn't think it'd be as bad as it was. You say Barnaby actually threatened you?"

"He came right at me!" Anthony declared.

"Well, he's further gone than I realized. I truly am sorry."

"Words," Anthony grumbled.

"You know, I have some fifty-year-old scotch back at the court that I could send you?" Lord Pool coaxed, and Anthony thawed.

"All right but, in the future, if there's any unwelcome news to be given, you do it yourself!"

"Agreed. Now, let's have a good stiff one." Lord Pool poured out a couple of glasses of aged cognac for him and Anthony.

"A toast," proclaimed Lord Pool.

"A toast to what exactly?" Anthony grimaced. "Me nearly being lynched?"

"A toast to our new endeavor—an endeavor that I am sure, in time, will prove successful," Lord Pool proclaimed with true conviction. "And to the hardest part being over. We've ripped off the bandage; it can't get any worse than it already has."

"Well, I'll certainly drink to that." Anthony took a hearty sip, and the two friends who were, after all, like brothers smiled and spent the rest of the night reminiscing about their schoolboy days.

Chapter Two

The next morning, Mary did not put on her nurse's uniform. It was not going to be needed in London. Instead, she wore the most becoming civilian clothes she owned. Mary caught the earliest morning train from Illhenny and rode in third class, impatiently kicking her heels the whole time as if it would make the journey pass quicker.

Once she arrived in London, she stopped to use the ladies' room, wherein she did something no one had ever seen her do in Illhenny—she applied cosmetics, including lipstick, to her face. She finished it off with the tiniest dab of a perfume that had been given to her as a present years before and which she only ever used for her London visits. It wasn't just about making herself as alluring as possible—the whole ritual was like shedding her skin. She'd transformed into another persona and it gave her an almost illicit sensation of freedom. Mary then hopped on a bus to a familiar neighborhood, casually rebuffing the advances made by admiring male passengers. She scampered up the steps to a third floor flat with her travel valise in hand and gave an impatient knock. It was immediately answered by a young woman with pencil-thin eyebrows and bobbed dark hair whose lips were painted a shocking shade of scarlet.

"Darling!" the woman drawled in a husky voice.

"My pearl!" Mary exclaimed as she collapsed into Phyllis's arms and hungrily ate at her lips. Then came the frantic struggle with buttons and shedding clothes across the flat. Nurse Grey and her married lover would be spending much of the rest of the day in bed.

When Mary was an adolescent, she thought something must be wrong with her because she had never liked boys. Not in that way, at least. She had become infatuated several times with pretty girls, but not once with a boy. She wondered if she had a man's soul that had somehow been transplanted into the body of a woman. It was only in the sixth form at school when Mary learned the truth.

Evelyn Raikes had had auburn hair and a love of reading. Mary befriended her and, while infatuated, resigned to not having things go any further. Then, one night, while staying over at Evelyn's place, Evelyn suggested they practice kissing. Matters quickly escalated. At first, they stayed top half only, but as they grappled under the sheets, territory in the nether regions was explored as well. Neither she nor Evelyn had any guidance in the matter; they'd never even heard of sapphic literature at the time. Yet somehow, they'd made their way, learning all kinds of things that can be done with fingers and tongues. Long, sweaty, and exhausting explorations yielded great rewards. As Evelyn once remarked at school, one was taught that a girl's body ended from the neck down; you'd never think the rest of her could be so useful. Or so pleasurable. But perhaps that was because other girls had to suffer the fumbling attempts of boys whose understanding of female anatomy was, alas, severely limited. Mary's affair with Evelyn had been a passionate one, even if short lived. Evelyn later moved on to romances with boys and ended up marrying a busman. Mary didn't.

Years later, while attending the Queen's Institute of Nursing in London, Mary soon learned there were a great deal of other women like her after all. And there were even places where these women could meet one another. A section in Lyons' Corner House in Piccadilly Circus became known as the Lily Pad, reserved exclusively for homosexuals. Mary had encountered a number of fascinating young women at such establishments with bobbed hair who dressed like boys. Often, these places were similarly popular with men who liked other men. Some of the men liked dressing in skirts and dresses, just as their female counterparts wore trousers and smoking jackets. They'd drink overpriced, watered-down drinks and listen to phonograph records, pairing up on the dance floor. Someone always stood lookout as well. That way, if the place should be raided, same-sex dance couples would change partners to appear to be mixed-sex pairs. Oh, it had felt good to be in like-minded company!

And sometimes, Mary and one of these other women would return to her companion's flat or find a cheap room. Like everything else, Mary found that with repeated practice comes better skills. She also learned to be inventive with tools on hand and came to appreciate the importance of attention to detail. Of course, her continued lessons in anatomy yielded fruit too. She became quite adept at therapeutic massage among other things.

Phyllis had been one of Mary's favorite dance partners. Mary had been assigned a post out of London, and Phyllis traded her maiden name for that of Mrs. Martin Graham, but neither of them saw any reason not to continue their intimate get-togethers. Indeed, Phyllis's husband, Martin, was relieved to hear his wife often entertained her old spinster friend while he was away, thinking it safer than leaving Phyllis all by herself, unoccupied. Phyllis always made a big show of getting the guest room ready when her husband left and, for the sake of verisimilitude, she and Mary were careful to muss the guest bed before the charwoman visited. Mary and Phyllis didn't spend the entire visit in the flat. They'd go out to eat, shop, and visit the cinema.

Mary had always loved London—just seeing everything and absorbing all the life, so unlike the quiet pace of Illhenny. But this time, something felt different. London was always a tough and dirty city, but something more was in the air. A toxic mix of fear and anger on the streets. There had, after all, recently been violence. Less than two weeks before, Oswald Mosley and the British Union of Fascists had attempted to march through London's East End, home to most of the city's Jewish population, in full Blackshirt uniform. A hundred thousand East Enders petitioned Home Secretary John Simon to ban the event for fear of violence. Simon refused to do so and even sent a police escort to attempt to prevent anti-fascist protestors from getting unruly. This strategy did not succeed. Rather, twenty thousand anti-fascist protestors, somewhere between six and seven thousand mounted Metropolitan policemen, and a couple of thousand actual fascist protestors all collided around

Gardiner's Corner in Whitechapel in what was a knockdown brawl for the ages.

The local neighbors generally sided with the anti-fascist supporters, or at least they were against the side of the police who had rubbish, rotten vegetables, and chamber pots thrown at them out of windows and rooftops. At the end, a hundred and fifty protestors were arrested, many of them claiming police mistreatment. Another 175 people were injured, including police, demonstrators, and civilian bystanders.

One week later, ten thousand Leftist demonstrators protested fascism in Victoria Park accompanied by five thousand policemen. Once more, there was bloodshed, this time brought about by a group of fascist youths attempting to snatch a red flag, resulting in razor slashings. Hundreds more fascists had gone on the war path in the East End, attacking Jewish homes and businesses.

The streets may have been cleaned by the time Mary got there, but tensions still ran high. You could practically smell trouble in the air; a sharp electrical current that could, at any moment, deliver a lethal shock. Mary didn't mention it to Phyllis, lest it spoil their romantic idyll, but she was quite frankly worried. Only once, one night over wine at a little café, did she voice any of her concerns.

"Phyllis," Mary started, "I read something the other day about how the government is now allowing girls of eighteen and older to work making three-inch mortar bombs."

Phyllis shuddered. "Can't say I'd want that job. Always afraid of one little accident and I'd be nothing but red mist. Wait, you're not thinking of applying for that, are you?" She looked truly alarmed.

"Oh lord, no," Mary protested. "But my point is, why is the government now allowing women to work in munitions factories again? They haven't done so since the Great War."

"Hmm, maybe they pay more attention to all those suffragettes and women's liberation types than we thought," Phyllis speculated.

"Or maybe they think there might be another war."

Phyllis gave a shocked giggle. "Oh, Mary! Don't be silly. Obviously, the political situation's a bit hot right now, but nobody in the English government wants a war."

"Well, that's true," Mary agreed. "But if Germany attacks—"

"For God's sake, why would Germany, or any other country for that matter, want to attack us?" Phyllis looked impatient. "Oh, please, all everyone talks about these days is European politics and it's just ghastly. Let's not ruin this, all right?" She clasped Mary's hand and gave her a pleading look. Mary relented and happily offered an alternative topic to discuss.

"You know, Phyllis, sometimes you could try visiting me."

"I don't think so, darling." Phyllis laughed.

"Why not?" Mary felt offended on Illhenny's behalf. "It may not be the most exciting of towns, but it's picturesque and the sea air is quite lovely. I could introduce you to some of my regulars."

"Introduce me as what?" Phyllis asked.

"As my old friend"—Mary looked her steadfast in the eye—"which you are!" The tips of Mary's fingers clasped Phyllis's hand.

"I don't know." Phyllis had a hearty gulp of wine. "It might be trouble. Do you even have a proper guest room?"

"No," Mary admitted, "but you wouldn't be sleeping there anyway."

"True, but where would we tell people I was sleeping?" Phyllis retorted.

"Well, women are known to sometimes double up in a bed without anything illicit going on."

Phyllis looked unconvinced. "I just don't see the point in taking the risk." With that, the conversation moved on to more pleasant matters, like whether Greta Garbo or Katherine Hepburn was the better movie star. The rest of the visit passed quickly without any outward conflict. Inwardly, though, Mary felt a strange sense of the bittersweet. However pleasant her time with Phyllis might be, it was always marred by the knowledge of how fleeting it truly was. Soon, Martin Graham would be coming back, and it was an unspoken rule that Mary would not be present when the man of the house was home.

*

Several weeks after returning to Illhenny, Mary received a letter from Phyllis explaining that the guest room in her flat was soon to become a nursery. The letter made no mention of her and Phyllis's long-time affair—perhaps Martin had been present when Phyllis wrote it. In any event, what was unwritten but all too clear was that Mary's visits were now over.

Well. It wasn't exactly a surprise. Deep down, Mary had always known this day would come, and so, she realized, must have Phyllis. Looking back on it, in all the years she'd been "visiting" with Phyllis, Mary had never once been introduced to anyone else Phyllis knew. If Phyllis didn't want Mary to meet any of her friends or acquaintances, it had been especially foolish for Mary to suggest Phyllis should meet anyone in Mary's circle. Their relationship had thus by definition been a transitory one. Still, that did not make the loss of it any less disappointing. She had come to depend on her private assignations, not just for the physical pleasures they offered but for the mental relief of having somewhere she did not have to keep any part of herself hidden. And now, that one form of escape for her was gone.

*

Though Mary couldn't confide her loss to anyone in town, Mrs. Simpson privately noted Mary Grey was wearing a long face. Mrs. Simpson wondered if Mary's visits to London had been to see a man and if her assignation had ended badly. She shared her speculations with other women in town who agreed her hypothesis seemed most likely.

"A shame, isn't it?" the vicar's wife, Dahlia Winthrop, proclaimed. "For a girl like Mary to never find a husband. It seems such a waste." And Dahlia would shake her head.

Meanwhile, Mary continued to write regularly to her mother. Only her mother. When Mary was three, her father had gone out for cigarettes and never returned. Mary didn't even remember him, and from what she'd heard he wasn't worth remembering. Her mother had rolled up her sleeves and went into business with one of her cousins as a seamstress. Eventually, they opened up a little shop together. Mrs. Grey never remarried nor showed any inclination to do so, and the cousin was a born old maid. Yet, despite her own life experience, Mrs. Grey had encouraged all her children to marry young, just as she had. Perhaps misery simply loved company. Then again, Mary's brother and sister seemed happy enough with their various spouses. Perhaps Mrs. Grey was frustrated Mary was the only one of her children not to provide her with any grandchildren. Or, Mary sometimes wondered, did her mother secretly suspect the true reason her daughter never had any male suitors? Mary didn't know and she'd never dream of asking her elderly mother such a thing.

Mary wrote to her mother, telling her so much about the other daily events of her life, yet this most crucial part of her life could not be spoken of. Sometimes she felt guilty, and other times she felt resentful. Perhaps it was all for the best, Mary reasoned, that she and her family lived in separate towns. It made it so much easier for her to keep her secret, and who knew? Perhaps they had secrets of their own to keep from her. Doesn't everyone deserve to keep at least some part of themselves locked away from the public eye?

That theory of Mary's was tested a bit by circumstance. Poor Annie Capman breathed her last breath in bleak November, and only Mary was there to attend her funeral service. Annie was buried in a plain wooden box, in a shallow grave, and what few possessions she'd had were burned for fear of infection. As Mary watched the flames, in the chill November air, she wondered exactly how Annie had come to such a fate. Annie had not been particularly forthcoming about her life before Illhenny, except to say she had no family, and Mary had not pried. As was the case with most consumptive patients, Mary deduced that Annie's life had been a hard one punctuated by loss and pain. But after Annie's death, Mary had questions. What if Annie had family somewhere or old friends and lovers? Should they not be informed of her death and of her funeral? Was it really for the best that Annie died among strangers? Surely everyone deserves to have their story remembered. Would anyone remember Mary's, or would she pass through the world completely unnoticed? Well, not entirely unnoticed; she'd certainly had some impact on her patients' lives, at least. She might not be remembered as the love of anyone's life, but there are worse fates than being remembered as a good nurse.

Except for Mary, the rest of Illhenny was left utterly unaffected by the death of Annie Capman and were far too busy seething about the proposed resort development.

Mary paid a follow-up visit to the Martins' home, feeling rather guilty that she hadn't done so before. To her relief, Mrs. Martin's sister, Amy, had arrived. Amy was a sensible looking middle-aged woman with firm lines around her mouth suggesting she brooked no nonsense from anyone. She was running the household like a drill sergeant and Mrs. Martin was already looking better. The twins continued to grow like weeds, and they roared as heartily as ever. There was, Mary noticed, still no sign of Mr. Martin, nor did anyone at the farm seem to miss him. Mary managed to get Amy aside for a moment to talk.

"You've done wonderful work here," Mary told her.

"Hmph." Amy received the praise gruffly. "Just needed some elbow grease was all. In a couple of days' time, I'll go on back to my post."

"Well, your sister is looking a lot better."

Amy gave a curt nod. "Most important thing was getting Helen to snap out of it, you know? Just had to be firm. Mind you, might have been easier if that husband of hers were any use." Her expression turned dark. "I did tell her not to marry him, but he was the only one who asked her, so she said she had to, and our mum agreed. As if marrying a poor farmer and having baby after baby ever did Mum any good! Me, I preferred to find me a good place and keep my freedom and my earnings for myself. I've never seen why any woman need marry at all!"

"I could not agree more," Mary replied with gusto.

Much to her surprise, as she was leaving the Martin farm, Mrs. Martin pressed a dusty old bottle on her.

"What's this?" Mary asked.

"Elderberry wine. I brew it myself." Mrs. Martin spoke with evident pride. "I'm famous for my homemade wines, I am! I realized I had some bottles that wanted drinking up and, well, I'm gonna send some back with Amy, but she can't carry them all home. And you've been such a help as well."

"No, really, I couldn't," Mary objected.

"It's yours." Mrs. Martin stood firm. "Anything you and Amy don't take might just go to my husband. Aye, actually, you better take two bottles. Molly, fetch the nurse another bottle! This time, some of the dandelion wine."

No such hospitality was extended to poor Anthony West. While neither Caleb Barnaby, who'd been warned off, or anyone else actively threatened him, he was always being treated with cold reproof. Anywhere he went for groceries or regular shopping, people had a way of scowling at him and saying just little enough to be not quite polite. And around the dock area, Anthony noticed an old sailor with a wooden leg who'd give him the evil eye. Except for Edgar Pool, Anthony found himself quite devoid of any sort of friends in Illhenny, and while if anyone had asked him, he'd have sworn he didn't care a fig for the opinions of some backward villagers, in reality, he felt quite lonely. To compensate, Anthony regularly had friends up from London to visit him, but because entertaining flashy Londoners fell suspect in the eyes of Illhenny residents, West unwittingly made himself even more an object of suspicion.

November rolled into December, and as a storm rolled in one cold night, Mary Grey came off a particularly long round of visits, exhausted and lonely. And hungry. Her stomach growled and she had blissful visions of steak and kidney pie or Yorkshire pudding topped off with copious amounts of ale. Visions that would remain unrealized. She didn't have a cook or the time to make such dishes herself. Once she got home, the best she could look forward to would be some homemade sandwiches and a nice pot of tea—assuming she wasn't too tired when she got home to make herself eat. More than one night, exhaustion had won out over hunger and she'd gone to bed without supper, huddled under a hundred blankets to keep warm, like the princess on the pea.

As she mused on all this, Mary felt the first snowflakes fall upon her skin. Oh well, it wasn't the first time she'd had to ride through snow, wind, and rain. At least she'd be home soon and in her own bed. There were times in her job when she hadn't even had that luxury but rather had to catch naps at the homes of patients and clean herself up as best she could between visits. And at least she could now sleep in a room to herself. It was a level of privacy she had not enjoyed in her childhood—when she and her sister shared the same bed—or in nursing school.

Florence Nightingale may have done wonders for nursing, but she hadn't made life easy for actual nurses. Hospital nurses had to live on-grounds, enjoying no sort of privacy or independence at all. They were, for all intents and purposes, prisoners, and the matron was the warden who invariably ruled with an iron fist. As a student nurse, Mary had to fight like hell for every day off and every overnight pass. At least as a district nurse, Mary enjoyed the hard-earned privilege of her own home, however modest it might be. And no bossy matron. It was, indeed, privileges like that which drew many candidates to district nursing despite its league of hardships.

Mary was almost home, and she'd be safely inside before the winter storm began in earnest. She was already eagerly anticipating hot tea in front of the stove when she heard from behind her the unmistakable sound of a car engine. She turned and saw immediately there was something wrong with the way the sporty little vehicle was moving. It seemed to sidle back and forth, and it was coming far, far too fast. She veered her motorbike off the road so quickly it went sideways. She fell onto a heap of frozen mud, and a huge hunk smeared into her hair. She began cursing at the car. The vehicle on the road did not stop or even slow down but continued at breakneck speed.

Mary picked herself up, slightly bruised, and her coat and uniform now covered in snow. She cursed as she started pushing the bike.

"You could have killed me, you idiot," Mary screamed. "You bloody idiot!"

The car didn't slow down, and there was no sign the driver had heard Mary at all. *What kind of maniac is behind the wheel?* Mary thought. Whoever it was had nearly killed her and might well kill themselves too. There was a bend in the road right before Griffin's Cliff and if the driver didn't slow down or use their brakes, they'd surely crash. And indeed, moments Mary later watched in horror as the car smashed into a copse of trees right off the road. At that moment, her own anger and pain were forgotten as Mary's professional instincts took over and she rushed to the scene with her torch and nursing bag.

Mary scrambled across layers of crunchy frost and bare branches covered in icicles that incessantly swatted her in the face. The trees lay right before Griffin's Cliff. From the top of the cliff to the rocks below, it was at least a hundred-foot drop. The car now lay at a crazy angle with the driver's side above the cliff and the rest hanging off.

There was a single figure in the driver's seat, and even though it was now dark and rain pelted her face, Mary detected a flicker of movement. She shone the torch into the driver's window, revealing a man bleeding from the head. He gave a low moan and then his blue eyes met hers and she recognized with a start that it was Illhenny's newest resident, the infamous Anthony West. He blinked at her, but he didn't speak.

"Mr. West, can you hear me?" Still no response. She continued, "I'm the district nurse. I'm here to help you. Do you understand what I'm saying?"

He slowly nodded his head.

"Can you move?" she asked him.

Again, he nodded.

"All right then, can you open the door for me?"

Slowly, Anthony moved his arm toward the door handle, and much to Nurse Grey's relief the door did, indeed, open. And not so much opened as swung off, but Mary could now get her arms and legs into the cab. For the first time, he spoke.

"It hurts." Anthony's voice was faint but clear.

"Where does it hurt?"

"My head. And my ribs. And my foot. My foot's stuck." His voice held a bewildered note, as if the whole situation was some kind of puzzle. Nurse Grey first examined Anthony's head and saw the bleeding was from a gash on the side, in the hairline. She determined that the injury was ugly but not immediately life-threatening. She then looked at his legs and saw one foot trapped under the accelerator pedal. She crawled forward into the cab of the car, her head near his lap, and then pressed his shoe.

"Can you feel that?"

"Ow, yes!"

"Good, can you move your foot at all?"

Anthony wiggled his foot. "Yes, but it hurts like hell."

"All right." Mary spoke as calmly as possible and tried to avoid thinking too much on the precarious position of the car. Did she actually hear the metal groan or merely imagine it? She quickly brought her scissors out of her nurse's bag. "I'm going to cut your shoe off to release your foot."

Mary hunched over awkwardly, having to lean across the driver himself to reach his foot, and he let out another groan from the extra pressure.

"Sorry," she apologized. Fortunately, the sharp scissors cut easily through cotton trousers and wool sock. The leather shoe was more of a challenge but, eventually, Mary was able to wrench it off. "Right, now, I'm about to lift the pedal. When I tell you to, I need you to pull your foot out. You may have to use your hands to help. It will be painful, but it has to be done. On the count of three. Ready?"

Anthony nodded and Mary gripped the pedal.

"One, two, *three*!"

The pedal gave way. Mr. West pulled as hard as he could and screamed from the pain. But the foot was out absent the sock. A deep wound was visible in the instep but there was no time to think on it. For now, it was clear the car was starting to slide and would soon go down the cliff. Mary grabbed Anthony by the arm and began to heave him out.

"Hey, I can handle it," he protested.

Mary rolled her eyes. West was breathless from pain and exertion, yet manful pride induced him to try to do as much of it as he could himself. The car gave a heavy groan and this time there was no question whether Nurse Grey imagined it. From the look on Mr. West's face, it was clear he'd heard it too.

"Maybe you should go," he told her.

Mary ignored his suggestion and rather caught hold of his jacket and dragged him out of the door, never minding that it would almost certainly cause him even more pain. As she did so, Anthony nearly fell on top of her, but they were out, gasping in the tree roots and dirt as the car made a final lurch. For a split second, they got a view of the underside of the engine, then down the car went, and they heard a huge splash from below.

Chapter Three

The first thing Mary did was dress Anthony's head wound with some cotton and a bandage. It'd do for now, but he'd need stitches later. His foot was badly hurt, but it was nearly impossible to do a proper examination under the circumstances.

"You're going to need X-rays," Mary told him, "and a hospital. We have to find some help." She started to stand up when he grabbed her by the wrist with such pressure it hurt.

"Don't leave me!" Anthony whispered, gazing into her eyes as he clutched her fingers into his.

"I won't. I swear, I won't." Mary kept her hand in his, but that raised the question of how they could summon help without her leaving his side. What she wouldn't have given right then and there for an alarm siren. Perhaps she could use the light of the torch to signal someone? But who would be able to see it from out there? And they couldn't remain here like this indefinitely. Hypothermia might already be setting in as it was. Mary feared she might have to leave her patient, if only momentarily, when much to her relief she heard footsteps in the distance. The sound of the wrecked car falling into the ocean had brought out curiosity-seekers despite the winter weather.

"Here!" Mary yelled with all her lungs, through frost and snow, as she waved the torch back and forth with her one free hand while keeping Mr. West's held firmly tight. "We're right here!"

The next hour was a confusion of villagers asking questions and people running and bustling about. Nurse Grey and Mr. West were both wrapped in blankets. An ambulance arrived, and Mr. West was put on a stretcher.

"Stay with me," he told Mary.

"Can I?" she asked the drivers.

"Actually," one of them spoke up, "I think they'll want to examine you at the hospital as well. Begging your pardon, ma'am, but you don't look so good either."

Nurse Grey looked herself over. She was, of course, completely covered in snow to the point of resembling a yeti, but moreover, to her dismay, her coat was now missing a button and her uniform had been badly torn.

"Oh dear," she sighed, "I'll have to order a replacement from headquarters. That's always a nuisance."

Mary rode along in the ambulance, to a nearby hospital that served Illhenny and a couple of other small hamlets in the area. Anthony West was taken away for X-rays while she was immediately instructed to get out of all her wet things and dry off thoroughly with a towel. She caught a glimpse of herself in a mirror and was jolted. No wonder the ambulance driver wanted her to come in too. Mary's wet hair hung wildly, mud was plastered to her hair, her skin was ashen, her lips blue, and her eyes were sunken and frenzied. She looked like a wild beast!

Taking off her clothes, Mary saw she was now covered in newly formed scrapes and bruises just starting to blossom. This came as a surprise to her because she didn't at present feel any pain. She stood for a time in front of the radiator, luxuriating in the heat as she changed into a hospital gown, and was loath to leave it. Eventually, Mary was visited by Dr. Harold Roberts. As district nurse, Mary had worked with him many times over the years. Dr. Roberts possessed a snowy-white beard and rosy cheeks that made him look remarkably like a portrait of Father Christmas. This, in addition to an amiable bedside manner, had made him a favorite with his patients. And he, in turn, loved his work, which meant, despite the best efforts of his wife and not-so-subtle hints from colleagues, he refused to retire.

"Well now, Mary Grey," Dr. Roberts addressed her by her Christian name, though he would have been most offended had she called him anything but "Dr. Roberts." "Do you want the bad news first or the good news?"

"Let's get the bad news out of the way."

"You're in for a lot of aches and stiffness come tomorrow and will have to take some bed rest. The good news is that nothing was seriously injured."

"What about Mr. West?" Mary asked.

"Ah, that's another story. Mild concussion with stitches to the head. Ribs cracked and his foot will need a brace for a time. Still, from what I've heard, he's lucky to be alive at all."

"He is, indeed," Mary agreed and gave an involuntary shudder at the memory. "He slammed straight into the trees and very nearly went down Griffin's Cliff." A thought struck her. "Has he said anything about what caused the accident?"

"He was probably speeding. You know how today's youth are behind the wheel," Dr. Roberts pronounced with evident disapproval for younger drivers.

"He was going very fast," Mary recalled, "but it was more than that." She remembered the way the car had swayed and how it had nearly done her in as well. "It was as if he'd lost control of the vehicle."

"Perhaps he was drunk," Dr. Roberts suggested. "Today's youth so often are."

Mary thought it a bit of a stretch to call Mr. West, a man who'd never see thirty again, a "youth," but then anyone beneath the age of fifty was, in the eyes of Dr. Roberts, a whippersnapper.

"Or maybe even drugs." Dr. Roberts' imaginings turned even more lurid. "There's no telling what sort of things his set get up to in London, is there?"

"His pupils were normal," Mary pointed out, "and I didn't see any signs he'd been drinking either when I examined him." Her mind flashed back to her moments with Mr. West as she'd rescued him from the car. The man had been in shock, to be sure, but there'd been no indication he was intoxicated. Lord knows Mary had enough experience patching up drunks at The Mud Crab to know the difference.

"Well, the road was icy, so maybe it was just an accident." Dr. Roberts seemed almost disappointed to admit to such a mundane cause. "Or possibly an attempted suicide." He brightened visibly. "A lot of Londoners are quite disturbed, you know!"

"He seemed perfectly sane to me," Mary told him drily, "and quite determined to live!"

"Ah, well." Dr. Roberts shrugged off the matter. "We've given him a sedative and he's out cold. In any event, we'd like you to remain overnight for observation."

Mary opened her mouth to object, but Dr. Roberts was too quick for her.

"How do you intend on getting home anyway?"

This gave Mary pause. She was now many miles from her motorbike.

"Well, I'm sure someone can give me a ride," she said.

Dr. Roberts snorted. "Take a look out of the window."

Mary did so and muttered, "Bloody hell." Snow flurries were coming down fast and hard.

"No one's going to be riding out in that. No sane person at any rate," Dr. Roberts opined.

Mary, begrudgingly, had to agree. Moreover, the adrenaline rush that previously sustained her had now ebbed and she was feeling as exhausted as she had ever been in her life.

"This'll give you a chance to get your sleep first." Dr. Roberts pressed his advantage.

"But what about my appointments tomorrow morning?" Mary wondered. "Oh dear, and I'm short a uniform now too."

"I've already called District Nurse headquarters and reported this to them. They're sending a relief nurse to take over for a day or two while you recover."

"My motorbike!" She sat up. "Good God! I left my motorbike on the road."

"Well, I'm sure someone can give you a ride back tomorrow."

"I'm not worried about that. I can walk back home if need be! But what if someone takes the bike?"

"Why would anyone want to take your bike?" Dr. Roberts pointed out logically, if not tactfully. "The thing's seen far better days."

Mary was unconvinced. Even if someone didn't steal the bike for itself, they might decide to salvage it for scrap metal. Or it could be damaged by the elements. But clearly there was no way to deal with the motorbike until morning. She begrudgingly consented to be put to bed, and her head had barely hit the pillow when she fell into a dreamless sleep.

When Mary woke up the next morning, she was stiff and muscle sore, just as Dr. Roberts had predicted. What she really needed was some time in a bathtub with Epsom salts. Or maybe some morphine. The hospital food was every bit as bad as she remembered from her time serving on the wards when studying to be a Queen's Nurse in London. Hungry as she was, Mary didn't touch the breakfast they offered her. Instead, she thought Mr. West might be awake by now and ready for visitors.

True, Mr. West was no longer Mary's patient. Technically speaking, he'd never formally been her patient at all. Nevertheless, the events of the night before had been so extraordinary, even in the life of a district nurse, that she felt an extra level of responsibility toward him. As a professional courtesy, she'd been left to sleep alone in an empty staff room on a cot bed with a pillow and blanket. She was still in a hospital gown, and she remembered her clothes from the night before were now unwearable.

Mary made her way over to the Casualty ward to find Mr. West. It hurt to walk.

Along the way, she passed the Children's Block and Female Chronic ward, filled with elderly ladies in the grips of dementia. Everywhere she went, Mary was greeted by the familiar hospital scent of antiseptic mixed with sickness and the din of patients complaining, nurses running to and fro. She felt a momentary pang of envy considering how clean and well-equipped the little clinic was compared to the places she worked out of. They'd even made efforts to decorate it with sprigs of holly and paper garlands for the holidays. Then again, she certainly had more autonomy than any hospital nurse did. And no Medea of a matron to report to.

Twice Mary was stopped by the hospital sisters, suspicious to see a patient out of bed. Nor was their suspicion lessoned when she explained she was there to see another patient. Only when she turned to her status as a fellow nurse would they permit her to continue. She decided it was time to ditch the hospital gown for something more professional. It took some coaxing and wheedling before she was loaned a hospital nurse uniform two sizes too large, under the strict proviso that it would be sent back once she had finished with it.

Because of his known association with Lord Pool, who, on news of the accident, had immediately called the hospital to assure them he'd cover the bill, Anthony West had been granted the luxury of a private room. When Mary found him, he was lying flat on his back with his eyes staring off into the distance. As she walked in, he started as if he'd been shot through with electricity.

"How are you feeling today?" Mary asked him.

"My ribs and foot still hurt," he informed her. "And I'd absolutely kill for a cigarette right now."

Anthony West, Mary noted, spoke in the distinct manners and address of the upper crust of British society. Under normal circumstances, she reflected, he and she would likely have never had any dealings at all. And here he was now, confiding in her like they were old friends! There was nothing like a dramatic rescue scene to do away with normal class distinctions.

"And," Anthony went on, "the food here isn't fit for pigs. Honestly, how do they expect anyone to recover when they give us such slop like that?"

"I know. I couldn't eat breakfast myself," Mary admitted.

"Precisely!" Anthony nodded. "And I can't say the robes they provide patients are any better. How I miss my dressing gown." He gave a melodramatic sigh and Mary hid a smile. "Other than that," he went on, "I've never been better. But I'm not the only one who suffered last night. How are you holding up?" Before Mary could answer, he interjected, "I say, couldn't they find you some civilian clothes? Or least a better fitting uniform?" He frowned.

"Well, it's only temporary. I'm going home later today and can change. And really, I'm quite all right. I was far more worried about you. But from what Dr. Roberts tells me, Mr. West, you're expected to make a full recovery."

"If I do, it'll be thanks to you. You're the only reason I'm still alive at all. And you don't have to call me Mr. West. My name's Anthony," he replied, still staring at her intently.

“I was only doing my job,” Mary told him firmly. “Do you have any family to notify?”

“My sister, Harriet. She’s staying in Cannes with friends.”

“How can she be reached?”

“The easiest way is probably by telegram.” He frowned. “Damn if I can remember the exact address. It’s in my appointment book at home.”

“I’ll find it,” Mary assured him. “I can personally stop by your house.”

“Thank you.” He smiled and added, “There’s also my uncle in Newcastle, though his own health’s so bad, I doubt the poor blighter could pay a visit. Still, he should be notified. His name’s Donald. Donald Harrington.”

“The name sounds familiar.” Mary’s forehead creased in thought.

“He’s the current owner of Harrington Steel. Founded by my maternal grandfather,” Anthony explained. Mary’s eyebrows shot up and she gave an involuntary gasp. Well, that certainly explained how such a young architect could afford such an expensive motorcar and why Harriet West could make trips to the Riviera. “Old Donald always wanted me to go into the family business, but I was never interested. Quite a disappointment for him, since Harriet and I are the only kin he’s got left. But the way I see it, there are so many other people in the world who actually have a head for business that it’s best to let them get on with running things and let the rest of us do things we’re interested in. After all, if I were running the factory, I’d either die of boredom or ruin the whole company. Or possibly both!”

Anthony chuckled and Mary smiled at him. Then all humor faded from Anthony's face and his mood turned somber as he stared at Mary with a strange intensity.

"Close the door," he ordered.

Mary did so uneasily. Patients often developed unhealthy fixations on nurses. In fact, she'd had it happen to her before and had some trouble convincing male patients they were not in fact in love with her, whatever they might believe. And she was even more certainly not in love with them. Admittedly, there seemed very little likelihood a gentleman like Anthony would take any romantic interest in her, but still, she'd have to be careful to establish boundaries, at least until his initial shock wore off. Many a patient who had proclaimed a hospital nurse their soulmate while ill was known to suddenly grow distant once they'd returned home to recover. What Anthony said next, though, shocked Mary to her very core.

"I don't want anyone else to hear what I'm about to tell you. Someone tried to murder me." He stated this as simply as if he were reporting on the state of the weather. For an instant, Mary thought she must have misheard him, but he went on. "The brakes failed. That's why I lost control on the road and nearly killed us both."

"Jesus," was all Mary could say. The events of the previous night flashed before her eyes and his explanation certainly did seem to fit.

"Are you sure the car was sabotaged?"

"I'm certain of it." West tried to sit up, and the effort caused him visible pain. "I'd actually just taken the car in for an oil change and a tune-up last week, and it was in perfect working order. And I've used the car since then without any problems, which means between that time and last night, someone sabotaged the brakes. Someone tried to kill me, and they damn well would have succeeded if not for you."

"If what you're saying is true then you should be talking to the police."

Anthony West gave a bitter laugh. "The police? Have you ever met Constable Evans?" He didn't wait for an answer. "The man's a blockhead."

"Now really," Mary protested, "the constable's a very nice man in his way and he does his duties just fine."

"Oh, I suppose he's all right for dealing with drunks at the pub, but not for something like this." Anthony waved his hand dismissively and, before Mary could say anything else in Evans's defense, he demanded, "Has the good constable ever even investigated a murder before? Or rather attempted murder?"

"Not to my knowledge," Mary admitted. "You'd have to go the police in Anchester for that. Or Scotland Yard."

"And I will." Anthony jutted his chin out as he tried to sit up, but with his injured ribs the effort was too painful. His shoulders sagged in defeat. "But I'm not sure the police will believe me. It would be one thing if the car hadn't gone off the cliff. I could have had it examined and proved the brakes had been tampered with. But as it is, I doubt they'll be able to salvage anything at all from the wreck. And without tangible proof, I'm going to have a very hard time getting the police to take me seriously. They'll probably assume I'm just trying to cover for driving drunk. Or they'll think me mad."

Mary stayed silent. There was a pause.

"Do you think I'm mad?" he finally asked her.

"No," she answered automatically, without hesitation. "I don't think you're mad at all." What she did not add was that she thought he'd just had a near death experience and was now lying in a hospital bed, heavily medicated. Mary knew all too well that such circumstances could prey on a person's mind and make them subject to fancies. Oh, she had no doubt there had been something wrong with the brakes, but that hardly meant foul play. As for the recent garage visit and maintenance of the engine, that proved nothing. So-called mechanics often fail to detect all sorts of problems with cars. There could have been an issue long in the making, which simply hadn't gone wrong until the previous evening. Or the brakes might have frozen up or something of that nature. But looking at Anthony's drawn face, Mary decided there was no point in saying any of what she thought on the subject. Right now, the young lad—and in the hospital bed, Anthony looked very young, indeed, almost childlike—needed someone to believe him and offer him reassurance.

"Good," he replied, "because I'm going to need your help finding whoever the hell's trying to murder me."

"Me? You want me to help you investigate an attempt on your life?" Mary was dumbfounded.

"Right now, you're the only person in that damned village who I'm a hundred percent sure doesn't want me dead."

Chapter Four

As a district nurse, Mary Grey had to fulfill multiple roles within the community, from midwifery to public health education to long-term convalescent care. She'd been trained for all those things at the Queen's Institute. Beyond that, while she wasn't officially assigned any such role in practice, Mary had more than once acted as a counselor or, as was the case with the Martin family, a social worker. She had even been deputized to act as a veterinarian by applying bandages and casts to the local animal population. Never before had she been called upon to act as a detective. Nor had she ever wanted to be one. The whole idea was preposterous. She was convinced there was nothing to investigate—just another vehicular accident, albeit an especially dramatic one. She was about to tell West it was impossible for her to do any such thing, but something in his face stopped her. Anthony West looked frightened—terribly frightened—and he was gazing on her as if he were a drowning man and she a life preserver. And she, Mary Grey, had made it her life's mission to help people.

"Yes," Mary told him, "I'll help you in any way that I can." For the first time since she had walked into his room, Anthony smiled. She took a deep breath and tried to organize her thoughts. For now, she'd just humor him about the whole thing and play along. Her investigating and finding nothing would be the easiest way for Anthony to realize his fears were groundless. Finally, she spoke. "So, the first question is, who on earth would want to murder you? I mean, obviously there's been controversy over the proposed development."

"Controversy?" Anthony repeated in disbelief. "Is that what you call it? My God, people here hate me!"

"I doubt it's that personal." Mary tried to soothe Anthony, but he had none of it.

"No! It is personal! I mean, I don't get the feeling that anyone here likes me really. Though I don't know why. It's not like I've done anything to them." Anthony assumed a look of self-pity. "But that Caleb Barnaby's the worst. He has it out for me. I saw it straight off when I first arrived. He's complained to me a few times about noise, and he even threatened me for it too. The other day, he said something about 'thronging me.' Though, the way that man drinks, I don't know how he can even notice any noise at all. He's the one I'd look into first," he said darkly. "There's another fellow too. Gnarly looking sort of chap with only one leg."

"Peg Leg Pete." Mary immediately recognized the description. "He's a local fisherman."

"Well, whoever he is, he's been giving me the evil eye too."

"Oh, that's just his face. Pete always looks out of sorts."

"Now, maybe that's true for Pete"—Anthony seemed only slightly reassured—"but that Barnaby fellow is a danger for sure!"

Meanwhile, Mary was thinking how the less-than-friendly reception Anthony had received in Illhenny had no doubt made him more paranoid and suggestive, which was understandable. Mary's duties gave her a certain standing among the locals of Illhenny, but she thought ruefully if anyone had even the slightest suspicion of where her true tastes lay, she'd be shunned far worse than Anthony. At best, she'd lose her job. At worst, she could lose her life. She was inclined to think Anthony overly sensitive, considering what a privileged status he enjoyed. Besides, this was Caleb he was talking about.

"I really don't see Caleb Barnaby as a murderer," she told Anthony bluntly. 'In fact, there isn't a single person I know in Illhenny who strikes me as a murderer.'

"Which is just the hallmark of a successful murderer! It's always the ones you don't suspect."

"In detective stories, perhaps, but we're talking about the real world here," Mary pointed out. "But I'll keep Barnaby on the list if it makes you happy." She added with the tone nurses use with patients they have to humor, "Assuming you're right and this is because someone is angry about the proposed development, wouldn't Lord Pool be a target as well?"

"It's probably a lot harder to get to Lord Pool or his Rolls-Royce. And the list doesn't end with Barnaby. He may have been the loudest, but there were plenty of other people at that meeting who shared his views." Anthony let his imagination run wild. "One of them might be the sort who keeps things bottled up and is all the more dangerous for it. Or maybe they just don't like me. Doesn't seem like anyone in the village does," he noted once more, morosely. As a man used to easy friendships and relative popularity, his outsider status in Illhenny had hit him very hard indeed, even before he'd considered it a danger to his life.

"They're not fond of strangers here in Illhenny," Mary admitted, "but that doesn't mean they'd try to kill them. But even if you're right and someone simply had it in for you, there's still the question of opportunity. Where do you keep your car?"

"I keep it, or rather kept it, in the garage." Anthony groaned. "Oh lord, it's going to be such a nuisance filing the insurance claim! And how will I get around in the meantime?"

Mary ignored the question of Anthony West's future transportation. "Going back to the accident, who has access to the garage keys?"

"There's no lock on the garage. The old lock was broken, and I never got around to having it repaired. I didn't think there was any hurry." In response to Mary's stare, Anthony became defensive. "Well, I keep the door from the house to the garage locked at least!"

"So, you worry about someone breaking into your home but not about anyone stealing your car?" Mary could not help but take a rather chiding tone.

"Dash it all," Anthony defended himself. "It's not like London, where we have car thieves on every corner."

"No, but according to you, Illhenny does have a cold-blooded killer," Mary pointed out.

"But until last night I didn't know that," Anthony reminded her. "I had no idea I was in any danger." Mary could see his reasoning.

"All right, never mind the unlocked garage. When did you last use the car? Before the brakes were tampered with," she clarified. "If we can establish a timeline then we can at least start eliminating possible suspects according to whoever has an alibi."

"That'll be difficult," Anthony said grimly. "I hadn't used the car since the evening before. The next day, Edgar, I mean Lord Pool and I had arranged to meet with some of the other investors. We had lunch together and visited the proposed site. Then, he dropped me off at home, and I stayed in working on plans. I didn't touch the car until the evening when I planned to visit a club in Anchester."

"So, the car was unattended all the previous night and then all day?"

"Correct."

"So, anyone really could have tampered with the brakes on your car?"

"Yes."

"And Illhenny's chock full of people with a grudge against you because of the proposed development."

"Also true."

"You're not giving me much to go on, are you?"

"Afraid not." Anthony gave a crooked grin.

Mary thought for a moment. "You really should call the police," she concluded. Anthony groaned. "You should! They have all other sorts of resources I don't have." They'd be in a far better position, Mary thought, to prove him wrong. "Because, right now, I have no earthly idea how to proceed."

"You could look around the garage! Ask questions in the village. They're far more likely to open up to you than me or the police. After all, you're one of them!"

"Actually, I'm not local at all," Mary corrected him.

Anthony blinked. "You're not? But you certainly seem to know everyone around here."

"Well, I have treated folks from at least half the families or households in these parts."

"So, they accept you then," Anthony said with triumph, "which means they'll talk to you."

"I suppose some of them might," Mary reluctantly admitted.

"Good! Also, could you stop by the house I'm renting?"

"I'm already stopping by," Mary reminded him. "I have to get your sister's address to wire her."

"Oh yes, but while you're there, I was wondering if you could, well..." He paused as if embarrassed.

"Investigate?"

'Well, that, too, but I was thinking you could pick up my dressing gown and cigarettes," he admitted sheepishly. "Perhaps a magazine or paper as well?" Anthony smiled. "Please? Please?"

"Very well. I'll get your things from your house. I'll even check out the garage for you as well, if you agree to contact Scotland Yard at the first opportunity."

"Cross my heart and hope to die. But I think my house keys are with my clothes and they took them."

Sighing, Mary flagged someone down, and she and Anthony negotiated with them for his keys to be retrieved.

The nurse had just brought them, and Mary was about to take her leave when in walked Lord Pool. Mary started. It was the closest physical proximity she'd ever had to a peer of the realm before.

"Edgar!" Anthony greeted him heartily.

"Clipper!" Lord Pool called out with equal boisterousness.

At Mary's obvious bafflement, Anthony explained, "Clipper's my old nickname from Eton." He turned to Lord Pool. "This is Mary Grey. She pulled me out of the car last night before it fell."

"So, you're the one we have to thank for this young devil cheating death once more." Lord Pool addressed Mary with bonhomie and then turned serious. "It was a damned good thing you were there, Miss Grey. Otherwise, our project would have been down an architect, and I doubt Anthony's sister would have ever forgiven me if her brother had died on a project I'd brought him to."

At Mary's look of incomprehension, Anthony said, "My sister, Harriet, and Lord Pool are engaged."

Mary's eyebrows went up, but she managed to murmur her congratulations.

"We're all just waiting for them to pick a date," Anthony added.

"At present, we are thinking sometime in summer." As Lord Pool stood by Anthony's side, Mary reflected on the strong physical contrast between the two men. While Anthony was shockingly fair and thin, his Lordship was dark, broad shouldered, and muscular. He'd have been perfect for a Heathcliff or a Rochester, and he was often cited in lists as one of the most desirable bachelors in

England. Though, apparently, he wasn't going to be a bachelor for much longer.

"Well, it's good to see you in such hearty shape since we can't very well marry without the best man." Lord Pool spoke with evident relief. "Don't think this means you'll get too long a holiday from work though." The men laughed together, and Mary politely said goodbye, letting them catch up.

A hack driver had been called up to take Mary home. Much to the driver's exasperation, Mary had insisted on first stopping at the stretch of road where she'd nearly been run over by Anthony's car. To her relief, the motorbike was still there, buried under several inches of powdered snow. Then came the matter of getting it home. Eventually, they had to attach it to the bumper of the cab before driving on to her cottage.

Mary lived in a little cottage supplied to her by the Rural Nursing Association. Once in her house, she changed into civilian clothes and had a proper breakfast. Thus fortified, if still bruised, she rode her bike to Anthony West's.

"Nurse Grey!" Dahlia Winthrop stepped right in front of her motorbike and, much to her annoyance, Mary was forced to stop. Dahlia was the vicar's wife. She was also the biggest gossip in Illhenny. She spent her days nosing about trying to collect tidbits, and then spreading venomous tales everywhere. Not coincidentally, her beleaguered husband, Reverend Winthrop, spent all his time either locked away in his study or walking along the shore. "I'm surprised they let you leave so soon after that horrible accident." Dahlia eyed Mary with fake concern. "My dear, you really do look a fright."

"I'm fine, thank you," Mary replied coolly.

"And what about poor Mr. West? I hear he's practically at death's door." Dahlia Winthrop didn't even try to hide her excitement.

"I spoke to him this morning, and he's expected to make a full recovery." Mary was all too glad to pour cold water on Dahlia's hopes. "In fact, I'm running a favor for him right now. If you'll excuse me?" Mary had to make a wild loop with the motorbike to escape the persistent Dahlia Winthrop. It would probably have been easier to simply run Dahlia over and the thought was tempting.

Finally, Mary was at Mr. West's home. She decided to first take a look inside the garage, unproductive as this was likely to be. Mary still did not really credit Anthony's suspicions of foul play. But he was her patient and thus her responsibility. If she at least tried to do what he asked and came up empty perhaps he'd give up his mad fixation with having her play detective. The garage was a plain wooden structure with a tin roof, which, minus a car, seemed very empty. There was a can of oil and a liter of petrol. There were shelves lined with tools, left for the use of whichever tenant currently occupied the home. These shelves were now covered with dust. Clearly, Mr. West was not a handyman, Mary observed with amusement.

In one area, the dust had been freshly disturbed. A pair of bolt cutters had been touched. Mary examined them with an old rag and found a fresh spot of grease on the blades. Her knees buckled and she counted to twenty to calm herself down. Until that moment, she had never seriously considered Mr. West's accusations. But here was proof that his story, sensational as it was, was true. Someone had entered the garage and used the clippers to cut the brake lines. *Or had they?* Mary stopped to think. There might be an innocent explanation for the use of the bolt cutters. She personally couldn't think of one, but that didn't mean there weren't any. Grease on the bolt cutters certainly wouldn't be enough to win a case in court. Nevertheless, it did give new credence to Anthony's wild suspicions.

She looked around the garage with fresh eyes. The problem was she wasn't sure what she was looking for. Sherlock Holmes would no doubt have been able to determine the would-be killer's shoe size and height by now, but Mary was having no such luck. There were no signs of tobacco ash, and even if there had been, she wouldn't have the faintest idea how to identify it. Neither were there torn-up bits of letters, no monogrammed handkerchief, no footprints. And she didn't have any fingerprint powder to dust for telltale prints. Another reason, she thought grimly, Anthony West really ought to have a police inspector in the room.

Mary was about to leave when her eyes detected something caught in the door—a single deep-blue woolen thread. As clues go, it wasn't much. It could have come from anything, including Mr. West himself. Still, it was the only thing she'd found in the garage that didn't look like it was supposed to be there.

Mary then went into Mr. West's new temporary home via the door from the garage. Stepping into The Laurels, Mary's first impression was that Mr. West had already managed to put his own personal stamp on the place. A number of modern art paintings and prints hung on the walls, which she was quite sure were not part of the regular décor any more than the personal photos. Pictures of Anthony on the beach with his arm around a pretty girl. A picture of a much younger Anthony with a much younger Lord Pool, both wearing their Eton school uniforms. Another picture of them from around the same time period, dressed in doublets and hose—obviously, they'd both been participating in some sort of play. A picture taken in a nightclub with an adult Anthony and several other young gentlemen at a table being entertained by some sort of dancer wearing a sequined skirt and nothing on her chest except some very carefully placed jewelry.

Lastly, Mary noticed a picture of Anthony with a young lady whose coloring and features were such a match to his she could only be Harriet West, the sister. Mary examined that photo with especially marked interest. Brother and sister looked so much alike they could have been twins. Perhaps they were. But while some would argue whether Anthony West could be considered handsome or not, no one would deny that his sister was quite beautiful in a strange, unearthly way, like a remote star.

Mary found a packet of expensive cigarettes in the sitting room, and in the disorganized shambles of his bedroom closet unearthed a plush navy-blue dressing gown and put them both in a leather traveling case initialed A.W. The appointment book proved the most difficult to locate. It turned out to be on the bottom of a pile of building plans and engineering reports. There was a "D" listed with an address in Newcastle. That had to be Donald Harrington. Another entry was marked "H". Harriet, the sister in France. Mary was going to simply copy the contact information for Anthony's relatives but then decided to take the entire appointment book.

Anthony might have use for it. She also found an empty envelope, which she put in her pocket.

On the way out of the door, Mary remembered to grab the morning papers for Anthony. The headlines were all a-flutter over speculation that Edward VIII might abdicate the throne of England to marry Wallis Simpson. A passenger plane in Croydon had crashed, killing fifteen out of seventeen passengers. In less relevant news from abroad, there was the ongoing civil war in Spain, and they'd soon be awarding the Nobel prizes in Stockholm. Interestingly, one of the prize recipients was not in attendance. Famed German pacifist, Carl von Ossietsky, who had been nominated for his work in exposing secret German rearmament efforts, had been refused permission to travel by the Third Reich. Mary found the story interesting, though rather remote. What, after all, did German politics have to do with the United Kingdom?

Mary then returned to the garage and, with a pair of tweezers from her nurse's bag, she removed the single bit of thread she'd noticed and carefully placed it in the envelope she had taken from Anthony's desk before sealing it and stowing it away.

She went straight away to the local telegraph office and sent Harriet West a short message explaining her brother had just been in a very serious collision and she should come at once. She sent another message to Donald Harrington explaining his nephew had been in a crash but would pull through. There was no mention of attempted murder in the telegrams; better, Mary thought, to save that revelation for a face-to-face meeting. Rather than try to find a car, she used her motorbike to make the trip to the hospital. She drove her hardest, eager to see Anthony again and tell him what she'd learned. Upon entering the hospital, there was ostensibly a reception desk to sign in, but Mary didn't bother to do so, nor did the bored looking receptionist object or make any notice of her arrival. Mary ran through the crowded halls, nearly colliding with one unwary visitor, straight to Anthony's room. It was empty. She grabbed a harried-looking student nurse laden with a pile of freshly scrubbed bedpans.

"Excuse me," she asked, "Where's Mr. West?"

"Mr. who?" The trainee was distracted by the number of bedpans which were really more than one person could manage, but Matron had thrust them all on her anyway. If she dropped a single pan, then Matron would make her clean them all again, which was simply tyrannical and, given the bedpans' purpose, utterly ridiculous. Who cared if they touched the floor? They were all going to be pissed in, anyway! Life for a student nurse was quite hard enough, thank you, without perfect strangers coming in and interrogating you. She glared at Mary with undisguised animosity, but Mary didn't flinch.

"The patient," Mary said. The trainee looked bewildered. "A fellow with white-blond hair brought in last night from a car crash."

At that, the trainee showed recognition.

"Oh him! They took away his body not half an hour ago."

Chapter Five

"Body? They removed his body?" Mary stared back at the girl.

"Aye, miss. It's what the porters do around here when a patient dies," the student nurse explained as if she were addressing a not very bright child. Mary's lips tightened and her back involuntarily stiffened, but she managed to avoid saying anything insulting and stuck to the matter at hand.

"But how could he have died? I spoke to him only a few hours ago and he was fine!"

"Well, he must have took a turn for the worse, mustn't he? It does happen around here, you know." She looked at Mary sympathetically. "I know it's upsetting though. Was he a close friend of yours?"

"I'd never spoken to him before last night."

"Ah, then."

An awkward pause stretched out between them.

"Excuse me, but I have to talk to whichever doctor was on call when he died."

"That would be Dr. Huxley, miss."

It took some time for Mary to track down Dr. Huxley—a harried looking fellow with thinning hair and watery eyes.

"How did Mr. West die?" she demanded.

"From his injuries. He was in a car crash last night."

"I know he was in a car crash," Mary answered back with lips curled up over bared teeth. "In fact, I was there when it happened. But his injuries were not life threatening. The doctor on call last night, Dr. Roberts, said so. And I was just here speaking with Mr. West only a few hours ago, and while he was in a lot of pain, he was perfectly coherent and on the mend."

"Well, there was probably some internal damage that went unnoticed. There often is, you know," Dr. Huxley countered. "Bleeding on the brain and so forth. I've seen it happen before."

"Who was with him when he died?" Mary demanded.

"No one. He was quite alone when one of the nurses went to visit him on her rounds. She called me in to confirm he was deceased. From the looks of things, it had happened very shortly before she entered the room. The body hadn't had time to cool. At least you can take comfort that he didn't suffer."

Mary was not comforted at all but rather assumed an expression as if she'd eaten a raw lemon.

"Will there be an autopsy?" she asked.

Dr. Huxley looked as astonished as if she'd suggested a trip to the moon to find green cheese. "Why on earth would there be an autopsy?" he sputtered. "We all know how he was hurt."

"To make sure his death really was from the injuries he incurred last night."

"But of course he died from his prior injuries," the doctor protested. "What else could it have been?" It was to his immense shock that the harpy glaring at him answered.

"He might have been poisoned. Or suffocated."

The doctor's jaw dropped. "Are you saying you think Mr. West might have been murdered?"

"I *know* Mr. West was murdered. He was the victim of a saboteur." Mary spoke with resolute conviction. "The only question," she went on, "is whether his murderer finished him off in this hospital or not. Now, if you don't arrange for a medical examination of the body, you can be damned sure I will."

Something so resolute, so vehement, in the district nurse's manner and speech gave Dr. Huxley pause. Old maids were a notoriously stubborn and troublesome lot. And district nurses, in Dr. Huxley's experience, could be particularly troublesome—came from them having too much independence and responsibility over their patients. Really, in Huxley's opinion it would be better not to have Queen's nurses at all but rather keep nurses where they belonged—in hospitals, under the authority and guidance of doctors. Male doctors, of course. Still, the fact remained that he had to deal with this particular district nurse, and noting the resolve on Mary Grey's face, Dr. Huxley quailed. She was exactly the sort of woman, he thought dolefully, to petition Scotland Yard and make official complaints and even go crying to the papers. Easier to have a cursory examination now and put the whole matter to rest.

Much to her frustration, Mary was not allowed to be present for the medical examination of Anthony's body, nor would anyone tell her anything about what they'd found. Instead, she had nothing to do but visit the main wards, where one of the windows now sported a beautiful bouquet of orchids. Mary wondered which patient's family had sprung for that.

It soon became evident that someone conducting the medical exam had found something because there was a lot of anxious commotion within the hospital and a call was made to the Anchester Police Constabulary. Not long afterwards, Inspector Ames was conducting an interview with a mortified Dr. Huxley in his private office as to why the whole thing couldn't possibly be his fault.

"It's not like there were any visible signs of violence," he told Inspector Ames for the tenth time. "And it's a hospital! People die all the time. If we investigated every one of them, we'd hardly have time to treat the living."

Inspector Ames waited patiently for the doctor to catch his breath and said, "I understand, sir, it was a nurse who suspected foul play?"

"A district nurse," Dr. Huxley stressed. "She doesn't even work here, but she came in and started making the most awful fuss." He looked quite put out about it.

"Rather a good thing she did, though, wasn't it?" Inspector Ames noted. "Otherwise, we'd never have suspected foul play."

Dr. Huxley did not agree it was a good thing at all Mary had intervened. Oh, it wasn't that he thought murders should go undetected. Not exactly. But really, if Mary hadn't said anything, well, the hospital wouldn't be crawling with police right now and everyone could have been spared a lot of trouble, couldn't they? But Dr. Huxley could hardly share such opinions with Inspector Ames, who then requested to see Mary.

"Oh," added Ames, "and I'll be wanting to talk with the nurse privately too."

Agitated and not a little annoyed at being dismissed from his own office, Dr. Huxley left and was replaced by a tall, well-built young woman of about thirty who reminded Inspector Ames of a statue he'd once seen of the Virgin Mary. He eyed her with interest. Her eyes were grave but something in the jut of her chin and the way she held her shoulders spoke of resolution. She, in turn, saw a middle-aged man of average height, average build, with hair neither dark nor fair. He was in every sense a very ordinary, even forgettable, looking man, except for having a bushy mustache and extraordinarily watchful eyes. She seated herself on the edge of a chair, her back straight and stiff.

"I'm Inspector Ames. I was going to ask you—"

Mary interrupted him, "So, the medical examiner did find something." It wasn't a question. "You wouldn't be here otherwise."

"You understand I can't give out any details just yet," Inspector Ames began.

Mary waved her hand. "Yes, yes, of course. But you do know he was murdered, right?"

"It would appear so, yes," Inspector Ames said cautiously. "I was wondering, though, what made you arrive at that conclusion?"

Mary Grey gave a bitter smile. "Well now, inspector, we should probably go to the canteen. I have a rather long story for you."

They went to the canteen and over a pot of strong hot tea, Mary went through the whole story—to Inspector Ames's growing amazement. When she reached the part about entering the garage, it was his turn to interrupt her.

"Wait, you invaded the crime scene?" He gave her a stern look. "That could be construed as interfering with an investigation."

"Well, it hadn't been declared a crime scene, now had it?" Mary argued. "And the deceased had given me his express permission to enter."

"Legally, you may be covered, but I think we both know, Miss Grey, you acted inappropriately. But go on."

Mary continued telling the inspector her discoveries of how the bolt cutters appeared to have been used and the thread she found.

"Wait, do you have that?" he demanded.

"Yes, I do," she admitted. He wordlessly held out his hand and Mary quietly surrendered the envelope with the fiber. Oh well, she already knew what it looked like. She then returned to her narrative and carefully omitted any mention of Anthony West's appointment book, which lay in her bag, but finished with her return to the hospital and discovery of West's death.

"And the rest you know." Mary shrugged wearily. "Whoever cut the brakes learned Anthony was still alive and came back to finish the job, which wouldn't have been all that difficult. That bloody receptionist—pardon my language—clearly makes no effort to keep track of who comes and goes around here. And since Anthony was in a private room, all the killer would have needed was a few minutes alone with him and a pillow. He couldn't have put up any struggle with his ribs broken."

"What makes you assume he was suffocated?" Ames asked. "He may have been killed another way."

Mary looked scornful. "The only other way to kill him without visible signs of violence would be poison, and if it had been poison, they'd have had to do a full autopsy and examination of all his organs and then run samples to a lab to be sure. No, the speed they sent for you would only have happened if the medical examiner found evidence of suffocation, which wouldn't take nearly as long."

"Well deduced," Inspector Ames noted drily. "It's been an awfully eventful twenty-four hours for you, hasn't it?" He cupped his chin in reflection. "You seem to be taking it all rather calmly?" His curiosity as to Mary's views on the matter seemed genuine.

Mary thought for a moment and then answered. "I've seen beautiful young girls die from sticking wire inside themselves to rid them of unwanted babies. I've treated shell shocked soldiers from the Great War who attempted suicide. I met a man who lost his legs in a mining disaster but who still felt them itch. I've seen wives beaten half to death by their husbands. I treated a drunk lad of twenty who I'd no sooner bandaged up then to have him taken away in irons by the police. Said he'd bludgeoned a man to death. And that was just while at the Queen's Institute for training. I've seen a lot more since they put me in the field. So, no, I'm not shocked."

Inspector Ames raised an eyebrow. "You've certainly seen your share of drama then," he observed.

"You know," Mary reflected, "the older I get and the more I see of the world, the more I think so-called melodrama is, in fact, often the real state of things. With all due respect to Austen and other writers of her ilk, real life usually doesn't fit into tidy drawing rooms."

"It certainly doesn't." He gave a hearty laugh. "Well, well, I think I'm starting to get an idea, Miss Grey, as to why you were the one Mr. West turned to. However, your involvement in this matter ends now," Inspector Ames instructed her sternly, as a father would a wayward child. "Now, in detective stories, amateur investigators may be the norm, but in the real world, all they do is muck things up for us real police. I can't have you crawling around crime scenes and disturbing the evidence. It only complicates my investigation and possibly endangers you. Do you understand me?"

"I do."

"Then I want you to give me your word that from now on you'll keep out of the matter."

"You have it, sir."

Inspector Ames gave Mary a shrewd glance. "I'm going to hold you to that, you know. If I see any sign you've returned to the garage or Mr. West's home, I'll bring a load of trouble down on your head, young lady."

"Oh, I'm not going back to Mr. West's home. Have no worries there."

"Then you won't mind giving me the house keys he gave you?"

Without a word, Mary surrendered the keys into Inspector Ames's hands.

"Am I free to go?" she asked.

"For now," he replied. "I might have more questions for you later."

A thought occurred to Mary. It seemed on the surface outlandish, but it couldn't be dismissed, and she had to ask. "And will you be questioning Lord Pool as well? He was the last person to see Mr. West alive."

"Actually, he wasn't. Lord Pool left when one of the nurses came in to change the bedpan and give Mr. West a sponge bath. She was the last person to see him alive before the other nurse found him dead."

"Oh." Well, that certainly seemed to leave Lord Pool well out of the matter.

"Believe me, though," Inspector Ames continued, "everyone who had contact with Mr. West today will be questioned, just as you were."

Mary was at the door when she turned around. "Oh, one more thing, inspector."

"Yes?" he asked suspiciously.

"Mr. West had a sister who's abroad. I just wired her, telling her about the accident, but she won't know her brother's dead."

"I'll see to it she's properly notified." Inspector Ames waved Mary to go.

"There's an uncle as well—" Mary continued.

"Goodbye!" Inspector Ames literally ushered her out of the door, which Mary considered rather rude of him. There was nothing for her to do but ride her bike home. Curiously enough, while she hadn't felt any of her injuries riding to the hospital to speak to Anthony, she felt every single one of them riding back. Her muscles had lodged a mass protest and she dry popped some aspirin. More than anything, Mary wanted to go home, yet she took a detour to the telegraph office, aching all the way. She sent another message to Harriet West telling her that her brother was dead. No doubt, someone would have notified her anyway, but it still seemed like the right thing to do.

Upon her arrival home, she finally took the long-needed bath with Epsom salts. As she bathed, her eyes ran over her own cracked plaster walls, but she didn't see them. Instead, she replayed the events of the last twenty-four hours again and again in her mind. The accident. Her talk with Anthony and the fear she'd seen in his eyes. The garage. Dr. Huxley. Inspector Ames. She tried to think of what she could have done differently. What vital clues she might have missed. She spent so long brooding in the tub, by the time she got out the water was ice cold.

After drying herself off and dressing, Mary paced around the cold, empty cottage for a while, like a caged lion. Her mind raced with a thousand different thoughts. Ordinarily, she was quite fond of her little cottage, with its simple secondhand furnishings and homey feel. Oh, it might not have seemed like much to some, but after growing up in an overcrowded flat, Mary found having a place that was all hers to be paradise. The old stone and rafters gave the little home a storybook feel; you could imagine it being home to the three bears or Little Red Riding Hood's grandmother. She had grown attached to the faded cream-colored plaster on the walls, cracks and all. And the little stove had become a beloved friend. Mary had even, over the years, found a few items to dress it up. A worn shaggy rug. Warm-colored blankets. Even an old watercolor of the seaside. But tonight, this usually welcome retreat felt cold and claustrophobic. Finally, she couldn't stand to be alone any longer. Even though it was snowing once more, Mary had to get outside, and after arming herself with wellingtons, a coat, and a large muffler, she headed out of the door.

Mary's destination, The Mud Crab, also the village inn, lay at the opposite side of the village square. It wasn't her usual habit to visit there, but tonight she felt the need for company, for noise, and most of all, a good stiff drink. The Mud Crab's current owners, Mr. and Mrs. Jones, were an odd pairing. He was thin as a soda cracker and she was the shape of a watermelon. Local wags had dubbed them Jack Sprat and his wife behind their backs. Though mismatched in appearance, the Joneses were a happy couple, and The Mud Crab did good business. It was, in its way, an institution as venerated as the town church. It went back centuries, passing from owner to owner, and always the chief watering hole of Illhenny. The old stone walls were decorated with various detritus that had washed ashore on the local beaches over the years—shells, driftwood, sea glass, the skeleton of a shark. There was even a hundred-year-old Baker rifle mounted as well, brought back by an Illhenny boy who'd served in the Napoleonic Wars.

Mary spied Mr. Martin still in hiding from his family. At the sight of Mary, he started and looked wary, as if fearing the district nurse might tell him to return to his wife. It was to Mr. Martin's considerable relief that Mary didn't approach him. Nevertheless, he paid his bill early and resolved to find another place to spend the night.

Mary found a seat by the fireplace and ordered a quaff of local cider and some of Mrs. Jones's delicious Yorkshire pudding. After she finished dining, Mary rested her eyes a while, soaking in the warmth of the fire, the smell of tobacco smoke, and listened to bits of conversation trilling in the air.

"Have to get that propeller fixed. Cost a pretty penny or two."

"She stopped him from going over the cliff, but he died anyway."

"If the King does abdicate, Bertie's next in line, but he can barely get through a sentence without stuttering."

"Someone will have to claim the body. Doubt they're gonna bury him here."

"I told that bloody fool the sea air here would ruin the wood, but he went and did it anyway, and, sure enough, it's already starting to warp. Why they can't stick to good stone or plaster—" Mary recognized the last voice. Caleb Barnaby sat over in one corner, giving her a cheery wave, which after a moment's hesitation she returned.

Looking around The Mud Crab, Mary realized anyone in the room could be the culprit. She might at that very moment be dining with a murderer. It was a terrible thought that sickened her. She'd made a mistake coming here, she realized. She should go. *But go where?* Her cottage now seemed unbearably bleak and lonely and any other place she went to would be full of suspects as well. Well, at least any place in Illhenny. Perhaps she could apply for a transfer? Move somewhere where she wouldn't have to be constantly on alert that she was living near a murderer. But murders could happen anywhere. And besides, to move would be a cowardly dereliction of duty on her part.

She was a district nurse. She didn't run from problems. She faced them head-on and tried to help. That's what she would do here as she squared her shoulders and jutted out her chin. She thought of her promise to Inspector Ames, but she'd promised Anthony first, hadn't she? For whatever reason, Anthony West had pleaded for her help in resolving the matter. Didn't that create some sort of obligation on her to at least try? She thought it did. It was perhaps curious for her to care so deeply when she'd known Anthony so briefly, but there was no denying the fact that Mary had been drawn into this affair, willingly or not, and she was now bound to see it through.

Oh, she'd keep her word in one sense—she wouldn't return to Anthony's home or garage. There was nothing she could do there anyway. But what she could do was keep her eyes and ears open and, in that, she thought to herself, she might even have an advantage over Inspector Ames. After all, she was familiar with the village. And a district nurse knows things about her community that even a policeman does not. She left The Mud Crab that night with new resolve in her step. One way or another, Anthony's killer would be brought to justice.

Chapter Six

Mary was awakened in the middle of the night by the ringing of the telephone. After considerable groaning, she managed to get up, put on her slippers, run downstairs, and, in a state of semi-consciousness, answer the phone. The message was brief. Mrs. Wilberforce had gone into labor a couple of weeks early and they needed Mary to come over immediately to help with the delivery. The Wilberforces already had three sons, and this would be their fourth child. Mary struggled into the one remaining uniform she had and was off on her bike. Next chance she got, she'd have to have it cleaned and pressed. Midnight calls and visits like these were not at all unusual for her, and as she rode through drifts of snow, she tried to clear her head of any remaining effects of the ale she'd drunk earlier. By the time she reached the Wilberforce house, she felt she was alert and sober enough to handle anything in the usual run of things.

"Where is she?" These were the first words out of her mouth when she saw Mr. Wilberforce.

"Upstairs. Second door on the left," he answered her. He wiped sweat off his brow.

A bloodcurdling sound like an animal caught in a trap came from above and Mary galloped up the steps. Mrs.

Wilberforce was a woman in her thirties with features now distorted by pain. She lay covered in sweat on a double bed, blankets and sheets all over the room. Once by Mrs. Wilberforce's side, Mary quickly established that the woman was fully dilated and having contractions less than a minute apart. Delivery would be very soon.

"What's wrong with Mum?" Mary turned and saw three young boys watching her from the hall. Their father was immediately behind them and, much to Mary's relief, he shooed them away. Mary returned to holding Mrs. Wilberforce's hand and urging her to keep pushing while she writhed in labor pains. Mercifully, the baby popped out quite suddenly with the placenta wrapped around it. In fact, it was so quick and smooth, Mary privately wondered if she'd even been needed at all. Mary cut the umbilical cord and then bathed the newborn and swaddled her as Mrs. Wilberforce lay flat in a state of utter exhaustion.

"It's a girl," she told Mrs. Wilberforce. "A beautiful, healthy baby girl!"

"A girl?" Mrs. Wilberforce whispered. At the news she seemed to come to life and even attempted to sit up a bit. "Oh, do let me see," she pleaded. Mary happily handed the newborn over to the still tired but now engaged mother, who carefully checked her child's sex and then gave a contented sigh.

"Three boys, one after another, but now, finally, a girl," she proclaimed. "At last, I can move into the spare bedroom and always be too tired for Tom. I have a baby doll to dress in pretty clothes, a faithful companion for my middle years, and a devoted nurse for my old age." Mrs. Wilberforce looked utterly pleased with herself as she delivered the speech, but Mary found herself feeling sorry for the little creature who would be raised with such a cross to bear. She also wondered if Mrs. Wilberforce had taken into account the possibility her daughter might marry and start a family of her own. Perhaps she planned to forbid it.

Then, of course, Mary had to deal with the soiled bed linens and disposing of the afterbirth. By the time she'd completed everything at the Wilberforce house, it was nearly dawn. Hardly worth going back to the cottage, but not yet time for her to begin her usual daily rounds. Instead, she went into the Wilberforce kitchen, put a kettle on the stove, began toasting bread, and frying up eggs and bacon. One by one, the Wilberforce sons and then their father all made their way downstairs to join her, having been lured by the sounds and smells of breakfast, and they all had a merry feast, punctuated with an occasional baby cry from the upstairs.

"Well, boys," Mr. Wilberforce told his sons around the table. "You now have a little sister. Her name's Lydia."

"But I don't want a little sister!" objected Brian, the eldest boy.

His brothers murmured their agreement, with middle boy Jack proclaiming, "Girls are silly!"

"Now, now, you know your mother's been wanting a girl for some time now. Indeed, there may be even more girls in the future. Or maybe another brother."

Fat chance of that, Mary thought, given Mrs. Wilberforce's plans, but she wisely held her tongue. After all, Mrs. Wilberforce might change her mind.

After finishing breakfast and leaving behind a lot of pamphlets on infant care that Mary suspected would go unread, it was time to visit Caleb Barnaby. It was a remarkably fine day—blue skies, white snow, and not too chilly. If she hadn't any murder to investigate, it would have put her in a cheerful mood, perhaps whistling a Christmas carol or two. As it was, though, Mary found it damned difficult to muster any sort of Yuletide spirit as she rapped on Barnaby's door. She had to knock several times before he answered, and when he did, he bore a large purple mark on his face.

"What happened?" Mary demanded.

"Tripped on me way home from The Mud Crab last night."

"I must say I was surprised to see you at The Mud Crab last night."

"Didn't know you were there either."

"I needed to get out last night."

"Hmph. Likely story. You've got some nerve telling me not to go out drinking, I tell you!"

"Well, I'm not the one with the face of a boxer, now am I?" Mary retorted crisply.

"It's nothing that a little whiskey won't cure!" Caleb philosophized and Mary rolled her eyes.

"I think it's better we get some solid food into you." At the mention of feeding, Ahab's ears perked up and he rose to attention.

Being free of any appointments after Caleb, Mary decided the rest of the day would be the perfect time to catch up on errands and social visits around the village and see what she could find out. First, however, she examined Anthony's appointment book. Much to her disappointment, she couldn't find anything that seemed the least bit sinister. It was all perfectly normal business, with only one entry that wasn't entirely mundane. About a week before the accident, Anthony had scribbled in *Take delivery. Mellors and Tania.* Now, that was puzzling. She knew of no one in Illhenny by the name of Mellors or Tania. Acquaintances from London perhaps? She put the information in the vault of her mind before stepping out.

She stopped first at the grocer, where she ran into Mrs. Simpson.

"Miss Grey." Mrs. Simpson's face lined with worry. "How are you holding up?"

"I'm perfectly fine," Mary assured her. Physically at least, it was true.

After putting in her order, she then proceeded to the baker, the butcher, the general store, and the local postmistress.

Mary purchased a couple of fairy cakes from the baker and asked if she might eat them on the premises. The large broad-boned baker, Verna Porter, readily agreed and as Mary nibbled on her first cake, she brought up the topic of Anthony West.

"No, Mr. West never came in here," Verna sniffed as she patted flour off her apron. "Suppose our rolls and seed cake wasn't good enough after what he'd had in London."

"And I don't suppose you've heard anything about him since he's been in town?" Mary asked.

"What do you think I am, a gossip?" Verna looked indignant.

"No, I just wondered—"

"Not like me to go around passing stories about people! Though, mind you," Verna leaned over and whispered conspiratorially, "Mr. West got some stories told about him. So's even I couldn't help but hear a few of them. Even though I'd never repeat anything."

"I see."

"Seems West knew all sorts of wrong 'uns in London."

"Wrong 'uns?" Mary asked.

"Fast folk," Verna explained. "London folk. Flashy folk with too much money. All wild types, always partying—even some artists and the theater crowd. And we all know what artists and theater people are, don't we?" Verna paused expectantly, so Mary gave a knowing "Ah." In fact, Mary didn't know what artists and theater people were, since she'd never met any and she doubted very much Verna had either. In fact, on reflection, Mary thought it might be interesting to meet some of them, but she didn't say that to Verna.

"Cocaine sniffers and perverts, the lot of them!" Verna scowled. "Not to say anything against his Lordship, but, well, he wasn't so careful in his choice of friends. Few men in his position are, are they these days?" She sighed and shook her head at the fallen state of the world.

Illhenny's butcher, Mr. Robinson, didn't look the part. Butchers are supposed to be beefy, heavyset men with ruddy complexions, but John Robinson was tall and lean as a picket, with skin so sallow it appeared he lived underground. No one could deny he was a good butcher, though, who could carve up a carcass quicker than anyone, and who, miraculously, had never once been caught putting his thumb on the scale. When Mary went to see him, he was chopping up an old ram for mutton and humming *I Saw Three Ships Come Sailing In*.

"Mr. West? All I knew about him was he liked sausages and steaks," Mr. Robinson declared, not looking up from his bloody work. "And he paid promptly. I'll give him that. Sometimes it's rich folk who put you off the longest for the bill. Look at the hall. They keep me waiting sometimes longer than anyone. By the way, Nurse Grey, could I interest you in buying some of this sheep's stomach? It's nice and fresh. Give you a good deal."

"It sounds good, but I'm afraid I never have the time to cook haggis."

Mary's next stop was the general store. As she walked in, a bell on the door pealed loudly and she saw Dick Townley in overalls, having a heated discussion with Purvis the clerk.

"Come on, lad, you know I'm good for it," Townley wheedled, but Purvis remained stone faced.

"I'm sorry Mr. Townley, but Mr. Harley's instructions were clear. I'm to give you no further credit until you pay your last outstanding bill."

"Now listen," Townley growled, but Purvis remained impassive.

"Furthermore, I'm to tell you that if you don't pay your bill with us soon, we will be forced to get the law involved in the matter."

Townley spent the next thirty seconds cursing Purvis, the store's owner, Mr. Harley, Mr. Harley's wife, his entire extended family, and British shopkeepers in general, before storming out of the store, making sure to slam the door as loudly as possible, which only served to make the bells peal all the more merrily.

Only then did Mary speak. "Funny, I saw Townley arguing with Mr. Legge the other day about an unpaid bill there as well."

"For a man on a gamekeeper's salary, Townley's inordinately fond of horse racing," the clerk told her. "There's no one in Illhenny who'll give him any credit anymore, and he won't be getting any pay raise from his Lordship either. He'll have to be catching his own food for a while."

"Ah." Interesting news, but, sadly, it wasn't going to be of any relevance to Mary's current investigation. She could at least enjoy being in the store. Always a hodgepodge of overfilled shelves, it was now bedecked with fake holly and tinsel, and an overwhelming smell of oranges and cloves perfumed the air. She carefully selected a fresh box of tea and some brightly painted cards of Father Christmas with a pine tree over his shoulder to send to various friends and family. Then Mary went on to purchase stamps from Postmistress Ferrars—a white-haired, pink-faced lady who was happy to talk, but could offer no news. Anthony had received plenty of mail from London, but Mrs. Ferrars had never seen anything from a "Tania" or "Mellors."

In growing frustration, Mary took a truly desperate step. She called on Dahlia Winthrop, who eagerly invited her in for tea, which they had in the stuffy parlor of the vicarage where every piece of furniture seemed to date back to the era of Queen Victoria. Needlework patterns hung on the wall, and Mary recognized one particularly intricate pattern as the handiwork of Mrs. Simpson. Mary had to admit the tea itself was quite good; it was served with milk and sugar, on delicate blue-and-white china. She was also offered an assortment of biscuits.

"My dear, it's just too, too awful!" Dahlia was practically panting with excitement as Mary nibbled on a chocolate biscuit. "Do you know the police have visited Anthony West's home and dusted for prints?"

"No!" Mary feigned shock, and Dahlia went on with relish.

"They're actually investigating the whole matter as a murder! Mind you, it's not so surprising, is it? What with the young man being from London and having such loose morals. Now, I'm not one for gossip—"

"Of course not," Mary assured her.

"But I happen to know for a fact that the young man had overnight visits from at least two separate women."

"No!"

Dahlia smiled and took another sip. "Oh yes! One of them had shockingly blonde hair that must have been bleached."

Mary instantly identified the unknown blonde as Harriet West.

"The other was a dark-haired little minx, with lips and fingernails painted bright rouge."

That one Mary couldn't guess the identity of. She filed it as a piece of information to track down later, possibly through Mr. West's appointment book.

"Now," Dahlia continued, "a young man who conducts his personal affairs so liberally is bound to get into trouble, don't you think?" She didn't wait for an answer but rambled on. "Perhaps he was killed by some girl he'd cast off? Or a jealous husband? Someone might have tracked him here from London!"

Mary had already considered this notion and privately discarded it. There was almost no chance any outsider could have come into Illhenny without being noticed. Dahlia's next words, though, were more germane.

"And he may have started making conquests here as well."

"Really?" Anthony had not mentioned any local romances to Mary when discussing suspects. Perhaps he hadn't wanted to talk about his private life. Mary could certainly understand that.

"Oh yes!" Dahlia's voice dropped down an octave. "Rosie Legge."

Mary's astonishment was quite unfeigned, and Dahlia beamed in satisfaction.

"Where do you get that from?"

"It seems Mr. West was a regular visitor at their tobacco store. Always in and out."

"Well, he did smoke," Mary pointed out.

"True, but he was observed on one occasion talking to Mrs. Legge quite animatedly and for rather a long time as well. Now, what I ask you could someone like Mr. West have had to discuss with someone of Mrs. Legge's station in life?" Dahlia paused significantly. "You know, I always thought Ronald Legge a fool, marrying a wife so many years his junior. More tea, dear? Oh, and did you hear about Thomas Rigby?"

"No, what?"

"Mrs. Rigby caught Thomas behind the butcher shop exchanging all sorts of dirty books and pictures with some other boys." Dahlia looked to Mary, eager for exclamations of shock and dismay, which Mary did her best to satisfy. Thus encouraged, she went on. "His mother boxed his ears red and exiled him to his room for the rest of the holiday, but he still wouldn't tell her where he got the nasty things. Probably picked them up at Eton, I'd say. Just another one of today's youth being corrupted. Indeed, I've told my husband it should be the subject of his next sermon." Then Dahlia went into a recitation of the various other misdeeds committed by her neighbors, until Mary pleaded an appointment.

Fortified with refreshments and new information, Mary was determined to make a visit to the Legges' shop. It was a tidy little place, and besides the predictable smell of tobacco, she noticed a definite aroma of wood polish in the air as well.

"Miss Grey," Rosie Legge greeted Mary with a puzzled frown. There were bags under her eyes as if she'd had trouble sleeping. "I didn't know you smoked. Don't get many women in this shop."

"I'm looking for a Christmas present for my father," Mary lied with ease. "Is there anything you'd recommend?"

"Well, we have some Virginians over here." Mrs. Legge began showing Mary various kinds of cigarettes and tobacco. Mary was wondering how to broach the topic of Anthony West when Mrs. Legge unexpectedly did it for her.

"They say you were there the night Mr. West crashed his car?"

"I was," Mary answered cautiously. "I also saw him the next day at the hospital." Mary tried to gauge Mrs. Legge's reactions. The woman had something on her mind and was clearly trying to decide whether to speak or not. Unfortunately, they were then interrupted by Mr. Legge.

"What's your business here?" he asked Mary abruptly.

"She's looking for—" Rosie began, but her husband cut her off.

"I asked her, not you," he retorted, and fixed baleful eyes on Mary.

"I'm looking for a present for my father. As a man, what would you suggest?"

"A box of Canaries," he answered her right away and grabbed a box. "I'll ring you up right now."

The price of the Canaries seemed steep, but it clearly wasn't the time to haggle. Mary paid for her purchase and exited the shop with Mr. Legge's eyes following her. Once she was outside, she had a last look through the window and the sight shocked her. Mrs. Legge's eyes were wide, and her mouth was drawn in an expression of absolute terror.

Chapter Seven

Mary returned to her cottage with overpriced cigarettes she had no use for and more questions than ever. She carefully examined Anthony's appointment book. There were references to meetings with someone identified only with the letter "L." *Possibly assignations with Mrs. Legge?* If there had been an affair, then that could be motive for murder. It was the best lead she'd come across so far. It would certainly go a long way toward explaining Mrs. Legge's look of terror. *Is she perhaps being abused by her husband?* Mary hadn't seen any visible bruises but, of course, sometimes men were smart enough to leave the face alone. If only she could have had a chance to examine the rest of Mrs. Legge's body. *Maybe I could try to offer to perform a physical examination?*

A knock at the door interrupted all such speculations. Usually, this signified a family member of a patient wanting her to come somewhere right away. *Complications perhaps with Mrs. Wilberforce?* Mary sighed and automatically reached for her coat, but to her shock, the person standing outside her door was none other than Harriet West. Her eyes were puffy, and her hair was disheveled, unlike the perfect coif she'd worn in the pictures, but it was definitely her.

"Are you Nurse Grey?" she asked in the same upper class accent her brother had. "The one who tried to help my brother?"

"I am," Mary answered quietly. "Come in before you freeze." She directed Harriet to sit in the more comfortable of the two chairs in the cottage's main room, and then put on a kettle. While waiting for the tea to brew, Mary examined Harriet more closely.

Harriet West was a very smartly turned-out girl. Her dress and jacket both looked like they'd come straight from the couture houses of Paris, and the look was completed with silk stockings and high heels of Italian leather that were now getting a bit muddy. Her hair was pinned with sparkling silver clips that matched her earrings. Mary also noted she had eyebrows a quarter of the size of what eyebrows naturally are. *That must take some careful pruning.* Her nails were expertly manicured, and her perfume—well, Mary thought her London scent nice enough, but what Harriet wore was on another level altogether. If past the pearly gates in Paradise there were an exclusive department store for angels and that store had a signature perfume, it would be the one Harriet West was wearing. To have such a person in Mary's little cottage seemed as improbable as seeing a marble statue in a bog. For the first time ever, Mary felt self-conscious about her humble living quarters, even if Harriet herself didn't seem to notice. She gave Harriet the best of her tea mugs and took a chipped one for herself. Harriet wordlessly accepted the tea and took a sip. As she did, she made a face.

"Sorry, but do you have anything stronger on hand?" she asked Mary.

“Not here,” Mary replied, “but I know somewhere we can go.”

Half an hour later they were seated at a private table in The Mud Crab. Harriet looked even more out of place in The Mud Crab than she had in Mary’s home, and almost every head turned to gawk. Harriet didn’t appear to notice, or perhaps she was simply used to being the center of attention. They found a table in the corner with dim lighting. After ascertaining that The Mud Crab didn’t serve champagne or any of the usual cocktails to be found in London, Harriet settled on ordering a classic scotch and soda while Mary put in a request for a good ale. As Mrs. Jones went to fetch their orders, Harriet pulled out an engraved cigarette case and lighter. Mary swiped an ashtray from a neighboring table.

“Mind if I smoke?” she asked and tried to light a cigarette before Mary could answer. Mary noted Harriet’s hands trembling. It took her several tries to successfully light her cigarette.

“Thank you,” Mary said to Mrs. Jones as she set down their drinks. “Oh, and I’ll take some supper as well. What about you?” she asked Harriet.

“I don’t really feel hungry, but I should probably eat something. I haven’t had a bite since this morning.”

“Bring her supper too,” Mary instructed Mrs. Jones, who was lurking at the side of the table.

The publican’s wife was clearly curious as to the identity of this fashionable outsider and why she was with Mary Grey. In fact, Mary’s presence was also unusual. Ordinarily, the district nurse might visit The Mud Crab once a month at most. To see her there twice in one week was unheard of. And her companion! Except for her puffy eyes, Harriet West could have stepped out of the society pages of a London paper. Illhenny almost never saw the likes of her at all, much less witnessed such a lady having a close conference with the district nurse. So, Mrs. Jones hovered around like a vulture circling a carcass. Mary first tried coughing and then became more direct.

"That'll be all for now, Mrs. Jones. Until the food, of course." Mrs. Jones did not try to hide her disappointment at being deprived of a taste of carrion. After she'd left, Mary turned to Harriet. "I'm so sorry about your brother. I didn't know Anthony very long, but what I saw of him I quite liked."

"Thank you," Harriet answered quietly, "and thank you for trying to save him."

Mary squirmed in her chair. "I didn't do much," she protested.

"From what I hear, you did," Harriet retorted.

"Well, it didn't do him much good in the end." Mary's tone was bitter.

Harriet, Mary noted, smoked a different brand from her brother. She also noticed Harriet's beautiful hands and her elegant, swan-like neck. Idly, Mary wondered what such a sophisticated beauty like Miss West would look like having an orgasm—not that she was ever likely to find out, but it was still an interesting question. *Does a woman like Harriet West even have orgasms?* You wouldn't think it to look at her; she seemed so cool and elegant. But Mary had found appearances could be deceiving on that score.

Between puffs of smoke, Harriet spoke. "When I got your wire about the accident, I came straight away by the first train. It wasn't until I reached the hospital that I learned I was already too late—and Anthony was dead. No one at the hospital would meet my eye, and then I had to talk to this police inspector, who asked me all these questions but refused to explain why. He just said the investigation was 'ongoing.'" She looked Mary directly in the eye. "I didn't know what to do, so finally I decided to call on you. Firstly, to thank you for what you did, but also because I wanted to know if you could tell me anything." Harriet's eyes pleaded with Mary's. Mary inwardly debated the matter. Certainly, Inspector Ames wouldn't want her sharing information, but it wasn't as if she were taking his wishes to heart anyway, was it? And Harriet deserved the truth.

"Anthony was murdered," Mary replied steadily.

Harriet sucked in a sudden gasp. "I knew it! I knew it! They wouldn't have been making so much commotion if it had just been a simple accident. But how..." Mrs. Jones had returned with their food and hovered within earshot.

"Not now. After we've eaten," Mary instructed Harriet. "You're going to need your strength. We both are. Thank you, Mrs. Jones!" Mary gestured for her to leave, which the older woman did, sulking. After Mary and Harriet had finished dining, Mary proceeded to tell Harriet everything. Harriet kept interrupting with questions and commentary but, eventually, Mary finished the tale. The dishes were cleared away and both women requested another round of drinks. Mrs. Jones did not need to be reminded again to leave. Apparently, she'd resigned herself to having to resort to the village grapevine for further information. Or maybe she thought she already had enough news to dine on for the days ahead.

Once she was gone, Mary handed Harriet the appointment book and asked her about the entries for "L." As Harriet flipped through the pages, Mary studied her wrists. Harriet's pale coloring and almost translucent skin made the blue lines of her veins all the more prominent. Mary remembered having heard somewhere that the phrase "blue blood" originally came from members of the nobility having marble-like complexions that made their veins visible in stark contrast to the tanned skin of those toiling in the sun. Now times had changed and many a working man was shut inside all day while a person blessed with money spent their time sunbathing. Intellectually, Mary knew all these things. But there was no denying the sense of something extraordinarily, well, Patrician about Harriet, whether she had a title or not. Maybe it was her expensive wardrobe but any number of women in equally fine clothing wouldn't have made the same impression as Harriet. Was it her excellent bone structure that made Harriet seem so special? Or the way she held herself? Mary made a conscious effort to stop herself from thinking all these silly thoughts and turned back to the matter of the murder and the identity of the mystery "L."

"Do you think it could have been Mrs. Legge?" Mary asked.

"No," Harriet replied promptly. "'L' stood for Laura Larrimor." At Mary's inquisitive glance, Harriet expanded, "A friend of ours who lives in London. She and Anthony were on very close terms."

"How can you be so sure?" Mary wondered.

"The dates! See, Anthony marked 'L' down two weekends ago when, I know for a fact, Laura came to visit him. Also, you'll see 'L' is a feature long before my brother ever came to this blasted place."

"Dahlia seemed sure Anthony was flirting with Mrs. Legge."

"Well, he very well might have been." Harriet gave a wry smile. "My brother did enjoy being the center of female attention. I wouldn't put it past him to have had an affair with a married woman and just have left it out of his appointment book."

"Which means, for now, the Legges stay on the suspect list," Mary observed. "What about this one?" She pointed to the reference to *Mellors and Tania.*

"I've no idea. I've never heard of either one of them. Maybe they had something to do with the resort project?"

"Maybe." Mary was doubtful. If Anthony had been meeting with other parties involved with the resort project inside Illhenny it almost certainly would have been talked about. Of course, even the arrival of two strangers like the enigmatic Mellors or Tania would have been noteworthy in Illhenny. It was, Mary thought, frightfully frustrating.

"And who was that one man, Bernard or something, who Anthony was afraid of?" Harriet asked.

"Barnaby. Caleb Barnaby."

"I'd like to look into him as well." Her lips tightened. "Maybe you can arrange an interview?"

Mary didn't care for the idea. First, she had trouble picturing Barnaby as a cold-blooded murderer, and second, she wasn't sure it'd be wise for Harriet to personally speak to any suspects. Things could get heated and overwrought. She quickly thought of a way around it.

"As it happens, I'll be visiting him tomorrow on my nursing rounds. I'll find a way to bring up Anthony and gauge his reactions. I could also try to find out his whereabouts at the time Anthony was suffocated."

Harriet blew a long stream of smoke. "Very well. While you're doing that, I'll see what I can dig up on my own. Maybe ask around the hospital. Even if the receptionist and logbook is useless, someone else might have observed people coming and going."

"Good," Mary said. "I'm sure Mrs. Jones could put you up for the night."

"I'd rather not stay here," Harriet mused drily as she looked around at all the natives in the room gawking at her.

"Understandable. I may not have a proper guest room, but I do have a spare cot," Mary suggested.

"It's very kind of you to offer," Harriet cut in, "but Edgar has already invited me to stay with him. In fact, I should probably call him now, to have his chauffeur give me a ride."

Of course, Mary remembered, Harriet was set to become the next Lady Pool. Naturally, she'd stay in the home of her intended. Mary was surprised and irritated by her own disappointment. Had she really been taking a fancy to the mourning relative of a murder victim she was trying to avenge? Perhaps she'd been on a dry spell too long. She walked home from The Mud Crab to spend another night in bed alone. In her dreams, Mary saw Harriet's elegant, manicured hands, and her long, sylph-like neck.

Chapter Eight

The next day at Caleb Barnaby's, Mary wondered how to bring up the topic of Anthony West when, to her surprise, Caleb brought it up for her.

"Heard you've been dining with the late Mr. West's sister."

"How did y—"

"Mrs. Jones told me," he answered. The virtues of living in a small village, where everyone always knew everyone else's business. "From what Mrs. Jones tells me, I gather the sister's quite a looker. A far cry from her brother, may he rest in peace." Caleb made the sign of the cross and tried to impersonate a decent, godly citizen. He wasn't especially successful.

"Actually, I think Harriet looks remarkably like Anthony," Mary replied. "They have the same coloring, for instance."

"Ah well, women look better with fair hair and skin than men do," Caleb opined. "On us men, it just makes us look like nancy boys. West certainly looked like one. Or maybe it was his clothes. Or maybe it was just the way he pranced about like Little Lord Fauntleroy."

"It sounds as though you didn't like Anthony." Mary wondered if she was being too direct, but Caleb Barnaby was not a man to take easy offense.

"Wondering if I done him in?" He laughed. "Ah, don't look so shocked. Inspector Ames has already been around asking questions, and I tell you what I told him. I didn't care for young West, but I had nothing to do with killing him. And any man who says I did is a damned liar!" Caleb spoke vehemently, with true conviction. In fact, his raised voice was enough to stir Ahab to open his eyes and survey the room warily.

"But you were angry with him at the meeting," Mary noted.

"Aye, I got a bit hot under the collar," Caleb admitted. "Mebbe I said a few things I shouldn't have, but you must understand, Illhenny's me home. I've lived here all my life, just like my father, his father, and his father before him."

"I've met more than a few residents who go back several generations. In fact, some of the people here seem to go back centuries."

"Aye! The people here have roots that burrow into the rocks themselves. Saltwater runs in our veins." Caleb demonstrated what had been a hitherto buried sense of the poetic. "And what that young lad was proposing was going to ruin it all."

"Some might have thought the new money and jobs would be a good thing," Mary proposed, "especially with the whole country in such a slump."

Caleb waved his hand. "Oh, it'd have brought in new money all right, but at what price? I'd take the slump any day. We've had hard times before and we still survived. But this could have destroyed Illhenny's soul!"

"Don't you think you're being a touch melodramatic?"

Caleb shook his head darkly. "You know how it is when these big developments go in. First off, they tear up the land, and the construction lasts for months—all that noise. Then the village shops all become quaint and cozy, selling the sort of souvenir rubbish the Londoners want. All the bother from swimmers and sunbathers starts scaring away the fish. Worst of all, the tourists and rich folks wanting to buy summer places come in and they kick all the old timers out. Illhenny would have become like all the other wretched tourist traps out there."

Mary had nothing to say to this. Every word Caleb spoke was true. It had happened and was happening in villages all over the coast. England was turning from a land with some of the most beautiful countryside in the world to a land overrun by suburban housing and roadside signs for Bovril. Caleb started coughing, and Mary fetched him a mug of tea.

"Perhaps I was a bit hard on the young fop," he admitted. "After all, him being from London, he weren't like to understand. It's Lord Pool who should have known better." His expression turned grim. "Him and his family been here for centuries. Now, his father, that were a man who respected tradition. He'd turn over in his grave if he knew what his son had planned. But the young Lord, well he's got expensive tastes, and the rents we tenants pay aren't enough. He wants more. Has his heart set on this project, he does." Caleb's mouth gave a bitter turn like he was biting into a lemon. "His Lordship will just find another architect. Hell, he's probably started looking already. And that's why you can be damn sure I didn't kill Mr. West. Because even I know it wouldn't have changed nothing." He sipped his tea and grumbled, "What is it with ye nurses and tea?"

"The warm liquid will do you good," Mary told him.

"Bollocks it will!"

Mary remained unruffled. "Maybe some broth or soup for you as well."

"Worse than nannies, ye nurses are! You lot are like nuns without the damn habits," Caleb grumbled.

"Actually, a lot of nurses over the years have been nuns. In fact, they were among the first recruits for the Red Cross."

"Doesn't surprise me one bit," Caleb retorted. "Nothing that would appeal more to God botherers than a chance to boss poor men and tell them it was all for their own good." But he quickly finished his tea and polished off his broth as well, complaining all the while about being fed like a child.

After her visit with Caleb, the rest of Mary's day was uneventful. She called on people down with the flu, counseled expectant mothers, and removed fishing hooks from the arms of careless fisherman.

Mary had just walked into her cottage when the phone rang. She sighed. She'd been hoping to get an early start on bed. *What is it this time? Another labor? An outbreak of measles?* She answered the phone and tried not to show the weariness in her voice.

"Mary?" It was Harriet West. "Oh, thank God. I've been trying to reach you since this morning! Do you never pick up the phone?"

"Only when I'm home. It's been a busy day," she explained.

"I have some news, Mary, and I have to see you again. The sooner, the better. Do you think you could come around tomorrow, maybe for tea?"

"I don't really get formal tea breaks."

"Well, what about after you finish your rounds? You can dine with us."

"Us?"

"Lord Edgar and me," Harriet explained.

"You want me to dine at Avenel Court?" It was as unlikely as a pig being asked to join the Sunday service.

"Yes. You do know where it is, don't you?"

"Yes, I'm familiar with the place." Mary didn't mention that the only time she'd been on the grounds of the property was to treat a gardener with pneumonia, and even then, she'd never entered the Great House itself.

"Good, see you tomorrow then, around eight o' clock." Harriet hung up.

It was only then Mary realized she had no fine frocks to wear to Avenel Court. Her mother had more than a few times dropped broad hints that Mary should stock up on a pretty dress or two "just in case," but Mary had never got around to it. Oh well, if she was just dining with Harriet, it really wouldn't matter. Well just her, Harriet, and Lord Pool but it wasn't as if his Lordship was likely to expect much from a district nurse. Assuming he even looked at her at all.

Well, maybe it did matter. Mary begrudgingly had to admit to herself she was not indifferent to Harriet's opinion of her appearance. She would like to show Harriet she could look nice when she put the effort into it. *But what good will it do anyway?* For someone of Mary's means, to try to appear chic or posh to someone like Harriet West was as ridiculous as a plain brown sparrow trying to impress a scarlet macaw. Nor was there any reason to think Harriet was the least bit interested in Mary in the first place. Indeed, she'd probably be horrified by the very idea. No, Mary realized with a touch of regret, there was no point in dressing up at all.

Chapter Nine

Mary had not wanted to risk being late to dine at Avenel Court and, in consequence, she arrived somewhat early, getting a curious glance from Dick Townley, the gamekeeper. As a girl, Mary had once been honored to visit the house of a Colonel Davies, the local squire, with her mother. Mary had always been impressed with the Davies' beautiful Georgian home. Avenel Court, though, made the Davies' mansion appear a hovel.

Avenel Court was considered one of the finest examples of Jacobean architecture in England, and it had been built on the scale of a palace. Lord Pool's ancestor, the first Earl of Illhenny, had nearly gone bankrupt building it and had, in fact, turned to embezzlement of court funds at one point before being forced to retire to his country estate in disgrace. Nevertheless, whatever chicanery had gone into building it, no one could deny the beauty of the building itself, influenced by French and Flemish designs, or the grandeur of the gardens. It was all very impressive, but Mary was more preoccupied with the ominous sight of gathering clouds.

Mary was greeted at the main entrance by a butler and maid. At that moment, her nose was red and starting to drip a bit. She hurriedly wiped it on her sleeve.

"The servant's entrance is around about that way," said the butler with the sort of elocution the King himself might have envied.

"What?"

"The servant's entrance... I assume you're delivering something?" the butler intoned.

"No, actually, I was invited to dine here."

Both the butler and maid looked askance. Clearly, guests to Avenel Court did not typically arrive on a motorbike. And while Mary had dressed cleanly and presentably, it was clear from a glance she wasn't the sort his Lordship usually entertained.

"I'm a friend of, well, an acquaintance, actually, of Harriet West's," Mary explained.

"One moment, please." The butler departed, and the maid's stare prompted Mary to try to comb her hair with her fingers.

A few minutes later, Harriet West was there. Her eyes were still red, but her smile was genuine, and she greeted Mary with warmth. Something in her demeanor gave Mary the impression she'd been at the cocktails earlier in the evening.

"Come in, Miss Grey! Come in and warm up."

"What should I do with my bike?" Mary asked.

"She can just leave it there by the door, can't she?" Harriet addressed the butler and didn't wait for an answer, but rather beckoned Mary to come in. And Mary did, indeed, just leave her bike by the door.

She now stood in a great room, which could fit three or four of her cottages. Massive stone works, vaulted ceilings, and, of course, a grand staircase. Her involuntary shiver as she walked in suggested that Avenel Court had either not adopted central heating or it was not at present turned on. Harriet saw the shiver.

"Now, Spode," Harriet ordered, "go and fetch Miss Grey a hot toddy, will you? In fact, bring me one as well. We'll be in the library."

Somehow Harriet navigated a maze of rooms and halls to a room with beautiful wood paneling, where shelves of books reached to the ceilings. Many of the books were hardbacks and bound with leather, though a closer inspection revealed that the vast majority of them were unread. Nevertheless, it was an impressive collection and Mary couldn't help but give out a whistle. Harriet raised an eyebrow.

"Sorry, I was impressed," Mary answered. "I suppose you're more used to it."

"I suppose I am." Harriet shrugged with indifference.

A cheerful fire burned in the grate, and after the cold outside Mary eagerly basked in front of it, warming up her face and hands.

"Have a seat," Harriet suggested and they both settled into two glorious old wingback chairs that looked as if they dated back to the days when Bonaparte was Holy Roman Emperor. Harriet tactfully passed Mary a handkerchief and a grateful Mary had a good wet blow. Spode returned with their drinks and after a small, tentative sip revealed the toddy to be delicious, Mary took a heartier swill.

"The others are taking cocktails in the lounge, but I pulled you in here so we could talk alone," Harriet explained.

Mary nodded and wondered which others besides Lord Pool Harriet might be referring to. So much for any hopes of dining with just Harriet and Lord Pool. “Oh,” said Mary, “before I forget”—she rummaged in her pockets and pulled out a rather disheveled brown paper package—“these are for you.”

Harriet hesitantly tried to unwrap the parcel neatly, but quickly turned to a full-throated assault of tearing and shredding. At the end, she was left with a box of Canary cigarettes. She turned her eyes wonderingly at Mary.

“Did you buy these for me?” she exclaimed.

“Oh no,” Mary answered hurriedly. “When I was talking to the Legges, I had to purchase them. But I don’t smoke, and you do, so I thought...”

“Oh, of course,” Harriet murmured. “I don’t think I’m familiar with this brand.”

Mary felt crestfallen. “I suppose you don’t want them then.”

“Oh, no, I’m sure I’ll like them once I try them. Or Edgar will.” Harriet rushed to reassure her. In doing so, she unconsciously grasped Mary’s hand. One of her fingers interlocked with Mary’s and, for a moment, it seemed color entered Harriet’s face. Or perhaps Mary just imagined it, for a second later Harriet pulled her hand back. Mary struggled to find a way to relieve the awkwardness.

“This is quite a place,” she said, looking around.

“It’s a bit old-fashioned for my tastes,” Harriet confessed. “I dabble in interior decorating and I prefer a more modern, streamlined look. I’ve been trying to convince Edgar to redecorate, but he refuses to do any alterations until he's got some spare cash on hand. He did say he'd like me to help furnish the new resort when it goes in." At the mention of the resort, Harriet's face darkened. "Would someone really kill Anthony just to stop him and Edgar from going ahead with the development project?"

"I don't know," Mary answered honestly.

"Edgar seems awfully suspicious of this Caleb Bartleby person." Harriet drained her drink.

"It's Barnaby, not Bartleby," Mary corrected her.

"I must have had him mixed up with Bartleby, the Scrivener."

"The who?"

"Melville. Never mind. Do you think the man's guilty?"

"I don't think so. Caleb may be a drunk, but he's not a fool. He knows full well killing Anthony wouldn't have stopped his Lordship from going ahead with the project. I still think it's worth looking into the Legges. There's something very wrong about those two."

"No." Harriet shook her head. "I've been doing some enquiries of my own, and Mr. Legge was working in his shop the day Anthony died. He's out of it. Besides, I've met Mrs. Legge and while I can see Anthony chatting her up a bit, especially if he was bored or lonely, I can't imagine an affair. She's not his type. Or rather wasn't...oh hell." Harriet's eyes began to water again, and Mary passed her a handkerchief. "God, I don't know what's coming over me. I'm not usually as sloppy as all this."

"You've had a shock and you're grieving. It's perfectly natural," Mary told her.

Harriet stared absently at the wall. Secretly, though, Mary wasn't entirely convinced the Legges were out of it. Mr. Legge may have been in the shop most of the day, but still could have slipped out long enough to kill Anthony. As for Harriet's assertion that Anthony wouldn't have made love to Mrs. Legge—well, could any sister really know her brother's taste in mistresses? For that matter, even if there hadn't been an actual affair, Mr. Legge might still have suspected the worst and hated Anthony for it. It wouldn't be the first time a man was so irrationally jealous he committed violence.

"Edgar's been so kind about letting me stay here, but really, I should be with Uncle Donald right now. Anthony was the closest thing he had to a son, even if he didn't approve of his career. And his health's been so bad already. This will probably finish him off." With that, Harriet polished off her drink. Spode appeared at the door. "Can I get another?" Harriet asked, holding up her glass. Mary was about to gently suggest that Harriet perhaps had enough when Spode spoke.

"Actually, madame, I came here to bring you and your friend to dinner."

Good, thought Mary. Getting food into Harriet might help sober her up a bit.

They made their way into the kind of dining room Mary knew only from books and picture shows. It was all there—the great table, the handsome linens, the fine china, flickering candles, glittering silverware, and sparkling goblets. Even a chandelier. Mary was directed to a seat at one corner of the table while Harriet sat on the other end. Besides Harriet and Lord Pool three other persons were present: A Lady Edith Ayers—a large woman with a mammoth bust and horsey face. The Honorable Freddie Cavendish—a slight young man with protruding ears—and finally, a Captain Henry Fielding. The last was a very fine-looking man with erect, military posture and a deep tan as if he'd spent some time abroad. The men all wore proper smoker jackets. Lady Edith was in a rich, emerald-green brocade and pearls. Even Harriet, Mary realized, wore what was actually a very fashionable pale-pink gown from Bond Street. Mary's clothes, which had seemed perfectly fine before now, felt cheap and shabby. Perhaps she should have got at least one proper dress from her mother's shop. Then again, Mary had a shrewd suspicion that the garments her mother sold wouldn't have passed muster here either. In a place like Avenel Court, even the maids would be in used silks and laces of finer quality than Mrs. Grey had ever touched.

Harriet was all the more striking for being at the side of Lord Pool. The physical contrast that had been evident with Anthony and his Lordship was just as present with the sister as well, but in a way that was quite becoming. Dark and powerful Lord Pool and fair and delicate Harriet made a beautiful couple. One could already imagine their wedding photos in the society papers.

"We'll be dining simply tonight," Lord Pool announced. Dining simply at Avenel Court meant salad, oysters, roast beef, followed by a pudding and fruit. There seemed to be a lot of people in uniform waiting on them. Hungry from the bike ride, Mary eagerly attacked her meal, thankful that she did at least know which fork to use with which course. Mrs. Grey had, for some reason, insisted on teaching her children genteel manners on the offhand chance they ever did some act of heroism that would get them invited to Buckingham Palace. Mary now silently thanked her mum. She had to admit the quality of the meal was quite excellent and she tucked in heartily—more heartily than anyone else at the table, but, of course, they hadn't had a full day of rounds to whet their appetites. Mary noticed with some concern that Harriet seemed to barely touch her food but was still drinking steadily.

Conversation seemed strained, and there appeared to be a tacit rule at the table that no one was to make any mention of the recent tragedy. It seemed that everyone at the table was aware of how Mary knew Harriet by their pointed refusal to ask about it. Nor did anyone speak of Lord Pool's development plans. Rather people spoke of the weather, the theater scene in London, sports, or the quality of the wines. Or at least everyone but Harriet and Mary did. Harriet was in no mood for idle chatter, and Mary didn't know a damned thing about cricket or vintages. At one point, much to her embarrassment, Mary had to ask to be excused to use the powder room.

"It's down that hall and to the left," Harriet pointed.

"Thank you."

Mary went down the hall and opened the door, and then involuntarily started. She was in a room filled with dead things. She stared. Foxes, rabbits, and birds who had once frolicked or flew carefree in field and forest had been stuffed and mounted all over the walls, with glass eyes now staring directly into Mary's soul. On one wall lay a glass display case filled with firearms ranging from pistols to rifles. The smallest of the guns was a dainty little pearl-handled revolver that could fit in a lady's clutch. The largest was an elephant gun. Mary quickly shut the door of the room to see Spode.

"That is the trophy room." He instructed her with a blank face, "The powder room is right across."

"Oh, thank you." Mary was flustered. Much to her consternation, Spode made a point of waiting until after Mary had finished in the powder room to guide her back to the main dining room lest she become lost once more. Not that Mary found the company of the dining room so engrossing, but it was still better than being surrounded by the work of taxidermists. She quietly ate her food and sipped her wine.

Lady Edith spoke up. "And my dear friend Honoria Wainwright of the Devon Wainwrights, you know, is having the most awful difficulties since her husband passed away. Those damned death duties ate up so much of the estate. Poor thing may have to sell Hawthorne House, which has been in the family for generations, and move into a cottage or a flat." She visibly shuddered. "Even I've had to move into smaller quarters. Why, the home I'm in now only requires four servants!"

"Seems to be happening to more and more old families these days," Captain Fielding observed. "Damned shame, it is."

"It's not just the damned taxes either," Lady Edith chimed in. "Everywhere you turn, things are getting worse. Communism and socialism are spreading all over Europe, and even in England we have so many problems with the unions these days. All this rot about universal education. It's all a campaign against our kind, you know," she proclaimed with true melancholy. "Why, things are so bad Lady Beatrice St. Vincent has had to marry a Greek shipping magnate. A Greek, I tell you. It's almost as bad as an Argentinian or a Turk. Though marrying into money may well be the only way for some of us to stay afloat these days. No matter if it smells like turpentine."

Lord Pool gave a loud artificial cough. He, after all, was marrying into money, and while Harriet certainly wasn't Greek, it was true her family fortune was fairly new as well. Donald Harrington could even be described as, well, vulgar, though fortunately, his niece and nephew had both received the benefits of a first-class education. Lady Edith may have been a distant relation but, at that moment, Edgar Pool would have happily sewn her lips shut. Still the blasted old lady kept going.

"We're a dying race, our kind. We're being replaced by buttonhole makers and commercial travelers, with their polygonal pince-nez, and their dentures." Lady Edith spoke with bitter vehemence and drained her glass, whereupon it was immediately refilled by Spode. "You mark my words, Edgar"—she turned to Lord Pool—"someday they'll be trying to knock down Avenel Court!"

"Not if I can help it," Lord Pool said with manly resolution. "This estate has been in my family for centuries, and I'd damned well do anything to keep it that way." There was a fire in his eyes, for Edgar Pool was a man truly and passionately devoted to his ancestral home. It was in his blood and attached to him as thoroughly as his own limbs. To lose Avenel Court would be as painful to him as an amputation—more so, in fact. At least if he just lost an arm or a leg, he'd have the comforts of home to bring him solace, and the reassurance of still having something to pass on someday to his future sons. Without Avenel Court, he'd be adrift as a boat lost at sea.

"Good to hear you say that, Edgar," Lady Edith commended him. "Mind you, if those damned socialists get anywhere, places like this will all be turned into hospitals and orphanages. You know that Hitler fellow and his crew in Germany may be crude, but at least they know how to handle scum like communists and trade unionists. Our own government is far too soft on them."

Freddie Cavendish decided a change of subject was needed to divert everyone from the dreaded topic of politics. He loudly cleared his throat and, in his desperation, turned to the only person who had neither spoken all evening nor seemed likely to fall out of her chair. "I understand you're the district nurse, Miss Grey." It was the first time anyone at dinner had directly addressed her, and Mary felt rather put on the spot. "I always thought that must be rather a rum sort of job."

"Rum how?" Mary asked.

"Oh, you know, going into other people's homes all the time. Sick people's homes, no less."

"Yes, sick people are the ones most likely to require nursing." Somehow, Mary managed to keep a straight face.

"Would make me dashed uncomfortable, I'd think! Sick people." He visibly shuddered. "Aren't some of them contagious?"

"They are," Mary confirmed. "You have to take precautions sometimes, especially with the tubercular cases."

"Consumption! Eww." Freddie didn't hide his disgust. "Do they actually cough up blood?" He sounded horrified and titillated at the same time. There came the sound of raindrops hitting windows.

"Yes. They do. It's quite painful for them, really. I do my best to keep them comfortable, even so—" Mary gestured helplessly.

"But it's so good of you to take care of those poor creatures," Harriet, who had previously been silent, suddenly spoke. "So kind of you to care for them, really. Me, I couldn't do it. I haven't the stomach for nursing. Or the kindness." She drained her drink and one of the footmen silently refilled her glass.

"This is hardly appropriate conversation for the dinner table," Lady Edith pronounced. "Especially now, when we should be trying to keep things cheerful, considering"—she coughed delicately—"recent events."

"What made you decide to take up nursing?" Harriet asked. It was the first time since dinner began that she'd said more than two words. Everyone seemed astounded, and then they all looked at Mary, who took a quick gulp of port.

"I suppose it all began with the bandaging," Mary began. "When I was about five years old, I fell and cut my arm rather badly. So, my mother cleaned the wound and bandaged it very thoroughly. I was quite impressed with how well bandaging solved my wound, and rather pleased with all the attention the bandage brought me. So, I decided to share the wonders of bandages with everyone else. Other children, dogs, cats. Anyone I found who sported any kind of injury, I'd simply take over. A little Mercurochrome and some gauze, and voila! The patient was good to go."

Harriet gave a little chuckle and rested her chin in her hand. She could just see Mary Grey doing exactly that. Mary continued her narration.

"In fact, I became so assiduous in my efforts that my mother finally decided we couldn't afford to buy bandages for the whole world. So, she instructed me to instead use whatever fabric we found in her rag bag."

"Rag bag?" Harriet asked.

"My mother owned a dress shop, so she had a basket of all the unused scraps of cloth," Mary explained.

"Your mother was a dressmaker?" Lady Edith asked. She said "dressmaker" in a way that made it sound like "sewer rat," while giving a quick once-over of Mary's attire, as if to wonder whether that was the best Mrs. Grey could produce for her own offspring. "How interesting! Was your father a draper as well?"

"My father abandoned his wife and children before I even knew him." That managed to shut up Edith, and everyone else at the table. Most appeared shocked Mary would bring up anything so sordid. Harriet was shocked as well, but also thought it rather explained a few things about Mary. "Anyway, thanks to the bandaging," Mary went on, "it became the joke of the family that I was destined to be a nurse. And so, I was."

"So, you had a calling," Harriet responded. "It's so clever of you to have a calling, isn't it? Seems like most people don't. At least not in my set. I certainly don't have any calling at all. Not that anyone ever expected me to. I was just taught to be pretty and please."

Again, there were some uncomfortable glances exchanged around the table. Harriet nattered on obliviously. "Now, Anthony has, or rather had, a calling," she hastily corrected herself. "He'd known for ages he wanted to be an architect. Even as a boy, he loved building models. All that precision and attention to detail. So patient with it all! Which is strange, because he usually wasn't patient at all." Harriet was clearly lost in memory, and Mary was transfixed by even this brief glimpse into Harriet's past. But the moment was broken by Lord Pool clearing his throat.

"Shall we adjoin to the drawing room? Perhaps have a game of cards?"

"Actually," said Mary, "I'd better be going. It's a long bike ride home."

"You're leaving?" Harriet cried out. "Oh, but you mustn't!" Harriet was distraught at the thought of being left with the likes of Lady Edith and Freddie Cavendish. Under normal circumstances, she could have borne it gracefully. She had loads of practice making polite conversation with people she'd rather not talk to. In fact, it sometimes appeared to be her primary occupation. But to do so now with her brother's killer on the loose was simply intolerable. Even Edgar's company felt suffocating these days. Mary was just about the only person Harriet felt she could stand, though she wasn't sure why. Perhaps because the district nurse was so utterly unlike anyone else she'd ever met.

"I'm sure Miss Grey has a very busy schedule," Lord Pool said.

Harriet felt an unjustified level of irritation with Edgar at that moment. Bad enough he was the one who'd invited all these dreadful people here in the first place. Now he was driving off the one person she wanted present. Really, men were so bad at picking up cues.

"I do have a full day tomorrow," Mary agreed, "and I don't play cards."

"But surely you'd prefer to spend the night?" Harriet asked anxiously.

Lord Pool looked up sharply in surprise and felt a twinge of disapproval at his fiancée's highhandedness on the matter of houseguests. It wasn't, after all, like Harriet was mistress of Avenel Court yet. Nurse Grey, surprisingly, was the one who remembered propriety.

"I wouldn't want to impose on his Lordship," Mary replied. "Besides, I haven't packed any spare clothes or toiletries for the night."

"But you can't bike home," Harriet protested. "Not in this weather! If you can't spend the night, then at least get a ride home!" Harriet turned her face expectantly on Lord Pool, who took the hint.

"Quite right. I'll have Andrews warm up the car for you.'

"But what about my bike?"

"You can put it on the boot end of the car."

And so it was that Mary Grey came to take her first—and in all likelihood only—ride in a Rolls-Royce. Her bike was awkwardly mounted on the rear end of the vehicle. She couldn't deny the interior was quite comfortable in black leather. The company, however, left something to be desired.

"It's quite good of you to give me a ride home so late," Mary said. "I'm awfully grateful for it."

There was no response from the driver's seat. Andrews, whom she had first observed outside Mr. West's home, was not a chatty sort of fellow. Perhaps, ordinarily, drivers were expected to be seen and not heard. Mary, though, found the silence a little unnerving.

"Do you like working for Lord Pool?" She made another attempt to engage him in conversation.

Again, no response. It was as if the man's tongue were cut out. No one spoke again for the remainder of the journey. When they reached the cottage, Andrews hopped out first and handed the bike to Mary, and then delayed not a wink before driving off into the night.

Chapter Ten

For the next couple of days, Mary's life went back to the usual routine of visiting farmers and fisherman. She popped the cork on Mrs. Martin's elderberry wine and found it to be delicious. She wrote to her mother, giving her a deeply edited account of the last few weeks that made no mention of police investigations or murder, but only of Mr. West's untimely death and that she'd been asked to call on Avenel Court. The last bit, she knew, Mrs. Grey would find very interesting, and she tried to give as good a description as she could of the house, the grounds, and dinner. She made sure to mention the presence of persons like Captain Fielding and Lady Edith Ayers. The last name in particular, she knew, would make her mother swoon. She regretted that Lady Edith hadn't proved more interesting in her conversation.

Another midnight call came two nights after dinner at Avenel Court. This time, it was to the house of Mr. Clode, the local blacksmith. His boy, Johnny, had the measles and his forehead was hot as a furnace. Mary spent hours dosing the boy and cooling him with water until finally his fever broke, and poor Mrs. Clode, who'd been up all night with Mary, wept with relief. Mary prepared to go home, but Johnny pleaded with her for a story before she left.

"Of course," said Mary. "Would you like to hear the story of *The Three Bears*?"

"I'm not a baby!" Johnny looked indignant.

"No, of course, you're not," Mary soothed him. "Well, how about the tale of the Cornish Merman then?"

Johnny looked contemptuous. "I don't want a silly story. I want a good story."

"A good story?" Mary felt a little grieved that neither the Brothers Grimm nor classic sea myths were considered "good stories" by her young patient. Modern children, she thought, were so much harder to please than they had been in her day. "What is a good story?" she asked, rather piqued.

"Tell me about Dead Sam!" Johnny looked enthusiastic.

"The story of Dead Sam?" Mary frowned.

"You do know it, don't you?" Johnny asked, doubt creeping into his face as to whether Mary was aware of anything of local importance at all.

"Yes, of course, I've heard it," Mary defended herself. "I'm just not sure I should be telling it to you."

Johnny made his eyes large as saucers, and, with a sigh, Mary relented and told him the tale of Dead Sam.

"Fishing," Mary began, "has always been a dangerous trade, and many a man who goes out at dawn to cast his nets never returns. Most of the time, they're claimed by the sea, but sometimes it's something worse. One night, long ago, there was the worst storm seen in fifty years.

Rain and wind hammered every building here. Some people's roofs blew off, and then they were left at the mercy of the wind and rain that battered them black and blue, and they nearly died of cold. The waters outside their doors were high enough to sail a lifeboat on.

"The next day, every man and woman in the village went out to see what had been damaged in the storm, and oh, the cost was high." As she told the story, Mary's voice became increasingly emotive, and she began gesturing dramatically with her hands. "Livestock had been lost or killed, and streets were flooded. A number of boats had been ruined or set adrift, and the church was now missing its steeple. And Sam, a local angler, had gone missing. Pieces of what had been his boat were found on the beach. Everyone assumed Sam had been caught in his boat when the storm came, and that the sea had claimed his body. They held a service for him in church over an empty casket.

"As they were concluding the ceremony, a local lad ran into the church, his face as white as mare's milk. The boy was screaming, so they had trouble understanding him. Finally, he calmed down enough to tell them he'd found Sam's body—or what was left of it—along some rocks while playing. A group of local men went at once to the place the boy had indicated."

At this point, Johnny sat up, a bit eager for what was the best part of the story.

"Days at sea had left their mark. The body was bloated and the features unrecognizable. Barnacles and fish had feasted on the limbs. There would have been no way to positively identify the corpse had it not been for Sam having an old tattoo on his chest. Still, drowned men had been seen before and would be again. What made the discovery of Sam's body so horrific was that the left side of his head had been shot clean off with a rifle. Sam had been murdered, and quite brutally at that. But why? There were no signs of robbery in his house. Indeed, they found a bag of coins under the mattress, undisturbed. Sam had no enemies anyone knew of, nor any heirs to profit from his death. They searched high and low for the gun and the killer, but they never found either. And to this day, no one knows who killed Sam or why."

Johnny listened, enraptured, as Mary told the whole tale. "So, the murderer got away," he said when she finished.

"The murderer got away." She nodded.

"So, he might still be out there." Despite the red spots and fever, Johnny looked visibly excited.

"Well, this was a very long time ago, so the murderer is probably dead now too." Mary punctured his hopes. "Now, Johnny, you really must try to sleep." As she said this it belatedly occurred to her that telling a child a frightening story was not the way to usher them into sweet dreams. So, to help things along, Mary gave Johnny a glass of warm milk with a teaspoonful of brandy, and in moments he was out like a light. Watching Johnny's peaceful slumber, Mary wondered if she should try the same technique herself. Then again, if she slept too deeply, would she be able to answer midnight calls?

As she left the Clodes, Mary thought about the story of Sam the angler in a new light. There had been a person who got away with murder. A person perhaps known in Illhenny, who had committed the worst of crimes and escaped punishment—rather living to the rest of their days a solid citizen, with no one around them aware of their dark deed. What had it been like, she wondered for the first time, for everyone in the community after Sam's death to know they harbored a killer among them, and with no idea who it was? Would history repeat itself with Anthony? For Harriet's sake, she hoped not.

Much to Mary's surprise, that very night, she came home late to her cottage to find Harriet herself waiting for her with a picnic basket.

"I hope you don't mind," Harriet explained. "I'm sorry, but I couldn't stand another night of Edgar's guests."

"I can certainly see that," Mary replied and then cursed herself for being impertinent in having spoken poorly of her betters before Harriet. Fortunately, Harriet herself seemed to miss the insult. Or maybe she didn't care.

"But I didn't want to be alone either," she continued. "So, I asked the cook at Avenel Court to make up supper for two"—she pointed to the basket—"and decided to come over." This request on Harriet's part had caused considerable commentary among the servants' hall at Avenel Court. Not that Harriet was aware of any of it. She had simply decided she had to see Mary once more, and left Edgar a note to that effect. But now, standing in Mary's doorway, Harriet thought she should have called first. "It's quite an imposition, isn't it?" Harriet anxiously asked her. "I hope you're not terribly cross with me."

"Not at all," Mary assured her. "I'm actually quite famished, in fact. Come on in and we can eat together. I'm sorry it's not very festive in here." She apologized for the lack of Christmas decoration.

"Perfect," Harriet replied. "I don't feel much in the way of the Yuletide spirit this year. It's been all I could do to keep from yanking holly off the walls at Avenel and smashing down the tree."

They went inside and Mary took Harriet's coat. Harriet today was wearing a simple yet still smart travel suit, and instead of having her hair pinned up as she had in the past, she now let it run free. Mary thought she liked this style all the better. Given the state of the chairs, it seemed more suitable to throw some old blankets and pillows on the floor, which lent an additional spirit of informality, and thus familiarity to the occasion. It was hardly up to the standards of Avenel Court or even The Laurels, but Harriet did not appear disappointed in her surroundings. In fact, she seemed more at ease than she had the night before. The basket contained steak and kidney pie for two as well as chocolate cake and a bottle of Chianti. Mary found an old tin can for Harriet to use as an ashtray while she smoked. Mary and Harriet both tucked in quite heartily, and Mary was relieved to see that at least tonight Harriet was showing a normal appetite. After the party, she'd worried Harriet might be switching to an all-liquid diet. But while Harriet enjoyed the wine, she was, Mary noted, drinking at a significantly more manageable pace than she had before. The two women spent hours talking and laughing together, like a pair of schoolgirls who'd known each other since the cradle. Harriet shared some especially scintillating gossip about Wallis Simpson.

"You'd think if you were going to give up a crown for a woman, she'd be the second coming of Helen of Troy," Mary mused, "but Wallis seems so, well, ordinary. I just don't understand it myself."

"No one else does either," Harriet observed. "The prevailing theory is she must know secret techniques of sensuality that you can't get from a more run of the mill prostitute." Mary laughed as Harriet went on, "Of course, it's so hard to get the real scoop on her since British papers are censoring themselves on the topic. But thankfully, foreign papers feel no such restraint on the matter."

"Ah," said Mary, "and what is the real scoop on Wallis?" She sipped the Chianti. Quite nice, if a little different than what she was used to.

"She's quite sympathetic to the Germans, you know. In fact," Harriet whispered, "they say she's been especially friendly with one German in particular. Von Ribbentrop."

"Name sounds familiar," Mary commented.

"That's because he's one of Germany's most important diplomats, and a personal friend to Hitler," Harriet informed her. "They say Wallis has been sharing her favors with von Ribbentrop and Edward both! Well, not at the exact same time, of course," Harriet hastily corrected when she saw Mary's expression. "She alternates between their beds."

"Oh my," Mary breathed as she sipped more of the wine. "Perhaps it's all for the best that Edward is abdicating. I mean, his poor younger brother may stutter but at least he's not a Nazi sympathizer!"

"Well, Churchill doesn't think so," Harriet commented. "He's all in favor of putting Edward back on the throne and dumping Bertie. Good thing Churchill isn't Prime Minister, or he and Bertie would have to work together. Good lord, could you imagine?"

"Would certainly make for some awkward state meetings," Mary agreed.

"But let's not spend the whole evening talking about politics. Tell me more about how you became a nurse."

"You really want to know?"

"Yes, I really want to know." Harriet was adamant. "Believe me, I wouldn't ask otherwise."

So, Mary told Harriet tales from nursing school, which Harriet seemed to consider as exotic and exciting as tales from a foreign land, or rather more exciting. Harriet had been abroad many times, and she'd always found army soldiers from India fairly tiresome, but Mary's world seemed fresh, indeed.

"But we shouldn't just talk about me," Mary proposed. "What about you? What's your life like?"

Harriet took a big swig of wine. "There's not a lot to tell really." It seemed an odd statement coming from one of England's leading socialites. "I'm a lily of the field. I toil not nor do I spin. I mostly spend my time going to parties." She gave a bored shrug. "Parties and shopping. And sunbathing on the Riviera, and galas with people with titles."

"Well, that's interesting," Mary told her. "Certainly more so than what goes on in a sleepy place like this."

"Not really. I'll let you in on a little secret, Mary. High society is no more interesting than common village life. Oh, there's more money involved, but deep down everyone's still awfully provincial. I mean, you saw how terribly dull Edgar's guests were the other night."

"They weren't thrilling company," Mary admitted.

"Yes, well, they're all that bad really—unless you're in a group with those Bohemian artist types, like Anthony was. He always was an adventurer, you know. As a boy, he used to love sledding down the main staircase." Harriet's face lit up. "Sometimes I'd even go with him. My God, we gave the servants a fright! I think that's where Anthony got his taste for fast riding from."

"What about you?" Mary asked.

"Oh, I was always in the back of the sled. I prefer to be the passenger," Harriet confessed.

"That's a bit limiting. I love being in control of my own way."

"Yes, but you're probably better at paying attention to the road. I'd much rather let someone else steer so I can think on other things."

"But then how can you be sure you're going in the direction you want to go?"

Harriet started. "I hadn't thought of that before. I guess I don't always know where someone else is taking me, do I?" She looked thoughtful. "I do at least know how to drive. Perhaps I should get my own car? I can certainly afford it. I just never got around to doing so because Anthony or Edgar or somebody was always on hand to give me a ride."

"You should definitely get your own car," Mary spoke earnestly. "You can't always count on other people for a ride, and it makes things a lot simpler. You wouldn't believe how much freer I've been since I got my motorcycle!"

"How did you get the motorcycle?"

"The Rural Nursing Association provided it."

"They do that?" Harriet seemed surprised. "Until I met you, I thought all district nurses were on regular bikes."

"Well, it's true many nurses still use regular bikes, and I've heard of one place so remote the nurse was actually riding a horse, but motorbikes are becoming increasingly popular," Mary explained. "They're faster and you can visit more places. In fact, the nursing magazines have even started giving advice on which models to buy and how to operate them." She worried all this information might be boring, but Harriet appeared impressed.

"Is it scary riding one?" she asked.

"Well, it was a bit unnerving at first," Mary admitted. "Took me a while to master it, and I had a couple of close calls. But once I got the hang of it, I found it was actually quite fun."

"Fun?"

"Well, not this time of year," Mary hastily corrected herself. "It's too bloody cold. Begging your pardon."

"Swear all you like. I'm not offended."

"Well then, the bike's not so good in winter, but when the weather's good, it's quite the experience! Racing along in the open air, smelling the sea."

"It does sound exhilarating," Harriet admitted. "You know"—she seemed struck by a thought—"perhaps once spring comes around, I could go riding with you sometime!"

Mary was dumbstruck. "You? Come on the motorbike with me?"

"Yes! I think it would be fun! If you'd have me, that is."

"Oh, I'd love to take you. But, well, what about his Lordship?"

"Edgar?"

"Yes, his Lordship might not want his future bride racing around on the back of an old motorbike. Indeed, by the time things do warm up, you might even be married and be Lady Pool. In which case, a motorbike ride would be even more out of the question for you."

Harriet listened to her with an expression of deep dismay, and then passionately cried out, "Oh, must we talk about the wedding? The date hasn't even been set yet. And with everything so crazy, I don't want to talk about it right now. Promise me you won't bring up the wedding again tonight?"

Mary promised and their conversation drifted onto other things. Mary explained to an astonished Harriet the full story of Mark Weston, born Mary Louise Weston, the Devonshire Wonder. Mary Louise had been considered one of the finest female athletes in England and even the world in the 1920s. She became the women's national champion in javelin throwing and discus and placed sixth in the Women's World Games in the two-handed shot put. Weston had been born with abnormal genitalia due to a rare condition known as disorder of sex development but had been assigned the role of female and been raised as a girl. Weston decided the original gender assignment was wrong, and in April and May of 1936 had undergone a series of surgeries at Charing Cross Hospital at the hands of the renowned physician L.R. Broster. The surgeries were a complete success, and the newly renamed Mark Weston had since married a woman named Alberta.

"Funny, isn't it?" Harriet noted. "Weston has, or rather had, your first name, and the surname is so close to mine."

"I hadn't thought of that. Well, I suppose they are common enough names here in England. I've often thought about how difficult it must have been growing up in a body that was all wrong. Everyone expecting you to be something you're just not."

"Well, at least Weston could fix that problem with operations," Harriet mused. "Sometimes, for the rest of us, it's not that simple." There was a real bitterness in her voice, and Mary was about to ask Harriet what she meant but was interrupted by a knock on the door. They both froze.

"Oh dear," Harriet said, "could that be a patient?"

"Maybe Lizzie Smith's gone into labor early," Mary speculated as she answered the door. Much to her consternation, she was met by the sight of Andrews, Lord Pool's chauffer.

"Miss West here?" he growled.

"Oh yes." Harriet picked herself off the floor, her hair mussed. "I suppose Edgar sent you?"

"He's worried." That was all Andrews said, but his expression was much more eloquent.

"I suppose it is getting a bit late," Harriet admitted, and Mary looked askance at the clock when she checked the time. How could so many hours have disappeared so quickly?

"Mary"—Harriet grabbed her hand and gave it a tight squeeze—"thank you for having me."

"It was my pleasure." Mary had never been more sincere.

An apologetic Harriet rode off with Andrews, and left Mary with the remains of dinner and the picnic basket.

That night, the cottage had never seemed emptier. Mary thought with envy of Mark Weston. She didn't think she'd actually want to go under the knife to become a man, but she would certainly enjoy the freedom it would bring her. And after all, Weston was now happily married and could even father children. What hope of family life was there for Mary? Harriet West and Lord Pool had each other. Her brother and sister both had families. Even Caleb Barnaby had Ahab. *Who do I have?*

That night, Mary dreamed she was walking along the base of the cliff where Anthony's car had gone over. It was broad daylight. The sun shone more brightly than it ever had before and the sea seemed bluer—a giant blazing sapphire against the beach, bleached white as bone. There was not a single cloud in the sky nor were there any birds. It was somehow quieter than Mary had ever known it. Not even the waves lapping at the shore made any sound.

She was searching for something along the beach. She didn't know what that something was, but she was certain she'd know it when she found it. Over past a dune, she saw a single rubber boot poking out. She raced toward it, knowing instinctively this was what she was meant to find, and noticing idly in passing there were no tracks of any kind in the glaring white sand. She wasn't even leaving any shoeprints in the sand herself.

Mary made her way around the dune and gazed in wonder at the sight she had found. She ought to have been frightened to see the corpse, but really, she was just interested. Seaweed had wrapped itself around the neck and torso like a shawl. Barnacles adorned the fingers and wrists like jewelry. The face had turned green-gray from days of decay, and the left half of it was missing altogether, having been shot clean off. But there was something recognizable about the features. And of course, there was no mistaking the district nurse uniform.

The body was her own.

Chapter Eleven

After its brief moment of excitement, life in Illhenny returned to its normal sleepy routine. Anthony West's body was released and was taken to a cemetery near Newcastle to be buried near his parents' graves, alongside the tombs of other Harringtons. Mary would have liked to attend the funeral service, but she hadn't the time nor the means for the trip. Lord Pool and Harriet had, of course, been there. Harriet remained in Newcastle with her uncle Donald while Lord Pool returned to Avenel Court and made preparations to continue with the development plans.

There were no breaks in the West case, or if there were the police didn't see fit to share them with anyone. Mary reflected bitterly how, unlike detective stories, in the real world, the police seemed damned determined to keep civilians out of investigations. It was all very well and good to take a vow to bring Anthony's murderer to justice, but another thing entirely to actually do it. She had no idea what to do next. Her only possible lead was the Legges, and she hadn't yet found a chance to speak to Mrs. Legge alone. The closest Mary came to excitement was getting caught in the crossfire of a snowball fight between the butcher's boy and the postman's son where she'd got powder all over her coat. Admittedly, there had been some satisfaction for Mary in retaliating, throwing snowballs back at both of them with such ferocity they fled crying for their mothers.

It was on the seventh day after the hideous dinner party at Avenel Court, and four days after Harriet and Mary's impromptu floor picnic, that all hell broke loose. Mary was calling on Peg Leg Pete, a local fisherman. If Peg Leg Pete had a last name, no one in Illhenny knew it. He was always called Peg Leg Pete, or just plain Pete. His landlady, Mrs. Rook, had been worried about Pete's cough, and it was she who summoned Mary.

"It's not pneumonia, is it, nurse? Or consumption?" she asked Mary anxiously.

"I don't think so," said Mary, much to the relief of both Mrs. Rook and Pete. "It seems like a simple case of the flu. A couple of days' bed rest should fix him up. But if he does get any worse, call in a doctor."

Mrs. Rook went downstairs to carry on with other business while Mary set about making the gangly, long-faced Pete more comfortable. She was settling him in with some tea and cough medicine, when he asked her, "Do you know how I lost my leg, nurse?"

"I heard it was during the Great War," Mary said cautiously.

"T'was. Hip deep in mud in France at the time, trying to avoid chewing on barbed wire. Now, I caught lice while I was over there, so I was itching something terrible. At one point, I stop to get a scratch in and fell behind. Sergeant starts yelling at me to move my arse. Then, the guy between me and sergeant stepped on a mine. They were both blown to pink mist and I took some heavy shrapnel to me leg. The doctors tried their best, but gangrene set in and they had to cut it off. Used a guillotine. No anesthesia, so they gave me whiskey." Pete's eyes stared off at something in the distance as he relived events nearly two decades old. Mary stayed silent. When dealing with survivors of the Great War, she'd found it was best to let them tell their stories in peace. "Perhaps it was all for the best, though," Pete concluded. "Since they had to amputate, I got to go home. Most of the lads in my regiment didn't." Then his gaze turned back to the present. "Sorry to bore you, nursie."

"You weren't boring me," Mary assured him.

"Don't know what made me bring all that up." Pete looked embarrassed, and Mary was about to tell him it was good for him to speak about such things to her when they were interrupted by Mrs. Rook. She was red-faced and wheezing heavily as if she'd run up the stairs.

"What's happened?" Mary asked. Mrs. Rook panted for another moment or two and then caught her breath enough to share the news that had made a stout landlady exert herself so.

"Lord Pool's been shot!"

While the news of the incident spread across Illhenny like fire, precise details were hard to come by. Some said Lord Pool had been in a duel, others claimed he'd been cleaning his gun. Some proclaimed him to be at death's door, others said it was merely a flesh wound.

To get an accurate account of the situation as well as save her sanity, Mary telephoned Harriet. "Oh, thank God it's you, Mary! It's Edgar. He's been shot."

"I heard that," Mary told her.

Harriet breathlessly added, "The police are treating it as an attempted murder!"

"I hadn't heard that," Mary admitted. There had always been the outside chance it could have been a simple hunting accident, but deep down, Mary realized she'd never thought it was just that. There was evil in Illhenny, and it had struck again.

"We're here, at Avenel Court, right now with the doctor." Harriet paused.

"Why not the hospital?"

"They sent him there initially for treatment, but his injury wasn't life threatening and he insisted on being allowed to return home to recover. Maybe it's better this way. After all, Anthony was murdered inside that dreadful place, and even though the police assigned Edgar a protective guard, who knows?"

"Well, he'd likely be far more comfortable at Avenel Court too," Mary mused. "He'll certainly eat better."

"Well, I was hoping you'd come here as well." Harriet added as an inducement, "You'll dine better, too, then."

"You want me at Avenel Court?"

"Oh yes, I'd feel so much better if you were here."

Mary couldn't understand why that would be so, but Harriet certainly sounded sincere. Perhaps she just needed a friendly face. Her uncle's illness, her brother's death, and now her fiancé being shot. It would be enough to drive any girl mad.

"All right, I'll drive right on over."

"No need to do that. I'll send Andrews round with the car to bring you here. Oh, and pack your things as well, to spend the night."

Harriet hung up before Mary could object.

Once more, Mary was riding in the backseat of the Rolls-Royce Phantom. Once more, Andrews was proving less than communicative. This time, though, as they approached the estate grounds, a number of police vans and constables were present. The constables appeared to be examining every blade of grass and speck of dirt on the ground. The Rolls-Royce was stopped once by someone with a sergeant's badge, asking who they were, but at the news that Mary was a nurse summoned by his Lordship's fiancée, the car was let through. Once at Avenel Court, Harriet rushed into Mary's arms while Spode looked askance. Harriet openly sobbed.

"There, there," Mary went, stroking Harriet's hair, comforting her. She felt a guilty thrill of pleasure to hold Harriet in her arms and to be so close, she could smell her perfume. "You said yourself his Lordship's injury wasn't all that serious."

"But someone wants him dead," Harriet wailed. "What if they try again? And after Anthony too? I can't bear it."

Mary handed Harriet her handkerchief and let her take a noisy blow.

"I think Miss West could use some tea, don't you, Spode? And maybe something for us to eat?"

"Of course." If Spode felt any resentment at being given orders by a mere nurse, he was too professional to show it.

"Oh," Harriet added, "and make sure Miss Grey has a room ready for the night, will you?"

Spode's left eyebrow lifted a fraction of an inch at that, but he nodded politely, and someone came to take Mary's overnight bag from her.

"What happened?"

"I don't know all the details," Harriet confessed.

"What do you know?"

"He was out for a walk when it happened. It seems it was all very sudden—no warning at all when he felt the pain. He was shot in the back, you see, which seems particularly ghastly, doesn't it? It's so cowardly."

"I doubt murderers are much concerned with fair play," Mary noted drily.

"No, I suppose they aren't. Once Edgar fell, Andrews started calling for help."

Much to Mary's relief, not only was Harriet calming down, but she showed no signs of having drowned her sorrows as she had the night of the dinner party.

"Tea, madame?" Spode arrived with the tea trolley and full service. Much to Mary's pleasure, beside the usual cakes and scones were sandwiches and little sausage rolls. She hadn't yet dined, and she eagerly filled her plate. Only then did she remember to ask Harriet when she'd last eaten.

"Not since breakfast," Harriet admitted.

"Then eat now!" Mary ordered, and Harriet obediently bit into a sandwich. "Leave the cart for now, Spode."

"Very well." Spode turned to go and then stopped. "Perhaps I could bring you ladies some sherry?"

"Yes, please!" both women said in unison.

After Spode left, Mary returned to questioning Harriet between bites. “Are the police sure it wasn’t just a regular hunting accident?”

Harriet grimaced. “I don’t know if they’re sure of anything right now, but for one thing, that spot of countryside was supposed to be quite clear of anyone else. Edgar had his red jacket on and could hardly be confused for a deer. And then, of course, it would be just too much of a coincidence, wouldn’t it? First Anthony, and now Edgar?”

“And both of them key to the resort project,” Mary said as her heart sank. “How bad was the injury?”

“The shot went straight through him, so there was no bullet to extract.”

Mary nodded. The missing bullet was probably why the constables were scouring the ground so carefully. Spode arrived with the sherry, which they eagerly gulped down as Harriet continued her narration.

“Thankfully, the bullet missed all the internal organs and arteries, so all Edgar needed was some patching up and a quick blood transfusion. Then he raised holy hell about them keeping him at the hospital, so, finally, the doctors agreed he could heal at home, as long as their instructions were followed to the letter.”

Given what had happened to Anthony West in that same hospital, Lord Pool’s objections had probably been wise, Mary thought.

Harriet went on, “The doctor’s given him something to help him sleep. Says what Edgar needs most right now is rest.”

“The doctor’s right. The best thing for Edgar is that he avoids being disturbed. And that they keep the wound clean. Gunshot victims are at high risk of infection.” She wondered if she should have said that. It wouldn’t do to give Harriet anything more to worry about right then. But Harriet didn’t seem worried. Instead, her face was steely and determined.

“No, Mary, the best thing for Edgar is that we find whoever’s trying to kill him. And I’ve found someone who can help.” Harriet looked excited as she went on. “A private detective. That is to say, a real detective with experience in murder.”

Mary was agape. It was not that she was unaware private detectives existed, but she’d always imagined them to be a rather seedy lot who spent their time taking compromising photographs. She’d never believed you could hire a private detective to do actual murder investigations, and even less idea of how you’d ever find such an individual.

“How—” she began.

“He was referred to me by a friend of my uncle’s,” Harriet explained. “A former policeman. They say he’s supposedly one of the best investigators in Europe.”

Mary stared at her, open-mouthed. “Who?”

Chapter Twelve

Franz Schaefer was drinking some truly dreadful coffee and brooding. He looked over the dingy little flat he now stayed in. Cheap furnishings held together by spit and prayer. Cracked paint. The impermeable musty odor. The paper-thin walls let in every sound from the other rooms and from the street. And in the East End, there were quite a lot of sounds. And smells. He thought longingly on the warm little flat he'd had in Berlin, situated on a quiet, tree-lined street, comfortably furnished, within walking distance to cafés and bookshops. But he reminded himself that, these days, the cafés were filled with men in jackboots, and the bookshops had all their "subversive" material burned. He sighed. In his case, he truly couldn't go home again.

Like most of his fellow Jews who'd fled Germany when the Nuremberg Race Laws came into effect, Franz escaped with little more than the clothes on his back. It was only through friends in British society that he'd been permitted an entrance visa into England at all. But it had proven difficult for him to find work. There was not much use, it seemed, for a former Berlin police inspector, however distinguished, in London.

So far, Franz's attempts to make a living as a private detective hadn't yielded him much except divorce cases and a couple of private thefts. He had to spend the first day of Sukkot hiding in a tree with a camera outside the window of a hotel room to prove adultery. Not that he had anyone to properly celebrate Sukkot with anyway, even if he had the day off. He missed his family. He missed his friends. He missed home, or rather he missed the Germany that had been his home until evil came to power.

In trying to build a client base in the United Kingdom, Franz had two marks against him: he was a foreigner and a Jew. Meanwhile, his sister, her husband, and their two children were still stuck in Germany. For now, they were trying to ride things out and keep their heads down in their medical practice, but the latest letter from Meike had made it clear things were getting worse for them every day—not that England was any land of milk and honey either.

Antisemitism, Franz reflected bitterly, was far from an exclusively German phenomenon. That very same morning, the Leibowitzs' shop around the corner from his flat had its windows smashed, goods stolen, and the words "Get out, dirty Jews" painted on the walls. Sometimes Franz feared England might go the same political way as the Rhineland had, and then where would he and his fellow émigrés go? Very few countries were welcoming fleeing Jews right now. Christians, in Franz Schaefer's experience, did not practice the so-called charity they preached.

These dark speculations were interrupted by a knock at the door. Franz was wary to answer it, lest it prove to be a bill collector, but then came a familiar voice, "Open up, Franz, it's me!"

Franz unbolted the door and admitted his guest, Sir Henry Carmichael. Sir Henry was a portly man of about seventy with a thick white walrus-style moustache who always wore good Harris tweeds. He did not, at first glance, seem to share anything in common with the slightly built, curly-haired man in his thirties with obviously Semitic features, wearing a suit that had once been quite fashionable but was now frayed around the cuffs. Yet, improbably enough, Franz and Henry were good friends. They'd crossed paths years earlier while working on the case of the infamous Count Rochford (who'd been no count at all) and the trail of crimes he'd left across the continent. It was Sir Henry who'd vouched for Franz when he applied for asylum. And it was Sir Henry who had more than once, discreetly, loaned him small sums of money to keep him afloat.

"By Jove, Franz," Sir Henry declared with his usual bluntness. "You look like something the cat brought in."

"The what brought in?" Franz was confused.

"Never mind. The important thing is I've got a job for you." Sir Henry's next words were music to Franz's ears. "There's an extremely wealthy young lady in need of your services." Franz's whole countenance brightened up, and Sir Henry nodded reassuringly. "That's right. This could be quite lucrative for you, old chap. Now, your client is Harriet West."

"I've heard that name before," Schaefer murmured. "Why yes, I believe I've seen her photograph in the society pages of the paper. A most attractive young woman, as I recall."

"She is. And she's set also to inherit the entire Harrington Steel fortune."

Schaefer's lips made an "O" as Sir Henry went on, well pleased with his news.

"Which means not only a big payday for you, but some useful referrals as well. Maybe put you up in a nicer place." Sir Henry glanced around the flat with evident distaste.

"That would have to wait," Franz noted. "What is most important now is that I send my sister, her husband, and their children some money to help them leave Germany. Things are getting even worse for them. Membership in the Hitler Youth is now mandatory, and hoarding wealth abroad is now punishable by the death penalty."

"Things over there do sound bad," Sir Henry admitted.

Franz's eyes grew darker. "My family must leave Germany soon before it will be too late."

Privately, Sir Henry thought this was a trifle melodramatic on Franz's part. Oh, it certainly wasn't good to be a Jew in Germany these days, he knew, but it wasn't as if they were all being rounded up and killed. Still, he sympathized with Franz's desire to be reunited with the rest of the Schaefer family.

"Well, look at it this way, old boy," Sir Henry soothed him, "a case like this will mean not only a big fat fee, but connections to some very important people in England. It could well be your family's ticket out of Germany."

"That it could." Franz looked more hopeful. "Is it a matter of adultery or stolen jewelry?" he asked, resigned. After all, what else did English socialites hire detectives for?

"Neither."

"Blackmail perhaps?" Franz asked hopefully. Blackmail would be decidedly more interesting.

"Even better." Sir Henry's eyes gleamed as he pronounced the next word. "Murder."

"Murder," Franz whispered and involuntarily licked his lips. He had not had the opportunity to participate in a murder investigation since his days in Berlin, and until that very moment had not realized how much he missed it. He thought he'd had enough of violence in Germany. And perhaps he had. But he had not had nearly his fill of puzzle solving.

"I thought that might cheer you up. Girl's brother was done in, though the papers reported it as an accident. And now, someone's taken a shot at her fiancé as well—who happens to be an earl. Like I said, Franz, this one's your golden ticket!"

*

An hour later, Franz and a battered suitcase were seated in a third-class railway car, headed toward some seaside town with a strange name he'd never heard of before. Still, he couldn't be called sad to be leaving the grime and poverty of the East End for a while. It was a remarkably fine day, and he enjoyed the views. The English countryside in winter had a cold, bleak sort of beauty in it. Everything brown and ugly was now covered in snow, making it look like something from a picture postcard. There were two station changes on the trip, and by the time he reached his destination it was already growing dark. Franz was the only passenger to get off at Illhenny.

The station itself was practically deserted save a bored looking man at the ticket office.

"Hello," Franz addressed the ticket officer. "Can I use your telephone?"

At the sound of Franz's accent, the Englishman scowled. *A German! And a German traveling along the coast at that time of night.* Dark suspicions ran through his brain, and he curtly refused to give Franz any assistance. His suitcase in tow, Franz took his first steps in the little English town and saw a weathered old man with a wooden peg leg, hobbling on the streets.

"Pardon me," Franz attempted once more.

"You're German, aren't you?" the man snarled.

"I am," Franz stated simply.

"It's thanks to you lot I'm a cripple." The man scowled and then spat in the street.

Schaefer kept his expression completely cool and neutral. Inwardly, he wondered if the situation would get physical. While Schaefer would prefer not to engage in fisticuffs on his first night in a new town on a fresh assignment, he also knew the importance of standing one's ground. Giving in to bullies only emboldened them. It was a lesson much of Europe had sadly yet to learn regarding the Third Reich. As the man continued to glare at him and inched in somewhat closer, Schaefer clenched his fist.

An engine throttle sounded, and a torch light blared at them.

"What is all this?" a strong feminine voice rang out in the same tone as a nursery attendant addressing a pair of naughty young charges. Franz made out the voice and shape of a young woman on a motorbike and nodded. The woman came better into view, and he saw she wore a gray uniform and had an intelligent, if worried, face.

"All right, that's you, Pete, and who's this?" Realization appeared to dawn. "You must be Mr. Schaefer!"

"That is correct." Franz wondered who this woman was and how she knew about him. She wasn't Harriet West. Even if Franz had never seen Harriet's pictures, he would have easily known this woman was no socialite.

"Wait, are you friends with a kraut now, nursie?" Pete asked incredulously.

"First of all, it's none of your business. Secondly, aren't you supposed to be resting?" the woman retorted.

"I figured a little fresh air couldn't hurt."

"Fresh air from The Mud Crab perhaps?" she answered tartly. "I swear, you're almost as bad as Caleb!" Schaefer did not know who "Caleb" was, but the amputee seemed affronted at the comparison.

"All I wanted was a chance to share a pint among friends. What's wrong with that?" Pete protested.

"It's hardly kind of you to spread the flu around, is it? Now, go back home!" The nurse spoke sharply.

Pete looked surly, but hobbled off, and then the nurse turned back to Franz. "I really feel I must apologize for Pete. He's not a bad man. He truly isn't! But, well, he left pieces of himself on the battlefields of France. Literally."

"I am well aware of the scars left by the Great War on men's bodies and souls." Schaefer shrugged. "At least he didn't call me a dirty Jew."

Mary wasn't sure whether to take that as a joke or not. The German had a face longer than the French Channel.

"I must say, Mr. Schaefer, it's a good thing to welcome you here. Things have become such a mess."

"Excuse me, but may I ask, who are you?" As he spoke, Mary stepped closer to him, directly under a streetlight, giving Franz a much better view of her. "You are definitely not my employer, Miss West."

"Oh no," she explained. "I'm Miss Grey. I'm a"—she hesitated a moment—"a friend of Miss West, who summoned you here." As she said "friend," a hint of color appeared in Miss Grey's cheeks. Schaefer observed it and filed it away for future use. Perhaps there was some tension there?

"But Harriet had to leave quite suddenly," Mary went on.

"My employer has departed before I have even met her?" Franz was stunned. Surely not even the English were this eccentric? Or maybe there was some secret behind Miss West's absence that made Miss Grey uncomfortable?

"Her uncle took a turn for the worse, so she's rushed straight off to be by his side," Mary explained. "She doesn't want to risk letting another family member die without her. I'm sure you understand."

"Ah yes," Franz answered. It was a simple enough explanation and Mary had shown no signs of embarrassment relating it. What then was the cause of her embarrassment? Well, he would find out all in good time.

"But I'm so sorry there was no one to meet you at the station," Mary apologized. "That was very careless of Lord

Pool. Though, of course, he is on opiates, so I suppose allowances have to be made. Have you eaten? Because I haven't! And I could do with a drink as well."

A short while later, Mary and Franz were seated in a pub. To Franz's mind, the beer was always inferior to that found in Germany. He had to push away the pint the landlady first served him in disgust as his mind turned nostalgically to the Oktoberfest celebrations he'd visited in Munich, or rather "Weisen," as the locals called it. Steins of real beer, endless pots of sauerkraut and bratwurst, music and yodeling on every corner. And the offerings of the Wienzelt! Franz sighed at the memory and asked for a glass of cider instead. That, at least, the British could do competently.

Mary ordered fish and chips for them both, and then added, "Mr. Schaefer here will need a bed for the night."

"It'll be payment up front," Mrs. Jones said, eyeing Franz's clothes, which had clearly seen better days.

Franz reached for his thin wallet when, much to his surprise, Mary pulled out her purse and paid for him. Mrs. Jones went off to put in their food orders.

"You don't look like you have much to spare," Mary told Franz.

Once upon a time, Schaefer might have taken insult at any suggestion he was a beggar but, as of late, false pride had become a luxury neither he nor his family could afford.

"Do you?" he asked her shrewdly.

"Not really," she admitted, "but Harriet will pay me back, and the Rural Nursing Association covers my room and board. No telling what expenses may come up for you while you're on the job. Besides, you're a stranger to our shores and the Christmas spirit is all about giving, isn't it?'

"I'm Jewish," he reminded her.

"Oh yes," she said, coloring. "Your lot don't go in for Christmas much, do they?"

"Typically, no. We celebrate Hanukkah this time of year."

"Hana-what?"

"Festival of Lights. Eight days of giving."

Mary still looked lost, and Schaefer inwardly sighed. Christians, he'd found, even kind Christians, seemed sadly unaware of any customs outside their own faith. "Not that it matters. I am not celebrating this year, having no one to celebrate with, and back in my homeland, all festivities are now being held in private synagogues instead of publicly."

"Oh, have public ceremonies been banned?" Mary was at least aware that the new German regime hadn't been good for its Jewish population, even if she had never really known what Jews actually did.

"They haven't been legally banned, but my fellow Jews in Germany have decided not to hold any, to try to avoid provocations. Many believe that if they keep a—how you say—low profile, they will be safe." Something in Schaefer's tone of voice suggested he was skeptical that this strategy would work. "In any event, any large public gathering of Jews in Germany right now would most certainly attract the attention of jackbooted thugs and blood would be spilled. So, no Hanukkah this year. Not that it will be missed as much as Purim and Rosh Hashanah were."

Schaefer sighed, and there was a long awkward silence as Mary wondered what on earth Purim and Rosh Hashanah were. She thought of asking but feared that would only deepen Schaefer's melancholy, so, instead, she tried another line of inquiry.

"Are you really a detective then?"

"Yes. Yes, I am."

"Well, that makes you the first detective I've ever met. At least," Mary corrected herself, remembering Ames, "the first private detective. How does one go about becoming one?"

"I began as an ordinary policeman in Berlin," Schaefer explained with a wry smile. "Somewhat to the disappointment of my family. They wanted me to become a doctor or a dentist. But the workings of the human body have never really interested me, and teeth even less so. Or if I was interested in the law, then why not an attorney? But no, I insisted on becoming a policeman, so that I could become a detective."

"Why?"

"It was my dream since boyhood. I was always taken with detective stories."

"Like Sherlock Holmes?"

"Well, Holmes has his charms, but I can assure you no one really knows how to identify two hundred kinds of tobacco ash! I prefer Sergeant Cuff from *The Moonstone*. And of course, I read a great deal about the Pinkerton detectives in the United States. Furthermore, all my life, I have enjoyed puzzles. There is something so satisfying when you put the right piece into the right place."

"And detective work is like solving a puzzle?"

"No, detective work is much more challenging because you don't always have all the pieces and you do not know what the final picture will be. For instance, I am now working on an assignment where I haven't even met my employer." Schaefer gave an amused half grin. "So, anything you could tell me would be a blessing."

Mary narrated the whole tale over fish and chips. Franz interrupted her a couple of times with questions, but mostly he sat and listened while she told her tale. He scarcely touched his food, but rather closed his eyes and assumed an expression of intense concentration. Only when Mary had finished with the whole story did Franz open his eyes and begin eating the by-then cold food.

At the sight of Mary's surprised expression, Franz noted, "I didn't want to miss any of what you were saying while chewing. But now, I must eat to keep up my strength."

"Ah," replied Mary.

"You have told me a very interesting story, Miss Grey," he told her between mouthfuls. Mary waited to hear more. Franz made no other comment but wolfed down the fish and chips like a starving man.

Mary stifled a twinge of irritation and asked, "I suppose the first thing you'll want to do is see his Lordship."

"Actually," Franz replied, polishing off the last of his meal, all but licking his plate clean. Fish and chips were not a favorite of Schaefer's, but he had had a long day and his diet as of late had been somewhat limited. "I am in no hurry to see his Lordship."

"You're not?" Mary didn't hide her surprise. "But he's the one who got shot!"

"And he didn't see or hear anything useful. Otherwise, we'd already know about it," Schaefer pointed out. "I first want to speak with Inspector Ames and learn what the police know of the matter."

"Sorry, but Ames won't talk to you. He doesn't like amateur detectives," Mary told him.

"Perhaps not, but as I have a letter of introduction from a former superintendent of Scotland Yard, he may make an exception for me. By the way, do you still have Mr. West's appointment book?" Mary passed it to him and then hesitated. She wanted to ask Schaefer if he'd keep her in the loop, as it were, regarding the investigation. Yet such a question might seem inappropriate. Much to her relief, Schaefer cleared up the matter himself.

"As a stranger to these shores, I will be relying on you, Miss Grey, to act as my local guide here in Illhenny. Also, I imagine locals might tell you more than they'd tell me."

"I'd be delighted to help any way that I can," Mary replied happily.

"Good! You've already been trying to get a sense of local feelings on Mr. West. I would also like to know what people have been saying about Lord Pool, particularly behind his back."

"I'll get on it. I'll even talk to Dahlia Winthrop again if I have to."

"I appreciate your dedication. Also, we can start eliminating suspects by finding out who has an alibi for the time of Lord Pool's shooting." All of this was music to Mary's ears. Clearly, Schaefer, unlike Ames, saw her as a potential partner rather than a hindrance to his investigation. She was beginning to take a liking to this sad-faced little German man.

"Your English is awfully good," she told him.

"My maternal grandmother was English. My grandfather met her when studying in London."

"So, you're a quarter English then?"

"Technically, yes, but to English eyes I am a hundred percent foreign. Moreover"—bitterness crept into his voice—"I do not know if my grandmother was ever accepted as fully English either. She was, after all, a Jewess. Now, if you'll excuse me, I think I'd like to retire to my room for the night, and I imagine you must be getting home as well."

"I do have a busy day tomorrow. As I do every day, really." Mary gave a sort of half grin.

"Ah, a healer's work is never done," Schaefer proclaimed. "Perhaps we can meet again tomorrow, at your cottage? Say, eight o'clock?"

"That would be perfect." Mary did not want the expense of going out every night, or the risk of being eavesdropped on.

"*Auf Wiedersehen*! Now, if you will politely excuse me, I wish to retire."

"Of course."

Mrs. Jones directed Schaefer to a stairway. "All the way up," she told him, "last door on the left. Here's the key." She left him to deal with his suitcase by himself.

The room in question was a narrow slit of a space, resembling a closet with a tiny cot and desk and chair wedged against the far wall. There was barely enough room between the wall and the bed to fit the suitcase. The mattress on the bed creaked, and the blankets were thin and moth-eaten. But Schaefer was so tired it didn't really matter. He didn't even bother to get under the covers before falling asleep.

Chapter Thirteen

"So, Sir Henry personally vouches for you, and he's asked me to show you every consideration. He says you're one of the best." Inspector Ames examined the German in front of him. They met at a tea shop called The Lilac Bush, which was painted white with blue trim. Inside, it was furnished with well-worn but comfortable furniture, and the lilac patterned wallpaper had begun to peel. The overall atmosphere was that of a sort of shabby gentility.

Ames ordered strong tea, Schaefer ordered black coffee, much to the consternation of the waitress. News of a German visitor had spread like wildfire throughout the village, and while he was reportedly a detective, suspicions were not assuaged. Inspector Ames did not suspect Schaefer of being a spy, but he still had doubts. At first sight, Schaefer didn't look very promising. Could this scrawny man with his hangdog expression really be the crime-solving genius Sir Henry had described? Still, he could hardly give Schaefer the brushoff—not when he'd been hired by the future Lady Pool.

"Sir Henry has been a most generous friend and benefactor"—Schaefer's lips turned up in the minutest direction of a smile—"but he is perhaps too free with his praise." The modesty seemed quite real and unfeigned. "I am here at Miss West's request to serve in any way I can."

"Hmm." Inspector Ames absently tapped his fingers on the table. At least the fellow wasn't arrogant. So long as he didn't get in the way, Ames might just be able to tolerate him. The waitress served them their drinks in delicate, dainty little china cups painted with flowers and vines that had begun to fade with use.

"Please," Schaefer said between sips of coffee, "can you tell me what you've learned so far? I would like a copy of the case files, but I want to hear it all in your words first, inspector. Begin with the beginning, as your Charles Dickens would say."

"Very well then." Inspector Ames recounted the results of Anthony West's autopsy and his first interview with Mary Grey while Schaefer drank his coffee. "Odd woman, that Miss Grey," Ames remarked, gulping down half his cup of now cooled tea. "Oh, I daresay she makes a good enough nurse, but rather pushy, isn't she? Old maids often are. Comes from not having a man, I say. Or maybe it's why they don't get a man." He chortled, but Schaefer did not join in, and the seriousness of his face cut Ames's laughter short. "What?"

"I think you should know that Miss Grey has become quite friendly with the late Mr. West's sister," Schaefer informed him.

"Has she?" Ames didn't hide his surprise. "Don't know much about Miss West, but from what I've heard of the circles she runs in, I wouldn't think she'd have much in common with a district nurse."

"Tragedy makes for strange bedfellows," Schaefer mused.

"I suppose it must." Ames shrugged and finished the rest of the cup of tea. "Now, back to the investigation. After talking to Miss Grey, we interviewed everyone at the hospital who might have seen something. There was a patient in the room across from Mr. West, said sometime after the Grey woman and Lord Pool were gone and he had another visit from the hospital nurse, a man entered Mr. West's room. He described the man as wearing a large hat, a long, black beard, and dark glasses." Ames snorted in disgust as the server poured him a steaming hot refill and he muttered a thank-you.

Schaefer motioned to his empty cup, and the server went to the coffee kettle.

"It sounds like our killer has a taste for the theatre," Schaefer mused as his cup was refilled with coffee. "*Danke schön*" he told the server, who skittered into the background at the sound of a foreign tongue, as if it might be some curse.

"Someone who spends too much time at the movies or cheap musical shows," Ames growled before blowing on his tea to cool it. "Still, it does mean we don't have a proper description of the fellow. The only relevant details we have are that he was of average height and carrying a large bouquet of expensive looking flowers. Orchids, in fact. Our mystery man goes in with the flowers, and comes out about five minutes later without them, but with the back of his head turned toward our witness, and leaves. The patient didn't think anything of it at the time. Only later, when the rumor mill in the wards started wagging on about West being murdered, did he realize the importance of what he saw. Bad luck he didn't alert anyone at the time," he observed dolorously.

"But certainly lucky for the murderer, and possibly even the witness," Schaefer replied. At Ames's raised eyebrows, he added, "In my experience, knowing the identity of a killer can be quite dangerous, and blackmailing one doubly so."

"Maybe so. Certainly sounds like our killer was being very careful not to let anyone see his face. We found a false beard and glasses in a dustbin outside the hospital. But we've had no luck tracing where they were acquired. They appeared used, like they came out of someone's old costume box. No telling how old they even are." Ames sipped the tea and now found it to be at an acceptable temperature.

"Did you try to trace the flowers?" Schaefer asked.

Ames looked offended. "Of course, we tried to trace the flowers! What do you think we are, a bunch of Lestrades? We canvassed every florist for miles around, but nobody in this area sold any orchids that day, which to me suggested the killer was from out of town, because where else but in a big city could someone buy orchids of all things and not be noticed?"

"Yes, that was a very big mistake on the part of the murderer," Schaefer agreed. "Very suggestive."

"Well, they were nice flowers at any rate. After they removed West's body, the nurses took the flowers to one of the public wards to add a little cheer."

"Which is why Miss Grey made no mention of them to me," Schaefer noted. "Because the flowers had been removed from the room before she had even arrived. Thus, she was deprived of an important clue."

"Well, it's hardly Miss Grey's job to be looking into this case, now is it?" Inspector Ames felt somewhat rankled. "This sort of thing's best left to coppers like us." He took a chocolate biscuit off a silver salver and began munching on it aggressively.

"Sadly, I am not a—how you say—'copper' anymore," Schaefer commented. "I am a stranger to these shores, and so I take whatever help I can get, whether it comes from official channels or not." Between sips of coffee, he tried nibbling on a scone. It was a poor substitute for puddingbrezel, and he wearily pushed it aside. Familiar food was only one of many things he missed about his homeland.

"Yes, well, she certainly had no business removing evidence from the scene, did she?" Ames retorted before biting into one of the scones.

"But Miss Grey did not remove the flowers," Schaefer objected.

"Not talking about the flowers," Ames retorted between mouthfuls of scone. Quite good, he thought approvingly, taking another bite. "But the thread. Now, I'm not going to argue her intentions weren't good, but I'd have preferred a pristine crime scene myself. Though, truth be told, even without Miss Grey's meddling, that one was a dead end," he reluctantly admitted. "Didn't find a single fresh fingerprint in that garage that didn't belong to West himself. My guess is the saboteur wore gloves while in the garage. Now, unless they were wearing actual mechanic's work gloves, doing the sabotage in the car itself might have meant taking off the gloves, and the possibility of a print on the car engine, but that was smashed to pieces on the rocks when the car went into the sea. Even if we could retrieve any piece of the car, any evidence would be washed away."

"Rather lucky for the saboteur," Schaefer commented.

Ames snorted in agreement. "Bastard got a trump draw there, to be sure. Hell, we can't even prove beyond a doubt the car was ever tampered with." He took a long sip of tea.

"But it can be proven that Mr. West was murdered?"

"Oh yes. The coroner found bloodshot eyes, a clear indication of suffocation. Moreover, he discovered a piece of pillow stuffing stuck in the back of the victim's throat. No question it was murder all right, and a cold-blooded job of it too. The hospital staff weren't happy to hear it, I can tell you. That Dr. Huxley seems scared witless they'll be blamed for the whole matter, and maybe they should be."

Schaefer nodded. "Yes, Nurse Grey gave me a vivid picture of your Dr. Huxley."

"I'll bet she did," Ames laughed. "No love lost there. He'd like to ban her from his hospital for life if he could, but that's a bit difficult with a district nurse."

"I would imagine," Schaefer replied drily. "I understand, though, Miss Grey found a piece of fiber in the garage?" After asking, Franz tried one of the biscuits. It was not as good as lebkuchen, but it was acceptable.

"We examined it and there was nothing unusual about it. Could have come from damn near anywhere." Ames looked doleful.

"Did you look into the deceased's finances?" Schaefer inquired, much to Ames's indignation.

"We went over all his accounts quite thoroughly and there was nothing wrong there at all. No outstanding debts, no signs of a gambling problem, or indication he was being blackmailed. The young man was quite well off and was due to be coheir of one of the greatest fortunes in England. Now, of course, his sister will get the lot of it. And she's the primary beneficiary as well under her brother's will. Normally, she'd be our top suspect, but she wasn't even in the country at the time of his death. Believe me, we checked. Now, originally, we were going with the theory that West's murderer was from out of town—some fellow Londoner." Ames polished off the last of the tea. The server came over with a teapot to refill it, but he waved her off.

"Oh? What made you think that?" Schaefer asked, finishing one biscuit and trying another of a different type.

"Well, in my experience, nine times out of ten, when a fellow gets murdered, it's by someone with a close relationship to the victim," Ames observed.

"That is certainly true," Schaefer agreed. The second biscuit was, he noted, noticeably tastier than the first.

"But the thing is, West hadn't really had any close relationships around the village." Ames threw up his hands. "So, I figured it had to be someone from the outside. He certainly had plenty of visitors. And, you know, a wealthy young man around town like that could have got into all kinds of trouble. Someone in business with him, some problem with his personal life, maybe involvement with drugs or adultery. That sort of thing."

"And were there any such troubles in West's history?" Schaefer finished his second cup of coffee. The server did not offer him a refill and Schaefer didn't ask. There is, after all, a point in which coffee serves not to keep you alert but to make you as jittery as a cat in a room full of rocking chairs.

"No, blast it, there weren't." Ames didn't hide his disappointment as he continued, "From our enquiries, we've gathered he was quite well liked in London. No jealous husbands or bitter jilted lovers in the mix. And there was no rummy political business that could have landed him in trouble either. We made discreet enquiries and he had no involvement with communists or socialists or fascists, or anything of that sort. Seems he preferred to stay out of politics altogether."

"A wise move in these times," Schaefer opined. "Though not always possible, I'm afraid, to stay completely apolitical. And I don't think the English government will be able to remain neutral for much longer regarding the affairs of greater Europe."

Ames listened to Schaefer's words with a growing impatience, and even discomfort. It had always been his policy, as an officer of the law, to stay out of politics, and he didn't appreciate some foreigner telling him otherwise, especially when they had a murder case to be focusing on.

As if guessing Ames's thoughts, Schaefer abruptly turned back to the investigation, "So, there was no indication of anyone in West's past who would want to harm him?"

"He didn't seem to have an enemy in the world. At least not until he came to Illhenny," Ames concluded. "Moreover, Lord Pool's shooting practically confirmed the matter was local, after all. Didn't take much questioning around here to show that resort project stirred up a lot of ill feeling."

"Like Caleb Barnaby?"

"He's of particular interest all right, but we can't prove his guilt either way. Fact is, anyone could have snuck into West's garage. We asked every single one of the neighbors and no one saw anything. The one time it would have been helpful for them to be spying on the place and no one had an eye on it!"

"What about Lord Pool's houseguests?" Schaefer changed the subject.

"What guests?"

The server was eying them coldly, wondering how long they would occupy a table without making any further orders, but Schaefer and Ames were far too engrossed in their conversation to notice this.

"Miss Grey reported several other persons visiting Lord Pool at Avenel Court."

"Wait, how would Miss Grey know?" Ames demanded.

"She dined there one night, at Miss West's request," Schaefer explained.

"Well, I'll be damned." Ames stroked his chin. "Guess they have become fast friends. But as it happens, all of Lord Pool's guests had departed the very morning he was shot."

"Really? Everyone leaves and then his Lordship is shot? Our perpetrator seems to have remarkably good timing."

"Does, doesn't he? There was no one at Avenel Court but the usual staff when we got there." Ames chortled, "Maybe the butler did it!"

Schaefer didn't laugh. "That is actually a real possibility. Long before my time, there was a case of a valet who packed up a suitcase of valuables and then killed his master before fleeing into the night. Unfortunately for the valet in question, an unexpected blizzard blocked the roads and spoiled his escape. He was caught, tried, and executed."

"Served him right, greedy bastard," Ames pronounced.

By this point, the waitress had resorted to tapping her foot in the corner while loudly clearing her throat. Schaefer was the first to take the hint.

"I believe the staff want us to leave," he told Ames, gesturing with a nod of his head.

"She can wait," was Ames's verdict. "Not like there's a crowd waiting to get in." This was true. The Lilac Bush was only two-thirds full, but the people seated at the other tables were all somehow different from Schaefer in his thread-worn suit, and even Ames who looked like a common bricklayer wearing his Sunday best. And Ames and Schaefer thus drew curious glances from some of the clientele. Ames, however, either didn't notice or, more likely, did not care. "And we've still got a lot to talk about. Let's get back to the greedy valet who killed his master." He leaned back in his chair, his eyes alight with interest.

"But that is the thing. It might not have just been greed. You see, the valet stabbed his master with a kitchen knife over a dozen times!" Ames whistled, and Schaefer went on. "Oh, robbery was clearly part of the crime but, to me, the extremely vicious nature of the killing suggested more personal motives as well."

"Like the valet had a grudge against his master?"

"Precisely. I've found resentments can pile up very easily among those who must do the bidding of others without speaking back."

"I've noticed it too," Ames agreed. "Your story reminds me of a case I once knew of a companion who slipped arsenic into her employer's daily cordial. At first, I assumed she was hoping to be in her employer's will but, in fact, she told me the bigger issue was she couldn't stand to keep listening to the old woman's boring stories anymore. But I'm afraid that won't work here. Even if one of Lord Pool's servants hated him, they could have had no motive for killing West. And West didn't keep any servants on hand at all. Just a charwoman who came in a few times a week. We checked her out, too, and she was working elsewhere when West was suffocated at the hospital."

"Very true, inspector. It sounds like you hit the—how you say—concrete wall then with Mr. West's death."

"Brick wall. *Brick*," Ames corrected him. "And yes, we have. At least until the attack on Lord Pool proved it's really all about the resort project."

"It would appear so, yes." Schaefer remained non-committal. "The cases must certainly be linked."

"And with Lord Pool's shooting, at least we have some hard evidence. We've found the bullet that hit his Lordship and the casings, so once we find the gun itself, we can match them."

"Assuming the shooter hasn't already abandoned the gun," Schaefer noted. "That would certainly be the most prudent course of action."

"Well, I've found criminals aren't a very prudent lot. In fact, most of them, in my experience, are downright stupid, so maybe we'll get a bit of luck for a change."

"Maybe."

"In any event, we're no worse off for having the casings than we were before. And the more crimes they commit, the more likely they'll slip up."

"That is certainly true. I should like to visit the crime scenes. With your permission?"

"There's nothing left to find." Ames seemed to take offense. "I assure you we didn't leave any stray clues lying about."

"I am quite sure you did not, inspector," Schaefer said soothingly. "I have every confidence that you and your men were very thorough, but I would like to see the locations anyway. I find it helps me to picture the events more clearly, like being at the cinema."

"Suit yourself." Ames sounded mollified. "I could give you a tour of The Laurels right now, if you like."

"That would be most kind of you, inspector!"

"Reckon it's time we were off anyway." The waitress had now been joined by the manager, both giving their table the evil eye. They'd probably, Ames thought with amusement while gesturing for the bill, be threatening to call the police on them as loiterers if it weren't for the fact that Ames was the police. The server handed him a bill, and Ames nearly choked at the sight of the total.

"For some tea and biscuits?" He was outraged. "This is highway robbery, it is!" Nevertheless, he started counting out coins. Schaefer reached for his own slender purse. Ames, eyeing Schaefer's rundown appearance, took pity.

"Don't bother, Mr. Schaefer. This one's on me."

"Thank you, inspector," Schaefer told him gratefully. "I do hope to repay your kindness later on, once Miss West pays me."

"Don't mention it," Ames brushed it off gruffly. "Overpriced and unfriendly in here. Someone shoot me if I ever darken the door of this place again," he grumbled.

As they walked out of the door, Schaefer added, "By the way, inspector, Miss West even had Miss Grey stay overnight at Avenel Court after his Lordship was shot."

"Did she now?"

"Miss Grey believes Miss West wanted her for reassurance, but once Miss West left to visit her uncle, Miss Grey returned to her own cottage." Schaefer paused. "Does that not strike you as peculiar? The nurse is only there when the injured man's fiancée is present, but when Miss West goes, so does Miss Grey, leaving Lord Pool alone?"

"Not exactly alone," Ames interjected. "His Lordship's got plenty of servants and his own private doctor too."

"It could be that," Schaefer mused.

"Well, you can ask his Lordship yourself."

Their first stop was The Laurels. Schaefer stepped inside the garage briefly and went directly to the tool shelf. The bolt cutters were absent, having been taken as evidence, but Schaefer seemed content to just look at the tools themselves, now gathering dust. He gave a curt nod and then left. As he and Ames stood outside the garage, Schaefer scanned his eyes in every direction. A woman standing in the backyard of a house on the opposite side stared at them, and Schaefer gave a friendly wave. The woman looked undecided for a moment before giving a half wave back.

"Mr. West had quite a few neighbors," Schaefer observed drolly. "Observant ones at that, yet nobody saw anything."

"Like I said, bloody bad luck." Ames gave another of his shrugs.

"Perhaps," Schaefer said. "Perhaps it is something more."

"Like what?" Ames asked, but Schaefer's expression was unreadable. A sudden thought struck the inspector. "You don't think someone saw something and then didn't say anything, do you?"

"It is possible," Schaefer told him.

"But for God's sake, why?"

"Sometimes, witnesses prefer not to get involved, especially if they are familiar with the people in question."

"Good God, man. You think someone would protect a murderer?"

"I've seen it happen before." Schaefer gazed away into the distance. "Either through misguided loyalty, a wish to be left alone, or sometimes because the witness involved thinks there may be something in it for them if they keep silent." He straightened himself and his eyes returned to the present. "Shall we go inside, inspector?"

They did so, and it soon became apparent that none of the late Mr. West's things had yet been moved.

"Suppose we'll have to release his things soon to his family," Ames speculated, looking over West's personal photographs. When he got to the one which included a topless dancer, he gaped a bit before putting it face down. Fortunately, Schaefer made no sign of noticing Ames's discomfiture, but rather took a look at the phonograph in the corner with albums of Ethel Waters, Duke Ellington, Louis Armstrong, and Ella Fitzgerald before moving on to West's bookshelves.

"Hmm." Schaefer wordlessly fingered thick hardcover texts on Bauhaus design as well as dog-eared paperback volumes by Graham Greene and Evelyn Waugh. "Mr. West was a young man of very modern tastes in both architecture and literature."

"Don't go in for that sort of thing myself," Ames commented.

"Modern architecture or modern authors?"

"Neither! I like good, old-fashioned English buildings, and good, old-fashioned classic English authors, like Dickens or Defoe. All these modern boxy buildings, and books about unpleasant people you don't care about, just leave me cold." Ames sniffed. "Even detective stories are better than that rot."

"Ah"—Schaefer raised a finger—"but remember, inspector, what is modern now is what will seem to be good, old-fashioned classics in the future."

Ames snorted. "I don't think anyone's ever going to call anything by that Virginia Woolf woman a classic!" he retorted.

"Interesting." Schaefer spotted *Pamela; or, Virtue Rewarded* by Samuel Richardson. "I would have said this was exactly the sort of book he'd like least." He picked it off the shelf and looked at it more closely. "Ah, the packaging is fake. Far from being an eighteenth-century morality tale, look what we have here." Schaefer held up a copy of *Lady Chatterley's Lover* which had been concealed within the cover of the Richardson novel.

"What?" Ames started. "This smut's been banned here in England!"

"So it has been. Hmm...for that matter, would young Mr. West have kept a copy of the King James Bible either?"

On examining the Bible, he discovered it had, in what was clearly an act of blasphemy, been hollowed out to hold a copy of *Tropic of Cancer*. Moreover, rifling through the works of Henry James and D. H. Lawrence revealed, in both volumes, little note cards of women in saucy poses without their clothes on.

"More pornography," Ames declared.

"Well, that's a matter of opinion, is it not?" Schaefer declared. "One man's art is another man's pornography. After all, there are some who would describe Michelangelo's *David* as obscene."

"Yes, well, Michelangelo didn't take these photos, did he?" Ames retorted. "And I don't think anyone's going to be putting them in a museum anytime soon!"

"Maybe not now, but in another thousand years such pictures could be considered priceless artifacts, inspector—perhaps all the more valuable because they were taboo in their own time."

"You can't be serious," Ames objected.

"You would be amazed the things I take seriously, inspector. Admittedly, the deceased himself didn't seem to value these articles much either. The photographs are almost an afterthought. The way they're placed here, it's like they were used as bookmarks. He took a lot of notes while he read too. See?" Schaefer pointed to pencil and pen marks in margins and passages that had been underlined.

"Certainly was engaged with the material, I'll give him that."

"It seems that when it came to literature, young West liked—how you say—forbidden fruit?"

"Seems like it. But whatever the young hound's taste in books, I'll be damned if I can see how it got him killed!"

"Ah, having possession of the wrong book, inspector"—Schaefer gave a bitter smile—"is exactly the sort of thing that can get you killed, as we Germans now know all too well." Ames was silent.

Schaefer then took a quick tour of the upstairs, casually flipping through West's closet.

"Certainly spent a lot on tailors, didn't he?" Ames noted with a certain disapproval. "Never considered it right for a man to make too much of a fuss in how he's dressed. Always makes him a poofter in my mind. Wait, are these real diamonds?" He held up a carved box containing a pair of ornate cufflinks that sparkled with a cold flame.

"I believe they are," Schaefer answered, and Ames gave a low whistle. "As you say, West was very nicely fixed." Schaefer gave the room a final glance. "I'm ready to go now, inspector."

"'Bout bloody time," Ames muttered under his breath.

Schaefer looked up abruptly. "Excuse me, inspector?"

"Begging your pardon, but I fail to see how we've made any progress here," Ames retorted.

"Perhaps we have, perhaps we haven't." Schaefer gave a non-committal shrug.

Once they were outside, Schaefer asked, "Can we see the scene of the accident? Yes, I know we definitely won't find clues there, inspector," he added, anticipating Ames's likely objection. "Still, perhaps you could humor me anyway?" He gave his ingratiating smile.

Past the trees, they stood on the edge of the cliff, right at the very edge, and Schaefer stared down at the waves crashing on the rocks below. He seemed mesmerized by the sight, and he was so close to the edge and leaning down at such an angle as to raise Inspector Ames's blood pressure. Ames cleared his throat loudly, and Schaefer took a step back, as if being released from an enchantment.

"Quite a way to fall, wasn't it?" Ames shuddered. "Can't say I fancy being this high."

"Nor do I," Schaefer admitted, which made Ames wonder why he had gone so close to the edge at all. As if he'd read the inspector's mind, he elaborated. "I wanted to get a picture in my mind." He pointed to his noggin. "I wanted to see what Mr. West would have seen in those moments he must have thought were his last. I wanted to see what his savior had to risk that night to pull him out of the car." Schaefer shook his head ruefully. "But, of course, this wasn't even the scene of the crime at all, was it?" He seemed to be speaking almost to himself. "The car was meddled with in the garage, and Mr. West was so brutally suffocated with a pillow in his hospital bed. *Hier ist kein Übel zu finden.* We can go back now, inspector. You were right. This place tells us nothing except that Miss Grey is a remarkable woman, indeed."

Ames looked up sharply at that. *Could it be the Hebrew kraut is sweet on Miss Grey?* Stranger things had happened.

Chapter Fourteen

Since Ames had a busy schedule, Schaefer went to Avenel Court alone, hitching a ride on a delivery truck. Spode, the butler, was less than welcoming. Firstly, because Schaefer was clearly a foreigner. Secondly, there was the nature of his visit.

"Well, Mr. Shay-Fur"—he enunciated the name carefully—"Avenel Court has been absolutely deluged with policeman and detectives of late." The butler managed to say "policeman" and "detectives" as if to imply they were vermin. "We've never seen anything of the sort here before. Indeed, I don't think we've ever even had a police officer step foot in this building before, in all the centuries it's been here." Spode sighed. "Times really are changing. First pay cuts for all the staff, then some of us were let go, and now this! Oh well, I suppose you better come in."

Schaefer was ushered to Lord Pool's bedside.

His Lordship, while still pale, was at least alert and sitting up, and didn't appear pleased to see Schaefer. "Harriet hired you?" He looked incredulously at Schaefer. "She never mentioned it to me."

"Well, your Lordship," Spode, who had remained on hand, chipped in, "was still sedated when she made initial enquiries, and then she had to hurry to her uncle's side."

"Yes, well, I still would have liked to have been consulted on the matter, you understand." Lord Pool sighed. Just another one of the ways Harriet's recent behavior bewildered him. Oh, he understood it was a trying time for her and that she was in grief, but she seemed so damned well cold to him as of late. Even now, he thought resentfully, while he lay in bed in pain after an attempt on his life, Harriet had gone off and left him. Yes, she had her uncle to think of as well, *but still!*

Lord Pool considered it not a little highhanded of Harriet to employ a detective without even consulting with him first. Moreover, he couldn't help but wonder at her choice of detectives. Not only had she hired a foreigner, but a Jew? Mind you, Lord Pool didn't have anything in particular against Jews. Compared to his fellow aristocrats, he was actually quite tolerant of them, but he'd never heard of a Jewish detective before either.

Perhaps she hadn't realized. They'd have to have a talk about it later. *In any event,* he thought, skeptically examining Schaefer, *the fellow's not going to get any money out of me!* "Well, I'm glad you're here," he said aloud. "Just between you and me, I'm not much impressed with the quality of the police work on this. They seem no closer to finding poor Anthony's killer now than they did on the first day."

"How bad is your injury?"

"Well, it isn't like the pictures, I can tell you. Getting shot hurts like hell," Lord Pool replied with emphasis, and Schaefer made sympathetic noises. "The doctor said my injury wasn't serious, but I can tell you, when I first woke up on the ground, bleeding and in pain, I thought... Well, I thought I might be done for." He shuddered at the memory of those terrible moments he lay bleeding. He flashed back to Andrews applying pressure to the wound and telling him to "buck up." Then the confusion of persons, as he lay there helpless, in a state of agony, praying the ambulance would be there soon. It was an ordeal his Lordship would not soon forget. He saw Schaefer's expectant face and continued speaking, "Fortunately, the doctor says I'll make a full recovery eventually, but a damned nuisance this is! Right now, even if I could leave the house, I'd not dare to with a shooter on the loose." He bit his lip. "It's a dark day for England when a man can't feel safe on the grounds of his own home."

"Tell me about the day you were shot."

"Not much to tell. I was just out stretching my legs a bit, when I felt something bite me in the back. I fell right there on the ground. Didn't see or hear anything." He threw up his hands.

"At what time did this occur?"

"Just after ten a.m."

"And how did you get help afterwards?"

"Andrews found me."

"The chauffer?" Schaefer asked. "Why was he not in the garage?"

"Don't know." Lord Pool looked puzzled by the question. "Suppose he wanted a little fresh air, eh? Wait, how did you know Andrews is the chauffer?"

"Miss Grey mentioned him to me. She told me she found him a capable driver, but not a very good conversationalist."

Lord Pool laughed. "Andrews is the strong, silent type all right. Reckon he learned it during the war, but he's always been a good servant though. Loyal, and you don't see that much these days."

"No, faithful servants are a dying breed," Schaefer agreed. "If you do not think it impertinent, I would like to know more about your relationship with the West family."

"Anthony and I were at Eton together, and we were quite close for a while. Then I went to Oxford and he went on to the Architectural Association School, but we kept in touch. These last few years, he was like a brother to me." Lord Pool became lost in memory and sadness. Anthony's loss had truly pained him and left a real hole in his life. Where once there had been laughter and camaraderie, there was now a dark shadow, and Lord Pool found it hurt him even more than the bullet.

"And he introduced you to his sister?"

"Yes. When I first met her, Harriet was still a child."

"But she grew up?"

"She did." Lord Pool smiled. "And well, we just sort of fell into it. The engagement, I mean."

"And love?"

"And love, too, of course." Lord Pool waved impatiently. "No man who ever got to know Harriet could help but fall in love with her. You'll understand when you meet her."

"It seems like the match was met with approval."

"Oh yes, Donald Harrington was over the moon about it before he became ill. Insisted ours would be the wedding of the decade! And Anthony was going to be the best man." Lord Pool turned solemn. "Now that Anthony's gone and poor Donald's on his way out, Harriet's not going to have any family left. Won't be anyone to give her away at the wedding. Not, mind you, that I'm even sure a big wedding would be appropriate anymore anyway."

"Probably not. So, as your future brother-in-law, it was only to be expected that you'd ask Mr. West to design your new resort."

"Blast the thing! I wish I'd never thought of the project. All the financing for it has been a nightmare of complications and red tape, and we haven't even broken ground yet!" Lord Pool brooded. "It got Anthony killed, and it nearly killed me too. Mind you, Caleb Barnaby's the one I'd look into first."

"Yes, his name has already come up in the investigation."

"Some investigation!" Lord Pool huffed. "I've put them on Barnaby's scent from the beginning, but have they done anything about him yet? No! Now I'm lying here, and he's out there, free to try to kill me again."

"Considering the present circumstances," Schaefer pointed out drily, "it would be most difficult for Mr. Barnaby, or any other villager, to attack you."

"While I'm here, maybe, but I'm not going to stay in this bloody house forever!"

"So, you are in no doubt that the proposed development was the motive behind the attacks on Mr. West and yourself?"

"Of course, I'm sure! What other motive could there be?"

"Someone perhaps with a long-standing resentment against Mr. West and yourself," Schaefer suggested. "Some old grudge or vendetta, unrelated to the development, but which you and West were both involved in."

"You can't be serious!" Lord Pool gave a half laugh. "What, do you think Anthony and I were on someone's list of enemies to take revenge on? That sounds like the plot of a bad novel."

"I have to consider every possibility." Schaefer shrugged. "And revenge is a classic motive for murder. It's why bad novels and some not-so-bad novels use it as a plot device."

"Well, you're barking up the wrong tree there. It's not like Anthony and I ever robbed an ancient tomb or drowned someone's son. I doubt Anthony ever harmed a soul."

"And have you?"

"No!" Lord Pool was indignant. "Well, at least I haven't done anything dramatic enough to warrant this—" He pointed to his bandage.

"So, you wouldn't mind then if I made enquiries into your past?" Schaefer asked with an expression of perfect innocence.

"Go right ahead." Lord Pool looked him in the eye. "You won't find anyone with a dark vendetta, I assure you. In the meantime, you're welcome to wander the house and grounds as much as you like, and you can ask the servants for anything you need," he generously offered.

"Your Lordship is most kind, but I prefer to stay at the inn."

"Suit yourself, but Mrs. Jones's cellar and pantry won't compare to mine."

"Perhaps not, but I will be closer to the townsfolk of Illhenny."

"Want to stay close to your suspect pool then, eh?"

"Something like that." Schaefer turned to go and then stopped, as if he'd just remembered. "Oh, by the way, your Lordship? Why is Miss Grey not here?"

"What?" Lord Pool seemed confused.

"Miss Grey. The district nurse."

"Well now, I have nothing against our fine district nurse, but I don't really need her, do I?" Lord Pool said dismissively. "I've got my own doctor here, and no shortage of staff to bring me tea and fluff my pillows." He gave a pained half-laugh.

"But your fiancée had Miss Grey here? Overnight, I understand."

"Yes, well..." His Lordship seemed uneasy. "Harriet wanted her here. She's had quite a few shocks of late, and well, I guess there's something about Nurse Grey she finds calming. Not sure I understand it myself," he admitted. "Funny how women take these fancies, isn't it? Anyway, she insisted on having the nurse in the room adjoining hers to give her support, and when the call came in about Donald's turn for the worse, she actually wanted to bring the nurse with her to the family estate! Never mind what anyone would think of Harriet bringing along such a guest. Oh"—he gave a dismissive wave of his hands—"she talked of how Nurse Grey might be so useful to poor Donald at this time. Nonsense, of course. The man's got an army of doctors and nurses looking after him. The only thing that stopped her was the nurse mentioning all the work she had to do in Illhenny and Harriet didn't feel it was fair to keep her from her duties." He rolled his eyes. "Honestly, I don't know what's got into her."

"Well, your fiancée has taken a number of shocks of late," Schaefer interjected soothingly. "It is a difficult time for her, and apparently she finds Miss Grey's presence reassuring." He thought a moment and then added, "Many people would. A most capable woman."

"Apparently," Lord Pool replied. "Certainly has a knack for appearing any time there's trouble around here, doesn't she?" He looked not a little put out by that, Schaefer observed.

After taking his Lordship's leave, Schaefer asked if anyone could show him where Lord Pool was shot.

"I'll send for Mr. Andrews," Spode said. "He's certainly free at present." Schaefer detected a definite tinge of envy to the butler's voice.

Andrews proved as laconic as Mary had described, keeping his communication mostly to grunts and an occasional "yes" or "no." Even those last two words had to be drawn out of him, and were done so with evident reluctance on Andrews' part. He clearly resented anyone trying to make him engage in speech. After walking past the Great House, the greenhouse, gardening sheds, and a gamekeeper's cottage, Andrews directed Schaefer to a certain spot with a pointed thumb.

"This is where Lord Pool fell?"

Andrews nodded.

"And you were the first to reach him?"

Another nod.

"And you were in the area because?"

"Was stretching me legs," Andrews replied. These four words were the longest he'd taken yet to speak.

Schaefer stood there and did a complete 360-degree turn, examining all directions. About thirty yards away he spotted an undergrowth of brush. "The shooter must have been hidden in there," he observed. He then laid his face down in the snow itself, apparently oblivious to the state of his clothes. He stayed like that for several moments before getting back on his feet and doing an inspection of the brush area itself. This was almost certainly unnecessary—no doubt Ames and his men had been over the area quite thoroughly. Still, Schaefer crept low among the bushes anyway and pantomimed firing a rifle. He then simply stood there a while, looking around in all directions, his eyes rapt like a man at a picture show at the cinema.

Watching the German go through such martial moves brought Andrews memories of the Great War, when he'd been killing Schaefer's countrymen like flies. A combination of boredom and force of habit made Andrews mentally size up Schaefer as an opponent in a trench fight. Not a big man, to be sure, but wiry, and, in Andrews' experience, the wiry ones were sometimes the most dangerous of all. The real question was whether the man was any good when the blood and the shit sprayed. Usually, Andrews could make up his mind about a fellow right quick on that question. This one had what it took.

This one didn't. The latter outnumbered the former. But Schaefer was proving more difficult to size up than usual.

"Oy! What you doing?" Schaefer was interrupted by a deep voice. Coming to them from the outer woods was a man in overalls with a long red beard streaked with gray.

"Excuse me, who are you?"

"Dick Townley. I'm the gamekeeper." The red-bearded man puffed himself up. "I'd ask the same of yourself, sir."

Schaefer looked hopefully at Andrews for assistance but found none. Finally, he said, "I am Franz Schaefer. I am a private detective."

"His Lordship hired you?" Townley looked at Schaefer with sheer incredulousness.

"No, Miss West did."

"Ah, yes. Miss West." Townley nodded sagely. "She's been having a bad time of it, hasn't she? Her brother dead, her uncle dying, and people jumping out of the undergrowth to take a shot at his Lordship! Don't know what the world's coming to. You know," he mused, "if only I'd been walking near here myself that day. I might have seen something. Might have seen all kinds of things I could have told the police." He shook his head sadly. "But I didn't see a bloody thing."

"Hmph." Andrews rolled his eyes.

"Well, best be off then," Townley proclaimed, "but Andrews, do pay my respects to his Lordship, will you? Let him know I wish him a speedy recovery. Nice meeting you, Mr. Schaefer." Townley enunciated each syllable of the name very carefully, and then wandered off.

As Townley retreated into the distance, Schaefer turned and said, “I, too, must be away. Thank you, Mr. Andrews, you’ve been most helpful. Don’t trouble yourself, I can find my own way back.” And then the German walked away whistling a Wagnerian libretto.

Chapter Fifteen

Sometime later, Schaefer had to admit to himself that perhaps he should have found a ride to town after all. Not that the walk itself was especially arduous, but he quickly realized that neither his shoes nor his coat was up to the task of a long trek on a snowy road. Even more ominously, there might be more snow to come. Clouds had been gathering as he began his walk back from Avenel Court, and he hurried his step, passing a gypsy's caravan on his way. Luckily, he reached the village square just as the first flakes began to fall. Instead of entering the library or bakery, which were both closer, Schaefer made his way to the tobacconist shop and greeted Mrs. Legge, whose crimson-painted lips formed a surprised "O."

"*Guten Tag!* I hope you don't mind. I thought I'd warm up in here." Schaeffer smiled ingratiatingly. "If that is all right with you, madame, of course."

"Of course," Mrs. Legge echoed.

"Danke schön."

Mrs. Legge didn't speak German and thus didn't know if she should take offense or not. She watched warily as Schaefer took a seat on a stool in the corner. Much to her surprise and relief, he never brought up Anthony

West. Instead, he made idle comments about the weather and about how he had just visited Avenel Court.

"Oh, you been inside, have you?" Mrs. Legge asked. "I never been in. Is it as grand inside as it looks outside?'

"Oh, it is. Though, I must say, it could perhaps do with a little modernization. Some of the carpets and draperies have become quite thread-worn."

"Ah, well, excepting yourself, men usually don't pay attention to that sort of thing. And there hasn't been a lady at Avenel Court since his Lordship's mum died when he was very little."

"Soon to be remedied when Lord Pool weds Harriet West," noted Schaefer. "A good match, huh? Title and money?"

"I suppose," Mrs. Legge answered, suddenly on guard again. Talking about Harriet might lead back to Anthony.

Fortunately, Schaefer moved on. "Speaking of decorating, I can see you've done some as well. That display case over there looks brand new."

"It was." Mrs. Legge beamed with pride. "Had it brought up from London, we did."

"Really? And what about that upper cabinet?"

"No, we hired a man in Anchester for that." Mrs. Legge happily spent a quarter of an hour telling Schaefer about all the little improvements she and Mr. Legge had been making to their home and shop in the past year or so. German or not, Schaefer was a very good listener, and when the weather cleared up long enough for him to take his departure, Mrs. Legge felt rather disappointed to see him go. She got quite an earful about it, though, from Mr. Legge.

"The German fellow? He came in here?" Mr. Legge looked apoplectic with rage.

"He was just trying to keep warm," she told him.

"You stupid cow!" He grabbed her roughly by the arm. "The man's a bloody detective! Why'd you even let him stay in the store? Why not throw him out, like we did with that nurse bitch?"

"Wouldn't that have looked more suspicious?" she countered hotly and shook herself out of his grip. "All but screams aloud we had something to hide, huh?" She didn't wait for an answer. "Since you threw out the nurse, I've been worried she'd call the coppers on us! Gave me a real fright, you did! Besides, he didn't say a word about Mr. West, or anything related to that business at all."

"He didn't?" Mr. Legge looked relieved, if not surprised.

"Nope, just talked furniture, he did. The kraut doesn't know a damn thing, and as long as everyone keeps their mouths shut it'll stay that way."

*

Schaefer returned to The Mud Crab and was greeted by Mrs. Jones with a beaming smile.

"Mr. Schaefer! So good to see you back, sir. Come sit down and have a cup of tea."

He did so, asking, "Have there been any messages for me?"

"Why yes, there have, sir. Miss West called. Her uncle passed away in the night. He's being buried day after tomorrow." Mrs. Jones practically warbled all this, happy as a lark. "Oh, and she confirmed that since you're in her employ she'll be paying your entire bill." Ah, now Mrs. Jones's good spirits and warm welcome made sense. "She also asked you be put up in the best room available. I've already taken the liberty of moving your things. By the way, sir, will you be having your meals out or dining in?"

"I would prefer to dine in."

"Then supper can be served at any time you like," Mrs. Jones beamed at him again, mouth wide open, displaying some truly hideous teeth.

Schaefer first used the telephone to make two calls and then retired to his new quarters, which were, indeed, a great deal larger and more comfortable. He admired the little sitting area with comfortable chairs and a warm-colored rug. An adjoining washroom had a claw foot tub. Best of all, there was a nice coal burning stove with a merry little blaze going. It was a scene meant for a gentleman to enjoy in an expensive dressing robe and slippers. Schaefer had neglected to pack a robe or slippers, but he enjoyed the suite, nonetheless.

Schaeffer made certain notes in his journal, took an early dinner, and then went to Mary Grey's cottage. Even though he'd never been there before and was a stranger to Illhenny, it was no trouble to find the place. The first bystander he asked pointed him right to it. He stood outside the simple dwelling and knocked. There was no response. He knocked again and called out, but there was no answer. He tried the door and found it locked, so he peeked in through the windows. But the house was dark and deserted. There was no sign of Miss Grey anywhere. He waited for over half an hour in the cold dark air before leaving. When Schaeffer came back to The Mud Crab, he was frankly worried. It was, he knew, too soon to make a missing person's report, but he considered calling Ames anyway, until reason reminded him there'd be no way to make a proper search until dawn in any event. He sat in the pub area and listened to bits and pieces of conversation around him.

"Are you sure he's not a German spy?"

"Propellor's broken. It'll cost a pretty penny to fix."

"A detective? She hired a bleeding detective? Doesn't sound like she's got much faith in Ames."

"We'll be having Christmas with my brother-in-law this year. God, what a long holiday that'll be."

"Bad enough to bring a detective into everyone's business, but a foreigner to boot! That Miss West sure is heavy handed."

"Gets harder every season for a man to make a living fishing."

"He's not just German. I think he might be a Jew as well. He looks like one, don't he?"

"He does look like a Jew, but I think he'd be better dressed. Aren't that lot supposed to have money?"

"Unfortunately, we Jews don't always have money." Schaefer unexpectedly joined the conversation and jaws all over the room dropped. "We do, however, have excellent hearing." For a while after that, the conversation in The Mud Crab became far more muted.

When Mary Grey appeared in the doorway, at a quarter past nine, bundled up like a bear, with a large muffler around her neck, Schaefer felt relieved both for her safety and also for the sight of a friendly face. He beckoned for her to join him, and she did so, oblivious to the stares around them.

"You weren't at your cottage," he told her.

"I know," she sighed. Her hair was mussed and there were dark circles under her eyes. "I've been with the gypsies."

"Excuse me. Sometimes I have trouble with English idioms. It sounded to me like you said you were with the gypsies."

"I was." At Schaefer's expression, she explained, "I'd just about finished my usual rounds when a young boy stopped me. Said his mum was in labor. I went into the caravan, and there was the mother, with four other children, all cramped into that little space. The father was off doing a job somewhere. I had to put all five children outside the caravan while I delivered their newest brother. Fortunately, it didn't take too long, and the father had returned by the time it was over and was waiting with the children outside. But then, of course, I had to explain to the mother she couldn't just keep the baby in the bed with her, because she might roll over and smother it. In the end, we had to put the baby in the drawer, and I'm not sure that once I left the mother didn't just return to keeping the baby in the bed with her after all." Mary delivered all this breathlessly. She held a hand up to her head, looking dizzy. Indeed, for a moment, Schaefer feared she'd fall out of her chair, but she seemed to rally.

"Are you well, Miss Grey?"

"I'm fine, just a little peckish. I haven't had supper yet."

"Mrs. Jones!" Schaefer raised his hand. "Please bring Miss Grey some food and drink. You can bill it to my room."

"Oh no," Mary tried to object, "you don't have to."

"You treated me last night. Besides, I am not the one paying. Miss West is."

Mrs. Jones delivered some cold mutton and a mug of ale. As Mary ate, Schaefer gave her an abbreviated account of his day. When he gave her a word-by-word account of his visit to the Legges' tobacco store, it put Mary's nose out of joint.

"Wait, you didn't even ask about Anthony? Or her husband's whereabouts on the day he died?"

"No, that was not my intent in going."

"Then what was your intent in going? If you don't mind my asking."

"To gather information," Schaefer said simply.

Mary waited for him to elaborate but he didn't. "What sort of information then?"

"Just general information. And what I found was very interesting."

Annoyed with Schaeffer's vagueness, Mary asked with some irritation, "And what exactly did you find?"

"Have you noticed the Legges have come into some money as of late?" Mary looked startled. "Their shop and home have clearly been improved upon, and Mrs. Legge wears good cosmetics and fine nylons. I would not have thought the tobacconist trade in such a small place as this was so lucrative."

"It shouldn't be," Mary whispered. "Damn, sorry, I mean, dash it. I'm such a fool. I didn't notice any of that myself."

"Why would you? It wasn't related to anyone's health and so it was not your area of expertise," Schaefer replied reasonably.

"But where's the extra money coming from?"

"I have an idea about that, but all in good time. By the way, when you stayed at Avenel Court, how did you find your room?"

"My room?" Mary was taken aback. "It was quite nice, I suppose. Good mattress and a fireplace. I didn't pay much attention to it, to be honest. So much else to think about."

"No matter. His Lordship asked me to stay at Avenel Court, but I declined. So, I wanted to know what I was missing."

"Not much, really," Mary assured him. "They tried serving me breakfast in bed, but I didn't really take to it. Just didn't seem right somehow, though it was excellent marmalade. The real homemade kind."

"I'll take your word for it. I prefer lingonberry jam myself, but it is impossible to find here in England." Schaefer sighed. "At least there is still beer." And he gestured for Mrs. Jones to fetch him another round. "By the way," he told her casually, "Mr. West had something hidden in his bookshelves." He went on to explain the illicit reading material Anthony had collected, and Mary listened with rapt attention.

"Are you, Miss Grey, familiar with any of the books in question?"

"No, I've never read any of them, but they do sound interesting." There was a wistful note in her voice.

"Yes, there is nothing like declaring a book forbidden to make it all the more tempting." Schaefer made an expression between a smile and a grimace. "Something Germany's current government does not seem to understand."

"Yes," Mary agreed heartily as she remembered her own experiment with illicit reading material. Once many years ago, someone had lent Mary an edition of *Urania,* a privately published journal that came out only two or three times a year. The first time Mary read *Urania's* head statement, "There are no men and women in Urania," she felt as if her head might explode. As she read on, the rest of the journal continued to challenge her long-held beliefs. "Sex is an accident" was a phrase the journal frequently used. It wrote about feminist movements all over the world and compiled information about successful sexual reassignment surgeries. You couldn't find the latter information anywhere, even in nursing school, Mary noted. *Urania* was not openly offered to the public because of its controversial nature. It was rather passed around by sympathetic parties and readers who were encouraged to send in their names to a register. Mary had mentally debated whether to submit her details. The journal was so interesting! But if her name were ever discovered on such a list, her career as a nurse would be over. Besides, how would she explain herself if she was ever discovered reading or in possession of such material? Reluctantly, she did not register. But *Urania's* status as forbidden fruit, no doubt, made it all the more tantalizing to those souls who did.

Then Schaefer's face turned grave, or rather graver. All the other customers of The Mud Crab, even Caleb Barnaby, had now departed. They were the only ones present as Mr. Jones started to close up the bar. "And Miss Grey? Take care. There is a most cold-blooded killer in your little hamlet. We do not want you to join the list of victims."

Something in his expression, even more than his words themselves, made her feel as if she'd been hit with a blast of wintry air.

Mary was especially assiduous about waving her torch everywhere as she rode back to her cottage that night. Once home, she was careful to lock and bolt every door and every window. It was some time before she fell into a restless sleep. In her dreams, she was pursued along country roads and Piccadilly's back alleys (somehow in the strange manner of dreams, Illhenny and London had all become one giant landscape) by a shadowy figure. The figure made no noise when it walked but had a cane that it tapped incessantly. Why the figure pursued her, Mary did not know, but she doubted its intentions were benevolent, and so she kept running from it, with nary a chance to rest as the relentless sound of the tapping cane followed her everywhere.

Chapter Sixteen

The next morning, Illhenny awoke not only to snow but hail as well. Anyone fortunate enough to be able to remain indoors thanked their lucky stars, and everyone unfortunate enough to have to go outside freely cursed the heavens. Mary Grey was in the latter category and the language she directed skyward would have shocked her mother and her superiors. She didn't care. Since coming to Illhenny, she had spent far too much time around rough seafaring men, and it had greatly expanded her vocabulary.

Upon visiting Caleb Barnaby, his first words to her were, "You look like a bear with all those layers on! A bear that's been rolling in a snowbank."

"And good morning to you, too, Caleb," Mary greeted him back. "Not exactly fit for Buckingham Palace yourself, are you?"

Caleb started to laugh, but it turned to a coughing fit so hard it seemed to rattle his ribs. Mary patted and slapped him on the back. His coloring, she noticed, was especially alarming, with a weird blue-gray tint to his skin.

"You seem much worse than yesterday." Mary's brow furrowed in concern.

"Ah, always happens when the weather's like this. Cold and wet seeps into me bones, is all. Nothing a good shot of whiskey can't cure!" He reached for the bottle only to have Mary grab it out of reach. "Hey!" he brayed. "What you doing now, nurse?"

"I'm afraid the situation now calls for something other than the whiskey, Caleb."

"Not more tea, tonics, and poultices," he grumbled. "It's worse than being visited by a bloody nun, this is."

"No, I'm afraid we're going to have to call Dr. Roberts," Mary informed him.

"But he'll charge me an arm and a leg! And really, what can he do for me you can't?" Caleb wheedled.

Mary remained firm. "You need more care than I can give you, Caleb. You might even need a hospital." She tried to break the news gently to no avail.

"A hospital? A hospital?" If she had suggested a stay in prison, Caleb Barnaby could not have been more horrified. In fact, prison would have scared him less. The death rates in prison were not as high as those in hospitals. And no British prisoner was ever forced to endure the indignity of an enema. Finally, and most importantly of all, it was much easier to get hold of cigarettes, alcohol, and other forms of contraband in prisons. Unlike sisters and matrons, guards and wardens tended to look the other way on such matters.

"You'd get round the clock care there."

"People only go to hospitals to die," Caleb moaned. "Well, I'd rather die in me own bed, thank you!"

"Well, I admit I would, too, for that matter," Mary confessed, "but if you go to the hospital, you might not die at all."

Caleb gave a loud snort, proclaiming his skepticism.

"I mean it! There's been a great deal of progress made in medicine of late. There's this new class of drugs called sulfonamides that can work miracles," Mary explained. "Look, let's just get Dr. Roberts and see what he thinks of the situation."

Since Caleb had no phone, it was easiest for Mary to walk to The Mud Crab and use the one there to alert Dr. Roberts. By happy coincidence, this would give her another chance to talk to Mr. Schaefer, or so she thought.

"The kraut's gone for the day," Mrs. Jones said the moment Mary entered. "Hired a car this morning at Miss West's expense so he could catch the early train. Said he might not be back until quite late."

"Did he say where he was going?" Mary noticed that Mrs. Jones had just started putting up holly and other Christmas decorations and wondered if that had scared Schaefer off.

"No." Mrs. Jones was almost as disappointed as Mary was. "Right mysterious about it, he was." What, she mused, was the good in having a foreign detective stay with you if he wasn't going to provide you with anything to chat about? Well, other than the fees he, or rather Miss West, was paying, of course. But still, a woman couldn't live on money alone, and any woman living in a small village knew gossip was the most precious commodity of all.

"Well, in any event, I do have to use the phone."

Mary called Dr. Roberts, who showed as much enthusiasm at the thought of visiting Caleb Barnaby as Caleb had shown at the thought of the doctor coming over.

"Caleb Barnaby, that old devil! He's the worst patient I've ever heard of! I'd be lucky if I ever see a penny in payment from him," Dr. Roberts complained.

"Nevertheless, you should see him, and I'd call sooner rather than later. He's really taken a bad turn and I think he might need the hospital."

"Small wonder with the way he drinks. By all rights, a man in his condition should have met his maker years ago," was the uncharitable, if not necessarily untrue, judgement of Dr. Roberts.

"Come now, doctor," Mary wheedled, "'tis the season to be generous and think of one's fellow man."

Dr. Roberts gave a martyred sigh. "All right, I might have a chance to drop by tomorrow, after I see another patient. No promises, mind you."

"Thank you, doctor." Mary's gratitude was unfeigned.

After the call, Mary took a deep breath and metaphorically girded her loins before continuing on her (very chilly) rounds, being pelted constantly by the hail. On days like this, she truly rued that the Association had not had the funds to provide her with a vehicle that possessed a roof. At least her patients were always generous in offering her tea and a seat by the fire if they had one. She attempted to make a follow-up visit to the gypsy woman and her newborn only to find the caravan had already left. No one to give her brochures on hygiene and nutrition to now. Not that there had been much chance the woman would have read them. She might not have been able to read at all. Many of the women Mary helped didn't. Honestly, sometimes Mary wondered why the Rural Nursing Association even bothered with the expense of printing the brochures in the first place. At least the gypsy woman had given birth plenty of times before and presumably had mastered all the basics. Mary gave a silent prayer for the family's fortunes before going on her way.

Postmistress Ferrars had slipped on slush and had a nasty fall. Mary gave her a thorough examination and determined that, while the old lady was much bruised and frightened, she hadn't broken any bones or sustained any head trauma. She put the postmistress to bed with tonic and a hot water bottle and firm instructions to stay off her feet for the next few days.

"But what about everyone's mail?" Postmistress Ferrars fretted. "This time of year especially, everyone's sending one another cards and parcels."

"Well, hasn't Annie Martin, the blacksmith's daughter, been assisting you?"

"Yes, and she's a good girl," the postmistress conceded, "but there are some things she can't do."

"Well, just have her do whatever she can at the post office the next few days, and let people wait for the rest," Mary advised.

"You're probably right."

"Of course, I am." Mary smiled back at her. "Now, let's get you comfortable, and I'll use your phone to call for Annie."

"Do the Martins have a phone?" Postmistress Ferrars wondered.

"No, but the Purvis family does, and they live only a few houses down." Mary made the call and was reassured that the village grapevine would immediately get to work delivering the message to young Annie.

Mary left the postmistress's home at dusk. The hail had mercifully stopped, but the air felt more chill than ever in the rapidly fading light. The steam of her breath wafted through the air like ghosts. The world was so quiet she could hear the snow crunch under her feet as she approached her motorbike.

Then, Mary heard something else coming from the hedges—a rustling sound. She dimly made out a pair of yellow eyes, full of malice, glowering at her. She screamed and cursed herself for not having a weapon on hand, and her knees gave way under her. She fell into the snow, landing right atop her backside. A large, white-faced barnyard owl flew out, hooting madly at the evening stars, with its claws stretched out before it as it flew across the moon.

"What was that?" Mary recognized the voice of Peg Leg Pete out on another of his rambles.

"Nothing, Pete. Nothing at all. Just took a little tumble," Mary called out, feeling quite embarrassed at her foolishness. She stumbled to her feet and wiped snow off the skirt of her uniform as best she could. At least Pete nor anyone else had seen the fall—she'd never have heard the end of it if they had. Mary hastily made her way to the motorbike and drove off.

Once home, after drying off and wrapping herself in a tattered old quilt, Mary parked herself in front of the stove to warm up. She had inevitably developed a bad case of cold urticaria, those itchy, red bumps you get when it's chilly. This had been a problem for her since she was a girl, and it was always such a nuisance with all the damned itching. Oh well, she philosophized, at least she wasn't one of those people for whom exposure to the cold easily brought on fainting and shock. If she were, not only could she never have become a district nurse, she might not have been able to live in England at all. But really, now more than ever, she had to help Schaefer find the killer, if only so she'd stop jumping at shadows—or rather jumping at birds.

That night, Mary dined off cold cheese and crackers and polished off the last of the elderberry wine. It really was quite good. She might ask Mrs. Martin for more once she'd finished the dandelion wine as well. *Perhaps Harriet might sample some of the dandelion wine?* Oh, how pathetic was that of her? Harriet West was a woman who drank French champagne, not homemade brews. Why was Mary so besotted with this woman so utterly beyond her reach? What was wrong with her? Was the loss of Phyllis making her throw herself at the next attractive girl she met? Mary considered the possibility. Certainly, the prospect of no more sleepovers with Mrs. Graham had left a hole in her life, but she instinctively believed Harriet's fascination for her went deeper. Something more of a biological or chemical nature, Mary felt. Whatever it was, though, shaking it wasn't going to be easy.

For the thousandth time, Mary thought of the night Lord Pool had been shot, when Harriet had needed her to stay the night. Their rooms had adjoined each other and shortly past midnight, Mary had awoken to find Harriet dressed in a light-blue silk nightgown and standing at the foot of her bed.

“Do you mind if I spend the night here?” Harriet asked.

“No,” Mary said, her heart pounding, and Harriet crept under the covers with her.

Harriet’s silvery hair lay in a cloud on the pillow with one lock absently lying on her face, near her mouth. Mary impulsively brushed the lock of hair back. As she did so, Harriet’s eyes opened once more and met Mary’s directly for a long moment. Nothing was said. Nothing more happened. When Mary awoke the next morning, Harriet had returned to her own room, but her smell lingered on the bedsheets.

Mary was deeply reliving those moments and trying to remember Harriet’s precise scent when she heard the phone ring. She sighed, assuming it would be another patient, and steeled herself. Luckily, there hadn’t been too much elderberry wine left; she still had a clear enough head to ride her motorcycle. Besides, might be good to get back to work instead of mooning on about society heiresses.

“Miss Grey?” Much to her surprise, it was Schaefer on the other end of the line.

“Where were you today?” she asked immediately. Detective work would also, she felt, have been a welcome distraction to her at this time. It would certainly be more dignified than shrieking at owls.

“Did you find out who Mellors and Tania are?”

“Later.” His tone was curt and there was a tautness in his voice that hadn’t been there before.

“What do you mean la—”

“Miss Grey, I’m at Avenel Court. There has been another murder.”

Chapter Seventeen

Dick Townley, groundskeeper of Avenel Court, lay on the floor of his hut. There was a gaping maw of skin, tendons, and congealed gore where his throat had once been. Ames saw a flash of white, and realized it was part of the neck bone that had been exposed. Townley's broad, amiable features had assumed the pallor of death and he was now frozen in a moment of complete surprise. He was ice cold and rigor mortis had already set in. The upper layer of skin was now just starting to separate from the body. Flies greedily surrounded the pool of dried blood on the floor. One of them sat on the corner of Townley's mouth, in a bit of spittle. It smelled of copper, the first hints of putrescence and, of course, feces and urine. That was another thing, Ames thought cynically, they never get right in the books. In the death throes, bladders and bowels often give way. Townley was lying not only in his own blood but in his own piss and shit. Well, at least he hadn't been dead so long he'd started to bloat. He was still perfectly recognizable, which was a mixed blessing. It made the matter of identification easier, but it also made the whole thing seem more personal somehow.

"All right, who found the body?" he asked brusquely, suppressing all thoughts of disgust or pity. None of it would do Townley any good at this point, and impartiality was a detective's best recourse.

"One of the cooks, sir," replied a very green looking Constable Evans, who had just been outside vomiting on the ground. Evans, unlike his superior, had not yet had practice in suppressing nausea. "She was set to meet him here tonight, she said. Seems like they had a little romance going. When he didn't answer her knocks, she walked in and found him like that."

"Where is she now?"

"She was in such a state, I sent her back to the main house, inspector," Evans admitted. "Told her to get a shot of brandy."

"Looks like you could do with a shot of brandy yourself," Ames noted. Evans looked shamefaced, and Ames added kindly, "It's your first body, isn't it, lad? I had trouble with my first too. You toughen up over time." Evans gave a weak shadow of a smile. "For that matter, I might do with a drink myself. Once I'm off the clock, that is. Well, I'll have to talk to the maid sometime, but there's no need to do it right this instant. Body's obviously been dead for a while. Leave everything in our hands now, lad." Ames gave Evans a manly, reassuring pat on the shoulder and sent the young constable on his way, feeling just a little bit better, but at the doorway, Evans paused.

"Could it have been a robbery, sir?" he asked Ames, almost hopefully.

"Doesn't look like there's anything around here worth stealing."

"No, but a tramp or gypsy or something like that?"

"Desperate man looking for shelter in a storm meets an outraged fellow defending his home and it ends in blood?"

"Yes!" Evans looked a bit happier.

"Ordinarily, that'd be my first theory, but I'm afraid it won't wash here, lad. Far too much of a coincidence with everything else that's happened." Evans's face fell at Ames's reasoning. "Get that snort of brandy, lad, and look lively. There's a very dangerous killer lurking about right now."

Poor Constable Evans was teetering as he went up to the Court.

Since the primitive hut was without any electrical lighting, it was clear that certain procedures would have to wait until the morning. Still, Ames had to go through the usual routines of removing the body and canvassing for any immediate clues. There was a noted shortage of the latter, except for one feature. Amid the pool of drying blood lay a small piece of torn paper. Ames carefully removed it and examined it under his torch light. It was the corner of a ten-pound note.

"Well, well, well," he murmured to himself, "now what were you doing with that kind of money, Mr. Townley?"

Ames walked back to the Great House, snow falling quietly and the stars cold and bright. It was exactly the sort of night and scenery, Ames thought, you'd see on a damned Christmas card. The cook, Mrs. Drayer, was a thickset yet handsome woman of middle years whose eyes were now puffy and red from tears. She could shed little light on matters. She and Townley had a long-standing arrangement wherein whenever she had the chance and inclination to come down to the cottage she would, for a friendly get-together. Townley had even given her a spare key and she was in the habit of letting herself in. But she hadn't seen him since two nights previously.

"Should have known something was up," the cook intoned bleakly. "Too full of himself, he was. Strutting around like a rooster cock. Talking nonsense about the two of us taking a holiday somewhere. I says to him, 'Dick, how we gonna get the money for that?' and he just laughed and told me not to worry my pretty head over such things." Mrs. Drayer shook her head, and her tears were replaced by an angry scowl. "Dick was always getting into some sort of scrape or another. I used to tell him, 'Look out now, Dick. One of these days, your sidewinding's gonna be the death of you.' And now it has." She started crying again, and one of the housemaids, armed with a handkerchief, took over comforting her while Ames awkwardly excused himself.

No one else in or around Avenel Court had seen Townley outside his hut since the previous day but, given the weather, no one had thought anything of it. And of course, any tracks that might have been left in the snow the day before were now buried underneath the fresh snowfall of today. Ames mused bitterly that even the weather itself was conspiring against the investigation.

"Excuse me, inspector." Ames heard a dry cough and turned to see the damned butler giving him another of his imperious looks. Another cliché Ames found irritating was "the butler did it," but after meeting Spode, he rather found himself hoping that this one would prove true just so he'd have the satisfaction of arresting the snooty bastard. He entertained a brief, beautiful vision of manhandling a handcuffed Spode into a police vehicle before asking, "What is it, man?"

Spode sniffed. "There's another detective to see you. A German." Spode stressed the syllables of the final word. "He's waiting in the study, sir."

Ames had not called for Schaefer, but he wasn't surprised by the private investigator's arrival. No doubt, the discovery of the body was by now being spread throughout the county, with the tale growing ever more lurid in each telling. By teatime tomorrow, Ames thought cynically, they'll be saying the man was decapitated. Townley's death would be a source of even more public titillation than West's had been.

"Should I bring him to you," Spode asked, "or send the man away?" The tone of his voice made clear Spode was all in favor of the latter.

"I'd like to see him actually." Ames got a perverse enjoyment at Spode's obvious disappointment. When Spode showed Ames to the study, the two men saw Schaefer standing directly in front of a painting of dogs tearing a fox to pieces, trampling snow and ice on the carpet, wearing a long black overcoat and in the act of hanging up the phone.

"Who were you calling?" Ames demanded gruffly.

"Ah, my dear inspector, I wish you good evening." Butter wouldn't have melted in Schaefer's mouth, but his eyes flicked upon Spode, who was examining Schaefer the way he would a cockroach.

"You're dismissed," Ames told the butler, who slithered off.

When Spode was safely out of view, Schaefer explained, “I was notifying my assistant of my whereabouts and that there’s been another killing. That was all.”

“I didn’t know you had an assistant,” Ames said.

“My dear inspector, I needed one. I am, after all, a stranger here.”

“Well, perhaps you do, but I’d prefer if you didn’t go around spreading any details about this murder to the public right now.”

“How could I do that? As of now, I don’t know anything. All I know is someone found someone dead while Lord Pool was on the phone with Miss West, and she, in turn, called me.” Schaefer stated this with perfect equanimity, but his eyes lay expectantly on Ames. The latter sighed and, against all normal police instincts, told Schaefer everything.

“The doctor and I both think Townley’s been dead since the previous night. Too bad the blasted snowfall this morning ruined any hope we had of finding footprints around the lodge itself.”

“And you haven’t found the weapon?”

“No sign of it in the lodge. Tomorrow, when it’s light out, we’ll look for it on the grounds. But I’ve got a hunch our killer took the blade with him.”

“Like he took the gun?” Schaefer asked.

“Certainly seems like a lad who’s attached to his weapons.” Ames gave a bitter laugh. “No signs of forced entry, which suggests Townley not only knew his assailant but admitted him inside. As for motive, I reckon Townley was blackmailing somebody. My guess, he saw something on the day Lord Pool was shot, and the damned fool tried to make a profit off it and got killed for his pains. The killer handed him a wad of bills, and while Townley was distracted, counting the money, in went the knife. The killer then takes the cash with him, but he missed that one tenner that fell in the blood."

"My deductions exactly, inspector," Schaefer concurred. "No doubt, Townley himself admitted his killer. The knife was in his throat before he even knew what happened."

"Too bad Townley didn't hear you speak on the dangers of blackmailing murderers."

"*Dummheit*," Schaefer replied.

"Eh?" Ames wondered.

"Stupidity," Schaefer clarified. "These would-be blackmailers. They always think they are so clever and that it can't happen to them, and it always does." He sighed and shook his head at the folly of it all. "If he had come forward to the police or to me when I saw him the other day, he would still be alive. But his own greed killed him."

"In the meantime, we've got another corpse on our hands and not a lot of evidence," Ames bluntly pointed out. "No one saw anyone go in or out of Townley's cottage the night he was killed. Oh, we'll dust for prints all right, but I'm betting we won't find any, just like we didn't at West's place. That's the problem with all these detective stories and plays—everyone these days knows to wear gloves or wipe away the prints."

"It could certainly be easier if today's criminals were less well informed," Schaefer conceded. "What about blood spray? Given the nature of the attack, it would have been virtually impossible for the killer to have avoided getting any blood on him."

"Probably would have been. But again, we'd need to find the bloody clothes to match! And that's assuming our killer didn't already discard the clothes somewhere or even burn them."

"That would have been the most prudent course of action for the killer," Schaefer noted before changing the subject. "What worries me most, inspector, is the way our killer seems to be escalating. Two murders and a shooting in such a short period of time!"

"At this rate, he'll be slaughtering whole families by Christmas."

Schaefer's eyes were intense and his speech rapid. He seemed to be thinking aloud, "And consider the shift in pattern of the killings."

"Shift in patterns?" Ames hoped Schaefer wasn't going to descend into some kind of German psychobabble.

"Don't worry, inspector, I am not a follower of Sigmund Freud," Schaefer told him, as if he'd read Ames's mind. "Maybe I read a little of Carl Jung, but I do not do so for advice in investigations. Still, this third killing is different than the other two, you see? More personal, more violent. Originally, West was to be killed in a vehicle accident. All the killer had to do was cut the brake lines of the vehicle and that would be that. An almost passive means of murder, like poisoning. The killer would never even face his victim directly at all."

"But he did have to face his victim," Ames objected. "West was suffocated."

"True, but that was not the original plan. West's unexpected rescue meant our murderer had to improvise," Schaefer countered. "Moreover, it takes neither strength nor courage to hold a pillow over the face of an invalid, who may well have been asleep when the deed was done."

"Even a woman could have committed that one. Can't rule out a woman using the beard and false glasses to disguise herself either."

"True! I thought of that but killing Townley was something else altogether. The victim was alert and on his feet. He was also, moreover, a strong, robust man."

"Would be hard to imagine a woman getting the jump on him," Ames reluctantly admitted, and Schaefer nodded.

"We are dealing with a perpetrator of considerable nerve here, inspector. A man of action. But that is precisely what the nature of West's murder would suggest we weren't facing." Schaefer waved his arms in frustration. "And then there was the shooting of Lord Pool."

"Downright cowardly, that one was," Ames growled. "Shooting a man in the back."

"*Ja*. On one hand, a long-range attack from afar. The very definition of cowardice. On the other hand, very audacious, was it not?"

"Audacious?" Ames echoed.

"It was, in many ways, extraordinarily risky. To try to sneak onto the great nobleman's property and assassinate him, all without being seen by anyone?"

"But he was seen. By Townley."

"Precisely!" Schaefer raised an emphatic finger in the air. "Again, it seems reckless, like our killer is not exercising any caution at all. And yet our killer, for all his mistakes, is still at large." Schaefer frowned, and his eyes seemed to be looking at something far in the distance. "These crimes are all related. They must be. But they are not—how you say—they are not consistent."

"They're not, are they?" Ames thought aloud. "Different styles, like you said, and different weapons as well."

"*Ja*! And in my experience, most killers tend to find a particular method that suits them and then they do not deviate. The poisoner sticks to poison. The strangler to strangling. And so on. But not this killer."

"Hmph," Ames grunted. "Maybe our killer's read too many bloody detective stories where people get murdered left and right in all sorts of ways without any rhyme or reason."

"Maybe. Life imitating fiction. Or perhaps, more than one hand at work in the matter?"

"You mean a pair of killers working together? Like Burke and Hare?" Ames was astounded. "Good lord, man, that would be the last thing we need around here."

*

Meanwhile, as Schaefer and Ames talked in the study of Avenel Court, Mary Grey had received another late-night call on the phone. She originally assumed it was Schaefer, but with a flutter of pleasure she heard Harriet's voice on the other end.

"I do hope I'm not disturbing you, Miss Grey," Harriet began apologetically. "I apologize for the late hour."

"No, not at all," Mary protested.

"But Edgar just called me and said there'd been another murder!"

"I know."

"You know?"

"Schaefer just called to inform me."

"He did? I didn't know you two were so close." Harriet's voice sounded inquisitive. If it hadn't been utterly ridiculous, Mary might have even wondered if Harriet was jealous.

"He just said someone else was killed, and he wanted me to be extra careful."

"Well, that's certainly good advice right now. It's why I was calling you myself."

There was an awkward pause, and then Mary added, "I was so sorry to hear about your uncle."

"Thank you," Harriet replied. "His funeral is tomorrow morning, and then there is the reading of the will. But directly afterward, I'm coming back to Illhenny."

"You are? But is it safe with the killer at large? And with two attacks so close to Avenel Court, and your brother having been so close to his Lordship..."

"Well, I'm not a witness or a participant in that damned resort project, so why would anyone want to kill me?" Harriet retorted. "Besides, no one's been killed inside Avenel Court itself, have they?"

"No, they haven't," Mary admitted.

"Which proves the killer must be someone on the outside who doesn't have easy access into the house. Otherwise, they could have simply finished Edgar off as easily as they did Anthony. So, I should be safe at Avenel Court. And when I'm not there, I'll be in public places."

"Well, it sounds like you've given this a lot of thought."

"I've had to." Harriet's voice cracked over the receiver. "And in any event, I can't stay away. I must meet Mr. Schaefer and find out what progress he's made on the case."

"Of course."

"And I wanted to see you again as well," Harriet added. "I've spent the whole time in Newcastle wishing you were here. You're such a comfort."

"Oh," was all Mary could say.

"So, I do hope to see you and Schaefer soon," Harriet concluded. "Now I have to go."

It was only after Harriet hung up that Mary realized Harriet had made no mention of missing Lord Pool during the call or asked about his welfare at all. Then again, Harriet could always simply call his Lordship himself and ask, and perhaps had already done so. It was possible to read too much into things.

That night, Mary carefully locked and bolted every door in the cottage and every window as well. She also put a kitchen knife under her pillow. It was only then she fell into a troubled sleep.

Chapter Eighteen

It was well after midnight by the time Franz returned to The Mud Crab. Mrs. Jones made no mention of the time or suggested his late arrival was in any way inconvenient. A testament, Franz thought, to just how much Mrs. Jones expected she'd be billing Miss West for. You can always tell the expense of an establishment by how well they treat you.

"You look half frozen, you do," Mrs. Jones scolded him.

"I could do with a drink," Franz admitted. "Something warm perhaps?" Visions of hot chocolate made with schnapps danced in his head, but he knew better than to expect any such delights here at The Mud Crab. The best thing he could hope for here would be tea perhaps spiked with a little whiskey.

"Know just the thing to cheer you up." Mrs. Jones stepped behind the bar a while and then came back with a mysterious steaming mug.

"What is it?" Franz asked her. "It doesn't look like tea."

"A bit stronger than tea." Mrs. Jones winked at him. "A hot toddy. Family recipe."

Franz sipped warily, but, to his surprise and delight, the drink was quite delicious if perhaps a little strong. With every mouthful of fluid, warmth and good humor seemed to flow through his veins. By the end of the cup, he felt a great deal more mellow than when he'd started, and his overall opinion of Mrs. Jones, The Mud Crab, and indeed, English public houses in general had significantly improved. Franz retired to his room, where a hot water bottle awaited him under the sheets, and instantly went to sleep.

The next morning, Franz breakfasted on black coffee, toast, and a hardboiled egg. He expected to have to bat off all sorts of questions about Townley's death (for it was inconceivable that Mrs. Jones had not heard the news by now), but he was pleasantly surprised to find her mum on the topic. Perhaps she realized how utterly impossible it would be for him to discuss the matter. Or perhaps she'd found someone else to fill her in on all such details, like one of Ames's constables. Franz suspected the latter was more likely than the former. As Mrs. Jones cleaned up after him, she asked with careful casualness, "Will Miss Grey be dining with you again this evening?"

"Perhaps," Schaefer replied. "Perhaps not."

"Hmm," was all Mrs. Jones said. It was enough. Somehow in that "hmm," she had managed to convey a world of commentary about how much the German visitor had been seeing of the district nurse, and was he perhaps mixing business with pleasure? Schaefer suddenly realized the main reason Mrs. Jones had not asked him about the murder was because right now her focus was on the possibility of a romance between the town's sole marriageable spinster and the exotic outsider. Inwardly,

Schaefer sighed. *Why is it in such small towns a man cannot exchange more than half a dozen words with a woman without setting tongues aflame?*

After breakfast, Schaefer met Inspector Ames directly at the morgue to hear the results of the autopsy. Dick Townley now lay on a cold metal table, carved up like a turkey, with various organs now removed into specimen bowls and jars.

There wasn't much Mr. Brown, the medical examiner, could offer. "The cause of death is obvious: a single, brutal thrust to the throat with a twist of the blade. He would have bled out right away. Interestingly, though, there are no signs of defensive wounds or any resistance."

"Which just proves he knew his attacker," Ames commented.

"It would seem so," agreed Brown. "As for time of death, I'd say about twenty-four hours, more or less, before the time the body was found."

"So, killed the previous evening, with no one the wiser," Ames thought aloud. "If the housemaid hadn't come by to offer him some warmth, it might have been days before we found the body. This way, at least we have some sense of a timeline."

"And I can tell you what murder weapon was used," Brown piped up, and both Ames and Schaefer sprung to attention. "And let me tell you, it wasn't a typical stiletto."

"Even I could see that," Ames grunted, "from looking at the wound."

"But it wasn't your usual kitchen knife either," Brown went on.

"Then blast it, man, what was it?" Ames burst out.

The medical examiner, resenting the way Ames was stomping on what ought to be his big moment, retaliated with a long, technical explanation about the size and angle of the entry wound, the tearing of the tendons, and the marks left on the bones, as Ames grew increasingly frustrated. Finally, as the inspector developed a throbbing vein in his left temple, Brown wrapped up with, "I'd say we were looking at a conventional cut and thrust knife, approximately six inches in length, single-edged, with a top leading false edge."

"Really?" said Ames, all pique now forgotten in light of the new tantalizing evidence.

"In fact, I happen to have on hand a knife that perfectly matches the marks of the wounds found on the victim. I keep a collection of such weapons," Brown said with evident pride, "for research purposes. Comparing different wounds, marks left on bones, that sort of thing. I've written at least five papers on the topic." He spoke with the enthusiasm of a schoolboy on what was clearly a subject near and dear to his heart. "Also, it's good to see for yourself how blood splatters."

"And the knife used to kill Townley?" Ames interrupted him. "What was it?"

Brown gave Ames a reproachful look at the inspector's attempt to rob him of his moment in the sun. He was not having that, and he continued his lecture as planned.

"Yes, the knife used to kill Townley. Well, to conduct my most fascinating research, I have, as I said, put together quite a collection of knives. It's taken me years to do it."

Ames was by now audibly grinding his teeth, but Brown went on, completely unperturbed. Schaefer found himself divided with sympathy for Ames's wish to move things along, and the fact that he really was keenly interested in the science of forensics. Perhaps someday he might read some of Brown's treatises.

Brown, meanwhile, went on, "I've procured my knives from kitchen supply stores, butcheries, and even the occasional pawn shop, which is, in fact, where I found this piece of work." With a flourish, he uncovered a tray holding a wicked looking blade with a wooden hilt.

"*Nahkampfmesser*!" Schaefer exclaimed.

"*Gesundheit*," Ames offered.

"No, that is the name of this weapon," Schaefer told them. "It is what we called them in Germany. They were assigned to soldiers in the Great War for close combat and trench fighting. They were designed to be used in tight quarters. The idea was they could be used to take out sentries quickly without alarming anyone with the sound of a gunshot."

Brown, having already prepared his own lecture on the history of *Nahkampfmesser*, felt a bit put out that Schaefer had been the one to say all this first.

"It's true that it didn't look like Townley even got a chance to scream," Ames mused thoughtfully. "You seem awfully familiar with it."

"I trained with this knife in the German army, but the war ended before I could be sent to the front."

"You realize saying that makes you our chief suspect, don't you?" Ames noted.

Schaefer ignored his attempt at humor. “May I?” he asked the medical examiner, who nodded. Schaefer picked up the weapon delicately and fingered the sharp blade. “As a policeman, I saw such blades used more than once in Germany. I did not expect to see one here in England.”

“Perhaps someone who served then?”

The medical examiner poured cold water on the idea. “Or someone who simply bought the blade in a pawn shop, like I did. But the good news is, if you should find someone with such a knife, we can conclusively prove whether it was the one that did in this poor bastard.” Brown nodded toward Townley and waited expectantly.

Ames ground his teeth but took the cue. “How?” he asked.

“From this!” Brown removed from some hidden pocket a tiny glass jar containing a single, minute piece of metal. “I removed it from one of the cervical vertebrae.”

“The what?” Ames and Schaefer said in unison.

“Neck bones.” Once more, Brown was happily delivering information. “It splintered off the knife during the ferocity of the attack, which means if your killer still has the blade, I can match the two perfectly.”

“That is good news.” Ames smiled for the first time during the entire meeting.

“It would certainly make things easier at trial,” Schaefer agreed. “Assuming the killer kept the weapon, of course.”

“Of course, the smart thing to do would have been to get rid of the knife altogether,” Ames couldn’t help but point out.

"True, but the killer then could easily have left the knife where it was, and simply wiped the handle of prints," Schaefer replied. "Instead, he took the knife with him. Now, maybe he simply disposed of it later, but it is still possible he kept the blade. Perhaps it had—how you say—sentimental value?"

"Strange thing to be sentimental about," Ames thought aloud. "Murder weapon and all."

"Yes, but I've seen some who do." A strange expression crossed Schaefer's face. "I wonder," he murmured to himself. "I just wonder."

"What is it?" Ames asked.

"Criminals often do use the same tools over and over again. In fact, some killers become almost well attached to their weapons. So maybe—"

"Maybe this isn't the first time our boy used a knife like this!" Ames interrupted him with visible excitement.

"I think we should make enquiries into other stabbings in the United Kingdom that showed any similarities to this one," Schaefer suggested. "Anyone attacked with a similar weapon, persons done in with a single savage blow to the throat. Going back, oh, as far as the Great War itself."

"Nearly twenty years of stabbings is a lot to look at," Ames looked dubious.

"Indeed, inspector. Fortunately, your lovely country is not an especially violent one. At least, not usually." Schaefer gave another glance to the sad pile of skin and flesh that had once been Dick Townley.

Neither Schaefer nor Ames had much of an appetite after visiting the morgue, but the latter thought he could do with a cup of tea and the former felt the need for coffee. They decided to visit a café, and Schaefer bought a newspaper on the way. Before entering the café, Schaefer stopped off at a callbox and phoned a number in London—with a very particular request—and then rejoined a thirsty and impatient Ames.

They were seated in the café. This place, unlike The Lilac Bush, had no pretensions toward gentility or even an official name, but Ames declared it to be a better value. They sat on chairs with battered old cushions at tables with peeling strips, and their orders were taken by a middle-aged woman with hair dyed an alarming shade of red who didn't even seem to notice Schaefer had an accent. The clientele here was a motley sort, consisting of shop clerks in uniform, typists with ink-stained fingers, elderly persons who seemed like they'd seen better days, a couple of young women whose garish makeup and fishnet stockings hinted at their profession, and even a strange looking fellow in the corner whose hair and clothes gave him the appearance of having been electrocuted. None of them gave Ames or Schaefer a second glance.

Tea and coffee and a mountain of kippers and toast were served on plain white china without any sort of fancy engravings or patterns on them, which was exactly how Ames preferred it, and he tucked in heartily to his meal. Schaefer, though, was distracted by the paper. He was flipping through the pages when he stiffened and hissed "*Scheiße*," slamming his hand on the table like a crack of thunder, and his coffee cup rattled and threatened to spill. The server and other customers all gaped, but Schaefer was oblivious to their stares. He looked like a man in need of something to punch.

"What?" Ames asked with real concern. "What's happened?"

Schaefer didn't answer but simply pointed to an article on the Spanish Civil War. Ames was bewildered. Why would Franco and Spain be of such concern to Schaefer? Then he saw a tidbit mentioning the presence of German troops in the area.

"Worried about your countrymen?" he asked Schaefer.

"No, I am worried about the world," Schaefer replied, and Ames stared at him aghast as the German went on. "Herr Hitler is spreading his evil farther afield, inspector. The fascists, their movement, spreads beyond Germany to Spain and other countries as well." Schaefer stared out of the frosted window, off into the distance. "What has destroyed my country will soon infect others. All of Europe will be caught in the storm, inspector. Not even Britain will escape that butcher's tyranny."

Ames felt cold and uncomfortable; less for Schaefer's words than for the vehemence with which he spoke them. Then the inspector, in grand English fashion, collected himself and soldiered on. "Well, even if you're right and a war is coming, that doesn't change the fact we've still got two unsolved murders on our hands," he declared. "Time to knock heads together, eh? See what we can come up with."

"Isn't that what we've been doing?" Schaefer asked.

"Come off it, man! We know the facts, now what we need is a suspect! A theory! Don't tell me you don't have anyone in mind."

"I might," said Schaefer, "have an idea. Just an idea."

"I knew it!" Ames was gleeful. "You've been looking like a foxhound following a scent for days. Well now, out with it."

"No." Ames began to protest, but Schaeffer snapped, "No! If I tell you what I suspect, one of two things will happen: you will think me mad, or you will I think might be onto something. Now, as for the first possibility, it doesn't help me at all if you think I am mad."

"I promise, I won't think you mad. I may not agree with your theory, but unless it's something like a ghost, I won't think you mad for it," Ames protested.

"I thank you for that, inspector, but then there is the second possibility. You may think me right. And if you do, that could be a problem for you!"

"What now?" Ames was baffled, and Schaefer's next words did little to illuminate him.

"For I have no proof of this theory. None! I might even be wrong," Schaefer admitted. "I do not think I am, but it is possible. I am waiting to hear from certain parties on certain matters. If they confirm any ideas I have, then maybe I can tell you what I think. But before that, no!" Schaefer was so emphatic, Ames knew it would be no use to press him further, but he wondered at his companion's behavior. Was it a German thing, a Jewish thing, or something peculiar to Schaefer himself?

"Well, in any event then, while you're waiting to tell me what you're thinking," Ames spoke with clear sarcasm.

"For your own good, inspector, I assure you," Schaefer cut in.

Ames ignored him. "I still have an ongoing investigation to conduct. While my men are out searching the estate, I think it's time I called on Caleb Barnaby again. And the Legges. Oh, don't cock your eyebrow at me, Schaefer, I heard the rumors about Mrs. Legge and young West same as you, straight from the lips of Dahlia Winthrop." Ames's mouth twitched as he spoke her name. "Nosy cat, that. Still, there might just be something to her hissing. I can't afford to overlook anything right now, can I?" Ames eyed Schaefer shrewdly, trying to gauge his reactions. Unfortunately, after his earlier display of emotion, Schaefer had recovered his usual aplomb. The German, Ames thought ruefully, would be a damned hard man to play poker with.

"No, inspector, you most certainly cannot," Schaefer agreed. "You would perhaps allow me to accompany you while you interrogate the parties in question?"

"Maybe. If you remember I'm the one who's going to be leading the conversations," Ames instructed sternly.

"My word of honor, I will stay out of your way." Schaefer crossed his heart.

"Will you?" Ames looked doubtful.

"If I ask any questions of my own, it will only be with your permission." Schaefer could not have been more obsequious if he'd been a courtier addressing a king, and it made Ames suspicious. What was the little German up to? But Ames's concerns were somewhat mollified by Schaefer's next words. "Oh, and my dear inspector, after we've questioned everyone, I must insist you join me for refreshment at The Mud Crab. On me! Or rather," he corrected himself, "it will be on Miss West."

"Then you can come," Ames generously agreed, privately resolving to order the best vintage The Mud Crab had in stock. The thought alone put him in a good humor for the interview with the Legges.

"Mind you," Ames confided in Schaefer, "I've got another little idea of my own."

"Oh?" Schaefer asked.

"It may sound crazy, but I'm not sure we can rule Harriet West out entirely."

Schaefer raised an eyebrow. "But does she not have an alibi for her brother's demise and that of Mr. Townley?"

"Oh, I don't think she did any dirty work herself," Ames declared, "but she could well have hired somebody else to do it for her."

"True," Schaefer observed. "She most certainly could have. She would have an obvious motive in the case of her brother, but why shoot Lord Pool?"

"Divert suspicion!" Ames declared. "Convince everyone West's murder really was about the damned resort."

"At the cost of her own fiancé?"

"Well, that's the thing. She might not have considered that such a loss."

Schaefer's eyebrows went up.

"I've had some constables chatting up the servants' hall at Avenel Court, and word is Miss West has been acting rather peculiar of late. She actually seems to be avoiding his Lordship's company. They don't think she was ever exactly head over heels about him to begin with. In fact, they describe her as a cool piece of goods. But lately, she's been downright frosty."

"I see. It could be strain."

"Could be," Ames belligerently allowed.

"Or perhaps now that she is sole heiress to the Harrington fortune it is possible Miss West believes she does not need his Lordship anymore? Especially if her family had been pushing the match on her," Schaefer speculated.

"Servants' hall have been wondering the same thing. They've been placing bets on whether the wedding will still take place. So far, they're leaning toward yes, for the sake of the title, but there are some contrarians who think there might be another man in the picture." He nodded knowingly. "If there is, that fellow could be a suspect!"

"Would you have any theories as to who this other suitor might be?"

"Well, I have asked around, but no one seems to know of anyone in particular," Ames admitted. "Problem is, a girl in her set is always surrounded by a lot of dashing male company, you understand, so it's hard to know for sure who Lord Pool's competitor might be."

"Well, that is a very interesting theory of yours, inspector, and I must admit it is not implausible either," Schaefer conceded. "Nevertheless, I hope you are mistaken."

"Why?"

"Because if your theory is correct then I am not going to be paid for this assignment after all."

Ames gave a start. "Hadn't thought of that," he admitted. "Would be a bit rummy for your end, wouldn't it?"

"To say the least."

"Well, we've still got other suspects to interview. Maybe we'll get lucky and one of them will be the culprit instead."

"Maybe." Schaefer gave a thin smile, but his eyes were troubled.

Caleb Barnaby was next. A constable waited downstairs while Ames and Schaefer called upon Caleb. One look at the old man made Inspector Ames blanch. The cough and sickly coloring that had so distressed Mary the previous day had only grown worse, and Caleb now looked more dead than alive. By his feet lay what was either a very large ginger cat or a very small tiger. At the sight of the strangers, the cat's ears laid flat, his back arched, his hair stood up, and he hissed like a cobra. Ames immediately made a mental note not to go near the blasted creature. Ames had heard it said that man was the most dangerous animal on earth, but to Ames's mind, whoever first coined the expression had never had to deal with a truly angry cat.

"Good lord, man, have you seen a doctor?" Ames asked aloud.

"Bloody bastard's coming around later," Caleb told him. "Maybe I'll get lucky, and he'll cancel." He reached for the whiskey, but Ames was quicker and pulled it away from him.

"You're worse than Nurse Grey," Caleb grumbled. "Can't an old man take his medicine in peace?" He eyed Schaefer shrewdly. "You're that German detective, aren't you?"

"I am," Schaefer confirmed.

"Never met a German before. In fact, never met any foreigners at all," Caleb noted and then gave Schaefer a quizzical look. "Wait, are you a Jew?"

"I am," Schaefer confirmed.

"Well, I'll be damned. Never met a Jew neither! Meet my first foreigner and first Jew on the same day. What a day for firsts, eh?"

"Might also be the first day you get arrested," Ames observed.

Caleb snorted. "I been arrested before, plenty of times! Drunk and disorderly, disturbing the peace. That sort of thing."

"All right, first time you might be arrested for murder."

"Well, that would be different," Caleb admitted. "But it wouldn't be true either."

Schaefer said nothing during this exchange but began examining the beautiful wooden figures on the shelves. He seemed especially transfixed with the form of a sleeping fox and, with his fingers, delicately traced the lines carved into the grain.

"I must congratulate you on your lovely collection of carvings, Mr. Barnaby," Schaefer said. Caleb snorted. "Did you do all these yourself?"

"Aye," Caleb replied, eying Schaefer warily.

"Then I commend you. You are a most excellent craftsman, Mr. Barnaby." Caleb puffed out his chest with pride. "Indeed," Schaefer continued, "looking at these figures, one would think you were a carver from the Ore Mountains."

"A carver from where now?" Caleb was confused.

Ames decided the whole conversation had gone decidedly off track and took command of the situation. "Mr. Barnaby, where were you the night before last?"

"I was here. All day and all night. Didn't have the energy to go out."

"Is there anyone who can vouch for that?"

"No, why? Wait, this doesn't have anything to do with Townley being killed, does it?" Caleb looked astonished and genuinely offended. As Caleb and Ames spoke, Schaefer, unobserved by either of them, had wandered to the windowsill and was looking outside with interest. Not that there was much of a view—just the waterspout and side of the building next door. And then, even that view was blocked when Ahab planted himself on the window and dismissively waved his tail in Schaefer's face.

"What would I ever want to hurt Townley for?" Ames made no answer but simply looked at him expectantly. Caleb got angry. "Look ye here, if you think you can make me some sort of scapegoat—" He collapsed into a coughing fit and Ames waited patiently.

When Caleb's coughing ceased, Ames went on. "Sounds like that doctor can't come here too soon, sir. And I truly hate to upset you in your condition, but we do have to look into every possibility. To that end, I have a constable downstairs who'd like to search these premises, sir, if you don't mind." He added that last bit hastily.

"I do mind," Caleb snapped, "but I can see I'll have no peace until you do. Let him come up."

"Thank you, sir. We'll try to make this as quick and painless as possible. Constable Evans!" Ames called out below.

Ames and Schaefer waited quietly in the hall.

"Don't like doing it myself," Ames admitted to Schaefer once the door was closed. "Feels like persecuting a man with one foot in the grave. But rules are rules, and Lord Pool's been after me to charge Barnaby since West died." He sighed. "This way, at least we can search his place and say we didn't find anything."

"True," Schaefer nodded sympathetically, but his eyes were distant. Ames had a shrewd suspicion that Schaefer's thoughts, right then, were focused more on the Rhineland than on Illhenny. "Besides, poor health is not necessarily proof of innocence. I knew a case in Berlin once." Schaefer got a faraway look in his eye. "A mousy little bookkeeper who worked for his father-in-law, who was a real bully, but the bookkeeper never even raised his voice at him. One night during Sunday dinner with his in-laws, the bookkeeper excused himself from the table. He returned with a pistol and proceeded to shoot everyone at the table, including his wife, who had a reputation for being something of a—how you say—a shraw? A shrow?"

"I think you mean shrew," Ames interjected.

"Yes, shrew. That is what his wife was known as. In fact, some of his neighbors would later declare themselves not surprised by the man murdering his wife but only that he hadn't done it sooner. Still, the level of his savagery that night shocked all who ever knew him. After the bookkeeper had emptied his gun of bullets into everyone else, his brother-in-law tried to flee for the front door, and so the bookkeeper pursued him and bludgeoned him with a candlestick."

"Well, that's determination for you," Ames observed wryly.

"*Ja*! But what happened next was perhaps strangest of all. Our killer then calmly finished his dinner before calling the police to turn himself in." Ames's eyebrows went up as Schaefer continued. "I asked what had possessed him to do any of it, and he said he'd been heartily sick of his wife and her family for years but had to swallow his rage. In the past week, though, he had learned he had an inoperable tumor. Knowledge of his impending doom made him snap and slaughter those he hated. After all, he was already under sentence of death. What more could the law do to him? On the day of his execution, he was quite cheerful and even whistling."

Ames had been listening intently. "You think the same thing might apply to Barnaby then? A man with nothing to lose wants to take a few others with him before he goes?"

"It is possible," Schaefer answered.

At that point, they were interrupted by a man carrying a black medical bag who reminded Schaefer of old pictures he'd seen of St. Nicholas. The man introduced himself as Dr. Roberts. "Nurse Grey called me here. Am I allowed to examine my patient, or is he going to be arrested? I'd hate to have come all this way for nothing," he added peevishly.

"We're just conducting a search, sir," Ames explained. "Expect to be done soon and then you can see Mr. Barnaby. And between you and me, I think he is in serious need of your services."

"I, too, have that impression," Schaefer added.

"What the bloody hell?" Caleb Barnaby's voice cracked out loudly. Constable Roarke was holding a hunting rifle.

“Where the devil did that come from?” Caleb howled.

“It was on top of the wardrobe, inspector,” the constable reported grimly. “Looks like the make of the weapon that shot Lord Pool, doesn’t it?”

“It’s not mine!” Caleb protested. “I’ve never seen it before!” He then collapsed into a violent fit of coughing. Dr. Roberts rushed to attend to him.

“Sorry to interrupt, Dr. Roberts,” Ames addressed the astonished looking physician, “but Caleb Barnaby, I am charging you with the attempted murder of Lord Pool and putting you under arrest!”

Chapter Nineteen

"But I can't believe Caleb's guilty!" Mary told Schaefer at The Mud Crab. That morning, she had paid a drop-in visit to the Wilberforce house and confirmed that Mrs. Wilberforce had now, indeed, moved into the guest room, much to her husband's bewilderment. The rest of her day had proceeded normally enough, until news of Caleb's arrest struck Illhenny like a lightning bolt.

"I share your opinion of Caleb," Schaefer replied. "And I do not think our good Inspector Ames truly believes him guilty either. Given the state of Caleb's health, it seems doubtful he could even have walked all the way to the estate at all, much less huddled in wait in a snowdrift to take a shot and then run home. But having found the weapon used to shoot Lord Pool in Caleb's possession, the inspector had no choice but to bring him in. The only reason Ames is not dining with us right now is that he had a host of formalities to deal with concerning the arrest. We even had to postpone our planned visit to the Legges." Schaefer paused before adding drily, "The good inspector has, however, made it clear he will expect the dinner promised to him at some point. Perhaps you could join us?"

"I'm not sure the inspector wants to see me again," Mary admitted.

Schaefer gave a faint smile. "I think you would find, madame, that his bark is worse than his bite. Oh, he does not appreciate interference in his investigations, but he's not so belligerent as to refuse any and all help. So long as you stay away from actual crime scenes, I believe he would tolerate your presence."

"Maybe." Mary looked unconvinced. "But that doesn't do poor Caleb any good, now does it?"

"No," Schaefer admitted, "and unless we can provide proof otherwise, the police will have to keep him in custody and, in all likelihood, bring him to trial, where he may well be convicted."

"But Caleb's so sick," Mary protested. "How's he going to survive a prison cell?"

"He's not in prison," Schaefer informed her. "Given the state of his health, Ames agreed with Dr. Roberts that Mr. Barnaby be hospitalized for the time being, with the proviso that a constable guard his room at all times."

"Well, that's one relief at least."

"To you perhaps, but I gather not to Mr. Barnaby," Schaefer replied drily. "He seemed more distraught about visiting the hospital than a possible murder trial, and he got very loud when he was told he couldn't bring a flask."

"Not even a murder charge can get Caleb to change his ways." Mary gave a wry smile. "Almost reassuring, isn't it?"

"Reassuring to you perhaps," Schaefer answered, "but I gather not to Dr. Roberts, who seems most aggravated not only to be caring for a suspected killer but by Barnaby as a patient at all. I think he would have almost preferred if we had taken Barnaby to prison, but the good doctor's conscience made him ask Caleb be hospitalized."

"Poor Dr. Roberts. I really do owe him for this. Still, I can't help but think it might be a good thing the police got involved in this case." At Schaefer's look of surprise, Mary clarified, "Getting Caleb to enter a hospital of his own free will would have been somewhere between difficult to impossible." Then another thought struck her. "And what about Ahab?"

"Who?"

"Caleb's cat."

"Ah yes, *der kleine Löwe*. No one dared touch it. I believe it was left behind at Caleb's quarters."

"Poor Ahab!" Mary sighed. "He must be dreadfully lonely. And hungry. Maybe I should stop in on him later."

Out of the corner of his eye, Schaefer observed Mrs. Jones watching their table like a hawk. "By the way," Schaefer informed Mary, "you should probably know that our regular meetings have been noticed."

"Everyone notices everything in a village," Mary replied.

"Yes, but in this case, it's gotten people to wonder if there isn't perhaps"—Schaefer coughed and tried to be as discreet as possible—"some sort of romantic connection."

Mary looked astounded. "Wait, they think you and I might be...But that's ridiculous!"

"*Ja*, but I thought I should warn you," he replied. "It could be embarrassing for you."

"Embarrassing?" Mary broke into a hearty laugh. At Schaefer's inquisitive look, she clarified, "People say all kinds of rot about unmarried women. I'm used to it." She got a conspiratorial glint in her eye. "In fact, I really don't mind if they link me to you."

"You don't?" Schaefer was surprised.

"Not at all!" Mary laughed. "In some ways, it's better to be considered a topic of scandal than just a frigid spinster. And in this, it's not even really a scandal, is it? I mean, neither of us are married. It probably enhances my reputation for people to think I have a suitor!"

"I see." Schaefer instinctively sensed there was more to it than that but didn't press the matter.

"But if the gun wasn't Caleb's, then how did it get there?" Mary wondered. A horrible thought occurred to her and she whispered, "Could the police have planted it themselves?"

"*Nein.*" Schaefer shook his head. "Ames is no villain, nor do I suspect young Constable Evans of any such—how you say—skulldigging."

"It's skullduggery."

"*Ja*, skullduggery. No, I notice the latch on Mr. Barnaby's window is broken, so it cannot be locked, and there is a good stout water pipe right outside. It would be simple for a fit man to climb the water pipe, enter through the window, and then plant the gun. Perhaps while Mr. Barnaby was out, or more likely when he was sleeping off his drink. What bothers me is, why do it?"

"Well, to frame Caleb," Mary responded automatically, and then felt silly for saying something so redundant. Schaefer clearly felt the same.

"*Ja, ja*, but why? Unless our killer has some personal grudge against Mr. Barnaby, it was a very foolish thing to do. The police weren't making any progress in finding Lord Pool's shooter. Why take the risk of being seen planting the gun?"

"Maybe the killer panicked? After killing Townley, they may have felt like the walls were closing in and were desperate to divert suspicion elsewhere."

"Probably," Schaefer agreed. "But there is so much that is inconsistent. Successfully planting the gun without being caught at it—that is the mark of a cool, clear-headed criminal. But yet, this is the same killer who shoots Lord Pool only once, giving him a non-fatal injury, and then flees the scene with the job left unfinished?"

"Maybe planting false clues is just easier than committing actual violence?" Mary suggested.

"Very possibly, but the killer had no such failure of nerve when it came to killing Townley," Schaefer mused. "In the meantime, I have yet to meet my employer, which I find most vexing."

"Well, you'll get to tomorrow. She's finally dealt with all the post-mortem arrangements for her brother and uncle, and she's coming back to Avenel Court first thing in the morning."

"Oh," said Schaefer with a single cocked eyebrow. "How do you know?"

Mary colored. "She rang me on the phone this evening to let me know." What Mary didn't mention was that, somehow or other, she and Harriet had ended up speaking together for nearly an hour, and Mary had very nearly risked being late to see Schaefer. Only after Mary had checked the time and made her excuses had Harriet reluctantly conceded that she should probably call Edgar as well.

"Wait, you haven't told Ed—Lord Pool you were coming?" Mary had asked.

"Not yet. I called you first." There had been a sigh over the phone. "But I suppose I must inform him too." And on that peculiar note, their conversation had ended.

"Well then." Schaefer made no open acknowledgement of Mary's blush. Privately, he thought to himself, *Ah. It is like that, is it?* He looked upon Mary with new interest. He had encountered many *Schwule* and *Lesben* in his work. Indeed, under the Weimar Republic, Berlin had been practically a mecca for homosexuals and cross-dressers. But that, too, had changed. Miss Grey, he realized, was perhaps as much an outsider in English society as he was, only better disguised. And it was perhaps better for her reputation if people did suspect a secret romance between her and Schaefer.

He wondered if his employer, Miss West, had any inkling of Miss Grey's feelings. In the meantime, he decided to discreetly avoid speaking of the matter aloud. Instead, he told her, "I greatly look forward to that meeting. In the meantime, I have some matters I must attend to privately." He gave a slight bow. "I bid you goodnight, madame."

Thus dismissed, Mary was left to ride home. She made a stop at Caleb's house. It was quite dark inside, and she fumbled around a bit before turning on a light. Then she called out, "Here, kitty kitty," several times and made seductive cat-enticing noises to no avail. Ahab refused to come out from wherever he might be hiding. Eventually,

Mary resorted to opening a dusty old can of sardines from the pantry, at which point Ahab appeared, hungry and demanding sustenance. She used the sardines to lure him closer and she let him eat first. He had nearly cleaned his plate when Mary grabbed him and stuffed him in her bag, experiencing some significant scratches and blood loss on the way. Ahab howled all the way back to the cottage with a ferocity and range which seemed extraordinary for a creature with such comparatively small lungs.

Once back at the cottage, Mary let the cat out of the bag, whereupon Ahab immediately ran around like a dervish to inspect every inch of the cottage before finally settling in on a high cupboard. From this protected vantage point, he began arching his back, fur raised upright, and hissing and spitting at Mary like a wild demon.

"I swear it's for your own good!" she told him. "I have no idea how long Caleb will be gone, or if he'll come back at all."

Ahab merely gave her a baleful glance followed by a loud shriek that promised future vengeance. Mary sighed and left milk out on a saucer before retiring for the night. She checked to make sure the knife was still under her pillow before she dared sleep.

Chapter Twenty

Mary awoke the next morning to an unexpected weight on the bedcovers. Sometime in the night, Ahab had crept in and deposited himself near her feet, enjoying both the softness of the bed and the proximity of a warm human body. Mary knew full well Ahab's new closeness was not motivated by any particular affection for her but, nevertheless, found his presence reassuring. It was the equivalent of having a giant, fluffy, vibrating pillow with her, and she luxuriated in it for as long as she could. Sadly, however, she had other commitments and so, reluctantly, she had to rise. She tried to do so without disturbing Ahab, but despite her best efforts, did not succeed in doing so. That his giant hot water bottle insisted on waking up at an ungodly hour in the morning, disturbing his slumber, was a great affront to Ahab's feelings, which he loudly protested.

"Oh, quit your bellyaching. Honestly, I should have just left you there with no one to care for you," Mary replied, at which point Ahab's eyes widened and his cries grew more plaintive as he impersonated a small, starving, kitten. Mary rolled her eyes but fed him anyway.

Before she went out on her rounds, Schaefer called and asked her to come meet him at The Mud Crab in the late afternoon. She'd checked her schedule and agreed to try to drop by, assuming there wasn't another emergency.

"Very good," Schaefer said. "Also, I will finally meet my employer. Miss West is arriving home today."

"Oh." Mary's heart gave an involuntary flutter at the thought of seeing Harriet again. "Well, I'm sure the two of you will have a lot to talk about then."

"Yes, but I think I would like to speak to both of you together at some point," Schaefer replied before hanging up, and Mary went about her rounds.

Caleb's arrest was all anyone in the village could talk about. Dahlia Winthrop, again, actually stood in the middle of the road to stop Mary on her motorbike and interrogate her about the matter, and it was only after she threateningly revved the motorbike's engine that Dahlia let her go on her way. Finally, at the appointed hour, she met Schaefer at a table in the back of The Mud Crab. She noted with amusement that Mrs. Jones was eyeing them with evident interest. Schaefer noticed it too.

"It seems our grand passion is the talk of the town," he proclaimed.

"If they only knew." Mary laughed. Then her expression changed, as if a candle had been lit from within her. "Harriet!" she called out.

In the doorway of The Mud Crab stood a young woman whose black silk dress only accentuated her gilded hair and pearl-like skin. Schaefer rose to his feet to finally greet his employer, but Harriet didn't even seem to see him. She said only "Mary" before walking to the table and clasping Mary's hands and then staring intently at her face. Neither spoke. Schaefer shifted from wondering if

Harriet West knew Mary Grey's feelings to wondering if Harriet even knew her own. The spell was only broken when Schaefer loudly cleared his throat.

"This is Mr. Schaefer." Mary pulled her hands away and flushed as she made the introductions. "Mr. Schaefer, this is Harriet West."

Schaefer gave a slight bow. He thought to himself the women had better learn not to wear their feelings on their sleeve.

"I am truly sorry, madame, for your losses."

"Thank you," said Harriet.

"I appreciate this is a most difficult time for you, but I believe I can at least provide you with answers. Please take a seat—" Schaefer gestured. "We have a great deal to discuss."

"The police have arrested Caleb Barnaby, but we don't think he did it," Mary summarized.

At Harriet's visible shock, Schaefer explained his and Mary's suspicions that the gun was planted before concluding, "A man in Caleb Barnaby's condition might conceivably be able to sabotage the car, but walking all the way to the grounds of Avenel Court and hiding in undergrowth to shoot his Lordship? And even if he had, it's inconceivable that Townley would have considered Barnaby worth blackmailing, or that Mr. Barnaby would have been able to launch such a vicious attack against Mr. Townley." Schaefer shook his head. "No, Mr. Barnaby is a convenient scapesheep, that is all."

"Scapegoat," Mary automatically corrected him. "It's goat, not sheep."

"Scapegoat," Schaefer repeated.

"If Barnaby isn't the killer, then who is?" Harriet's words stopped short the English lesson.

"We don't know," Mary admitted. It almost physically hurt her to say it. "But I don't think we're any closer to figuring out the truth than we were at the beginning. Isn't that right, Mr. Schaefer?" She addressed the detective, but rather than respond to her statement, his eyes drifted to Mrs. Jones who was now eagerly approaching them, breathless and red in the face.

"Mr. Schaefer! There's someone called Sir Henry on the phone who wants a word with you."

"Excuse me, both," Schaefer hurriedly told them, "but I have been expecting this call, and it is of grave importance that I answer."

He left the table and disappeared to the area in the back where Mrs. Jones kept the telephone.

Schaefer was at the phone for a long time. Mrs. Jones eavesdropped, but, disappointingly, the German was mostly listening rather than actively conversing. He made a few questions, like, "When?" and, "Where?" but as Mrs. Jones couldn't hear his answers, she found it all deeply unsatisfying. Finally, he said, "It is as I suspected then. Please call Inspector Ames and inform him of everything you told me." And then, much to Mrs. Jones's frustration, he hung up the receiver.

When he returned to the table, he addressed Harriet and Mary. "Ladies, there has been a—how you say—breakthrough. I believe I may be close to apprehending the person responsible for these heinous deeds." Harriet's mouth swung open, but before she could speak, Schaefer continued, "For now, I cannot answer any questions. Forgive me. But all will be explained in time."

Then, to the amazement of all three women in the room, Schaefer walked upstairs without another word.

"Well, that's a bit rude," Mrs. Jones concluded.

"That's an understatement," Harriet declared, her face going scarlet. "For what I'm paying him, and he just up and won't tell me anything! The bastard!"

"Mr. Schaefer is definitely an odd one," Mary interjected, "but he really does seem to know what he's doing."

"Does he?" Harriet's voice dripped with scorn. Mary put a reassuring hand on her shoulder, which Mrs. Jones thought awfully forward of the district nurse.

"I know he's been taking the case very seriously. Now, I'm not sure what's going on right now, but it won't do any harm to wait just a little longer to see what he tells us."

Harriet bit her lip in frustration but gave a reluctant nod.

"How's his Lordship?" Mrs. Jones asked, and Harriet gave a start and her expression turned guilty.

"Oh dear, I really should go check on Edgar, shouldn't I?" She didn't wait for an answer but turned to leave. "You will be there tomorrow, won't you, Mary?"

"Of course," Mary promised, before forcing herself to add, "Give his Lordship my best wishes,"

Harriet left. Then Mary departed, too, leaving Mrs. Jones in a state of resentful bafflement about everything.

*

When Mary arrived back at the cottage, she found Ahab waiting for her with a cross expression.

He cried out loudly as she approached him.

"You must want to be fed," Mary guessed, and put out some more food and water. Ahab quickly attacked the bowls. Upon finishing, he began aggressively circling Mary's ankles while butting his head against her knees. Mary took the hint and got to work, giving Ahab a good head scratching followed by a full body massage. On the third belly rub, Ahab unchivalrously bit Mary's hand, and she called a halt to the proceedings and retired to bed. Once more, Ahab curled up with her and, once more, he was welcome, even if he wasn't the bedmate Mary would have chosen. For the first time in days, Mary's sleep was restful and untroubled.

The next morning, she awoke with a spring in her step, and was preparing breakfast for herself when the phone rang. Mary ran down the list of possible callers. *Patient, Schaefer, or Harriet?*

"Hello?" she spoke into the receiver.

"Mary, it's Dr. Roberts. Caleb Barnaby died in the night." A long moment of silence followed. "Mary, did you hear me? Are you there?"

"Yes, of course, I heard you," Mary answered mechanically. "Caleb's dead. How did it happen?"

"Peacefully. In his sleep. There's no question of foul play in this instance, you know. There was a constable guarding him all night, and he was already sick as a dog. It must have just been his time."

"Yes, it probably was. Thank you for telling me." Mary hung up the phone, lost in thought, only to have her reverie broken by a loud, angry series of meows. Ahab was impatient for breakfast.

"Your master's gone," she told him. Ahab was unresponsive. "Would you even care if you did understand me?" Another howl from Ahab. "All right, all right, I'll feed you. I suppose life must go on, I guess."

After feeding Ahab, Mary tried calling Schaefer to inform him of the news.

"The kraut's out. Again," Mrs. Jones answered. "Left with Inspector Ames this morning. And no, they didn't say a damn thing about where they were going. All secretive, they was, about it. You'd think it was a matter of life and death or something that they keep quiet."

"Actually, since it's a murder investigation, it might well be a matter of life and death," Mary pointed out.

Mrs. Jones's only response was a loud snort before asking, "By the way, nursie, is it true old Barnaby's dead?"

"How did you kn—" Mary started and then sighed. 'Yes, yes, he's dead. The doctor just informed me."

"Any chance he was done in?" Mrs. Jones asked hopefully.

"No," Mary answered before she slammed down the phone.

Without Caleb, the rest of Mary's rounds were very light and uneventful, which turned out to be more a curse than a blessing. She found herself with nothing to do by early afternoon—nothing to occupy her mind as time dragged on, maddeningly. Perhaps that played a role in what came next.

"Nurse Grey!" Mary had been idling outside on the main village green, trying to decide where to ride her bike next, when she heard the unwelcome sound of Dahlia

Winthrop. She had somehow appeared out of nowhere and chased Mary down like a lion attacking a gazelle.

"Yes?" Mary turned to her, stone-faced, as Dahlia gushed forth.

"Oh, did you hear about Mr. Barnaby?"

"I heard." Mary's voice and demeanor could have frozen beer as Dahlia went on.

"Oh, isn't it all so ghastly?" Dahlia panted with excitement. "Another death here in such a short space of time! And so wretched for poor Mr. Barnaby to die alone like that after being arrested." She lowered her voice, "Mind you, it may have spared him the noose." At this something snapped and Mary's hand by its own volition met Dahlia's face in a vicious slap.

For what might have been the first time in her life, Dahlia was shocked into silence as the left side of her face, where Mary had struck her, began to turn red. Mary said nothing, either, but turned and made her way to the motorbike to ride off along the cliffs and clear the blood pounding in her head. The sound of Mary's palm meeting Dahlia Winthrop's face had echoed throughout the green, and her action was witnessed by at least four onlookers. By the end of the day, the story would be over all of Illhenny, and several neighboring villages as well, of how the district nurse had assaulted the vicar's wife before riding off into the sunset. It had actually been some hours before sunset when the incident happened, but in the legends to come it would be reported as happening as the sun went down. The whole event became a scandal—nearly enough so as to rival the murders themselves. Some telling the story would shake their heads and wonder what sort of women the Queen's Institute was accepting these days. After all, shouldn't a district nurse be above such behavior, no matter the provocation? For other inhabitants, though, the story made Mary rise greatly in their estimation. As Peg Leg Pete put it, "That Winthrop bitch has needed a good belting for years."

Mary, when later examining her feelings, felt not the least bit sorry for slapping Dahlia. She couldn't, however, claim any great satisfaction from it either—not with Caleb dead and so much other misery afoot. That night, as she sat alone in her cottage, lost in thought, idly stroking a purring Ahab in her lap, the phone rang. The unfamiliar sound sent Ahab hissing and sputtering across the room while Mary reluctantly answered it. Was it a patient or someone from the Rural Nursing Association, chastising her for slapping a vicar's wife? So deep was her melancholy that even hearing Schaefer's voice on the other end didn't serve to cheer her up.

"I've been in London much of the day," he explained.

"London?" This, at least, roused in Mary some surprise. Ahab watched suspiciously from the corner as Mary began talking to the strange black metal object in her hand. "You just came here from London, and you run back down again?"

"The inspector and I had to make some enquiries."

"Enquiries? What sort of enquiries?" At that point, Ahab decided Mary was paying far too much attention to the telephone rather than him and began stalking her heels and butting his head against her shins. Frustratingly, Mary ignored him, and seemed entirely engrossed by the peculiar sounds from the black metallic beast.

"Valuable ones," Schaefer told her. "I cannot explain now, but the inspector and I are now in possession of information that is most illuminating. We have—as you English say—chipped the case."

"Cracked the case," Mary corrected him. "Cracked it. But wait, have you really? You mean you kno—"

"Precisely. That is why I called. Miss Grey, I ask that you and Miss West meet me tomorrow at Avenel Court. I have found her brother's killer."

Chapter Twenty-One

Avenel Court hosted a grim gathering the next day. Mary Grey was there in uniform, straight from a follow-up visit to the Wilberforces, and took a seat in the corner. Harriet in a Parisian dress and Lord Pool in a Savile Row suit sat together on a loveseat, and Mary thought with a pang how good the two of them looked together. But Harriet was distracted and kept nervously drumming her fingers while giving frustrated glances at Schaefer. Lord Pool was still pale and drawn from his recent shooting, with an indefinable sense of weariness about him. Inspector Ames was there, glaring at everyone rather balefully. And Schaefer stood quietly by the fireplace, warming his hands over the blaze. There was snow around the folds of his coat and flakes melting in his hair as if he'd been for a long walk outdoors. A parlor maid came around and served tea to everyone in the room except Schaefer, who waved refusal. Minutes ticked by and the others sat and sipped their tea, but Schaefer did not speak or even turn toward them. Rather he appeared enraptured by the flames until Ames loudly cleared his throat before saying, "Shouldn't we be getting on with it?"

"Ah yes, inspector. Please forgive me. I was doing a final—how you say—sweep outside earlier to settle some things in my mind. Unfortunately, I got quite chilled doing so. A most unfortunate time of year to be doing detective work."

"I'll say," Mary muttered. "Murder so near Christmastime. It seems especially horrible, doesn't it?"

"In my experience," Schaefer remarked drily, "homicidal impulses do not go away simply for the sake of Christian holidays."

"Blast it, man, what's all this about?" Lord Pool cut in. "I don't mean to sound rude, but you've gathered us all here and I don't know why! Caleb Barnaby's dead. What's the point of any of this?"

"The point," Ames interrupted gravely, "is that Caleb Barnaby was not the person responsible for either murder or for shooting your Lordship. The person who committed those acts is still very much alive." Ames paused as Lord Pool stared at him, open-mouthed. He'd never admit it, but he actually quite enjoyed the drama of the present moment. *No wonder such scenes are always being written into those damned detective novels.*

"But what do you mean Barnaby wasn't the shooter?" His Lordship sputtered. "You found the gun on his property!"

"Yes, but it had been planted there," Ames explained. "The whole thing was a frame-up job. Oh, and by the way, we've cleared the Legges of any involvement in the murder, but they might still have legal problems."

"What sort of problems?" Mary asked sharply.

"They're smut dealers," Ames told her flatly. "They've been selling dirty pictures to folks all over the village. West was a regular customer of theirs too."

"He didn't just buy photos from them but banned books as well," Schaefer explained.

Ames snorted with bemusement. "That's what they've been hiding this whole time."

"The references in the appointment book Nurse Grey found were to Mellors and Tania," Schaefer cut in. "No one could find any such persons in Mr. West's actual circle of acquaintance because they did not exist. They are literary creations. Mellors is the gamekeeper and paramour of Lady Chatterley in *Lady Chatterley's Lover*, while Tania is the narrator's lover in *Tropic of Cancer*. Mr. West's use of their names for his dealings with the Legges was, thus, a sort of code."

"More like a private joke," Harriet said with a faint smile. "Anthony would have thought it funny to refer to books as assignations, wouldn't he?" She said it softly, as if to herself, and seemed for a moment lost in memory before looking concerned. "Oh dear, I do hope the Legges don't get in too much trouble for something as silly as that! Lord, I've read a few naughty books myself."

"You have?" Lord Pool looked surprised and intrigued at Harriet's disclosure. Mary felt the same way but could hardly say so in front of others. But then his Lordship's mind turned to more salient matters.

"But if Barnaby didn't shoot me, and the Legges didn't have anything to do with Anthony's death, then who?" he asked almost plaintively.

"Ah, well, Schaefer?" Ames gestured toward the little German and, as if on cue, Schaefer finally turned and gazed at them all. Did his eyes linger on Harriet in particular, or was that Mary's imagination? And then he spoke.

"To paraphrase your Mr. Dickens, we must begin with the beginning. The violent events that have shaken this little village began with the murder of Anthony West, or rather with the attempted murder of Mr. West. Some person unknown entered the garage of The Laurels and cut the brake lines on his car. The original plot was clearly to have Anthony West die in an automobile crash with the hope that it would appear an accident. The police were never supposed to become involved in the matter at all. But thanks to the intervention of our good Nurse Grey"—Schaefer nodded to Mary and kept narrating—"this plan did not succeed. Mr. West was left injured, but still very much alive.

"A second attempt had to be made to finish the job, and this time, alas, Mr. West perishes. But again"—Schaefer raised his voice, cracking it like a whip—"no one was supposed to suspect murder! The intention was almost certainly that the hospital staff would assume Mr. West was simply one of the many trauma cases who took a sudden turn for the worse. After all, Mr. West had only confided his fears to Nurse Grey. There was no reason for anyone, at that point in time, to believe there would be any suspicion of foul play. But once again, Nurse Grey intervened by demanding an autopsy."

Schaefer again nodded at Mary, who felt awkward at being the focus of all this attention. "Yes, Nurse Grey was the—how you say—wrench in the gears? But for her there never would have been a police investigation at all. But when the person who instigated this whole affair realized their efforts to make Mr. West's death look accidental had been in vain, this person panicked." Schaefer's face darkened. "And as an animal is always most dangerous when cornered, inevitably more blood was spilled. There was no rhyme or reason to shooting Lord Pool here." He nodded in his Lordship's direction. "It was simply a desperate reaction born out of panic, but Dick Townley was a witness. And then he had to be silenced as well."

Mary started at this. "I'm the reason Lord Pool was shot, and Dick Townley killed?" she asked incredulously.

"In a sense, yes," Schaefer replied gently, "but no more so than Inspector Ames is the reason for it. And neither you nor the inspector bear any moral responsibility in the matter in the eyes of God or that of the law. The guilt, I assure you, lies elsewhere." He let his words hang in the air before speaking again. "After every crime, the first question one asks is what was the motive? Who would benefit from the victim's death? In the case of Anthony West, there was one very clear beneficiary. His sister."

"Me?" Harriet looked stunned.

Mary gasped.

And Lord Pool angrily growled, "How dare you!"

Schaefer remained stoic. "It had to be considered. After all, her brother's death made Miss West sole heiress to an enormous fortune. And because her brother died before her uncle, she was spared having to pay double death duties on the estate. People have been known to kill their own flesh and blood for far lower sums than those at stake in the matter here! Even the fact she hired me was not enough to clear her. She may have done so as a ruse to divert suspicion. But I was able to clear our fine *fräulein* of any involvement in the matter. For while she had a strong motive, she did not have the opportunity. She was, indeed, in France at the time of her brother's demise. And she also has an unimpeachable alibi for the time when Dick Townley was slain. So, then I asked myself, was there anyone else who might have stood to gain from Miss West being the sole heiress to her brother's fortune? Why, yes, there was. Her fiancé, Lord Pool."

His Lordship rose to his feet and veins bulged in his face, but Schaefer's recital went on. "And independent enquiries determined his Lordship could certainly use a double share of the inheritance. His family fortunes are in decline, yet his Lordship maintains an expensive way of living. Considering the size of his debts, and what with taxes and death duties, it would be no small matter for him to have Harriet receive all the Harrington money instead of only half. And, of course, his Lordship did visit Mr. West on the day of the accident. It would have been quite easy for him, at some point, to enter the garage unnoticed and sabotage the brake line. Thus, motive and opportunity. Then there was the fact that the saboteur used tools already present in the garage. How could the perpetrator have known they'd be available? Why not bring their own tools? The use of tools on site suggested to me we were looking for someone already familiar with the contents of Mr. West's garage. And of course, his Lordship owned The Laurels and was the one to rent it to Mr. West. Then, there were the flowers."

"The flowers?" Mary repeated.

"The expensive orchids left in Mr. West's room by the person who smothered him. They did not come from any local florist, and to drive them all the way from London would have been too much trouble and they'd likely have wilted on the ride. I concluded then they must have come from a private greenhouse in the area. But the only such thing in the vicinity of Illhenny is the conservatory here at

Avenel Court." Schaefer walked to a window and drew back a curtain. In the distance, one could see the conservatory glass shining in sunlight on snow, like a cold diamond.

"Should have thought of that myself," Ames chimed in, shaking his head. Lord Pool was sitting utterly immobile, the blood drained from his face.

"But his Lordship was shot!" Mary cried out.

"Precisely," Schaefer replied. "He was shot in the back. And such an injury cannot be self-inflicted. It is physically impossible. Also, it seemed most unlikely that a man recovering from a gunshot wound would have the vigor needed to dispense with Townley."

"Exactly!" Lord Pool muttered. "I couldn't have shot myself or killed Townley!"

"And you didn't," Schaefer cheerfully agreed. "You had your chauffer perform both tasks, just as you had him smother your friend. You never would have had the courage to do it yourself." You could have heard a pin drop in the room. "As I told the inspector earlier, there was an inconsistency to the manner of these crimes. That's because there were two different parties at work in the matter. Your Lordship and Andrews. But Andrews is not his real name. He's had several over the years, and his criminal record is a long and colorful one, including assault with a knife and suspicion in at least one murder; a very dangerous man, indeed, but also quite useful to you. When you decided to kill Anthony West, he was your accomplice. Or maybe accomplice is the wrong word since he almost certainly did all the work. It was he who cut the brake line on Anthony's car, wasn't it? He didn't even have to enter the garage from the outside and risk being seen. He went in directly from the house."

"Andrews was coming out of the house when I passed them by," Mary remembered.

Schaefer nodded. "Ordinarily, a chauffeur wouldn't come inside the house with his master, but no doubt you found some excuse. Perhaps he might have simply asked to use the lavatory?"

"This is madness! Utter madness!" Lord Pool protested, sweat pouring from his brow. He turned to Harriet. Harriet said nothing. Her face was a frozen mask. "Harriet! Harriet, you know me! You know I'd never hurt Anthony!" He tried to take her hand. She snatched it away as if she were extracting it from a bear trap. Then, she slowly and deliberately stood up from the loveseat and walked to the other end of the room, by Mary's side. Without thinking, Mary gripped Harriet's hand as Harriet put her head on Mary's shoulder. Lord Pool looked stunned as Schaefer continued his speech.

"Mr. West suspected nothing, even after the crash. When you learned he was still alive, you visited him to find where his room was, and made sure you were seen leaving. Then, you had Andrews go into the hospital disguised with a beard, deliver the flowers to Anthony's room, and let him finish the job. No doubt, he preferred to do it in person anyway, given his background. The idea to stage the initial killing as an accident was, no doubt, your Lordship's. You were terrified of any sort of investigation or suspicion. But, unfortunately for you, Anthony's death was listed as a murder after all. And with detectives asking questions and rumors flying all over the village, you panicked." Schaefer shrugged. "You were especially concerned about Miss West. You'd detected a certain coldness in her manner toward you of late. You feared she suspected you. Actually, the problem was your fiancée's affections had transferred to someone else."

Lord Pool, whose attention had temporarily shifted to Schaefer, turned his gaze once more to Harriet and Mary, and a strange bitter sound chortled from his throat. Schaefer did not pause in his narration.

"And so, you devised a reckless gambit. You had Andrews shoot you in the back. Being careful, of course, to miss all vital organs. Then, he miraculously found you so quickly and called for an ambulance. It all went off perfectly, except Dick Townley saw what happened. Ironically"—Schaefer's face darkened—"I was a witness of sorts to what transpired next. Townley was not someone who would be admitted to your Lordship's sick bed for a private audience, but his hints to what he might have seen, made to Andrews, had the intended effect. Once more, Andrews was the go-between, sent to Townley's cottage with the money, and we all know how that ended."

"You've no proof," Lord Pool told him flatly. "Just a bunch of guesses and theories."

"Actually," Ames spoke up, "we can make a damn good case against Andrews already. We've searched his apartment. There was a bloody shirt and knife among his belongings. And as was said, he has a criminal record."

"You've got nothing against me!" Lord Pool sputtered.

"Not until Andrews implicates your Lordship in the matter," Ames agreed, "but we're confident he will. Don't see any reason why he'd protect your neck when he's sure to get the scaffold himself. Should make for an interesting trial though. When's the last time England's even tried a peer for murder? What a mess this one will be."

"Being unfamiliar with English law, I will take the inspector's word for that," Schaefer chimed in.

At that moment, Lord Pool's eyes locked with Schaefer's. They stared at each other for a full thirty seconds. Then, Lord Pool said, "At least have the decency to give me a moment to myself," and walked out of the room.

"Wait, are you going to let him get away?" Harriet gasped.

"We've got men guarding the house," Ames assured her. "He won't be going anywhere."

"No," said Schaefer grimly, his face suddenly shadowed, and he spoke with a strange weight. "No, he won't."

It was not even a minute later when they heard the gunshot.

Epilogue

Newcastle, February 1937

“My God, after all this, that blasted resort project’s still going through?” Mary Grey was incredulous.

She, Harriet, Shaefer, and Ames were all seated in a private room at one of Newcastle’s better dining establishments. It was the first time they were all reunited together in one spot since the revelations at Avenel Court. Shaefer was looking better than he ever had at Illhenny. He’d benefitted from having some decent meals since then and had even invested in a couple of new suits, one of which he wore this evening. Harriet of course, looked fit to appear on the red carpet at a film premiere wearing a light-blue silk chiffon gown and pearls. Mary was wearing an outfit she had bought with Harriet while shopping. She had wanted to keep her purchases simple and out of her own pocket. Harriet thought Mary needed a whole new wardrobe. Eventually they’d compromised, with Mary letting Harriet buy her a couple of new suits that were respectable looking but by no means overly posh. It had been with the greatest of difficulty that Harriet got Mary to agree to one very simple black dress for those extremely rare instances when she would go out. She was wearing that very dress tonight. Ames had put on his usual garb, utterly indifferent to how he'd appear.

The room they were in was exquisitely decorated, even opulent with its thick jeweled carpets and wood paneling. But Mary did not feel nearly as ill at ease there as she had at Avenel Court. Partly this was Harriet's pervasive influence which was getting her more accustomed to the finer things in life. But mostly it was because she was far more at ease with her current company. And the fact that none of the servers at this restaurant were staring at her the way the servants at Avenel Court had openly gaped at her helped as well.

"All these murders and they still plan on going ahead with the resort?" Mary was truly outraged.

"Apparently the economics of the idea still make sense," Harriet remarked. "And no, they're not worried about bad publicity. In fact, they think Illhenny's new notoriety may actually be a selling point."

"Bloody vultures," Ames growled. "Mind you they might be right. Look at all the folks who tour Whitechapel because of Jack the Ripper. Hell, they're probably already building his Lordship's effigy for Madame Tussauds." Ames chortled and then looked abashed as if suddenly remembering what a difficult topic Edgar Pool might be for Harriet West. But Harriet seemed unperturbed. She took another gulp of wine and continued to narrate her most surprising news.

"Well, the resort won't be going through exactly the way they originally planned. My brother's designs, however beautiful, will not be realized. The new investment team thinks there's no reason to go to all the expense of building his planned improvements."

"So, no one will lose their homes then?" Mary wondered. "Well, that's one relief at least."

"Well, actually someone has already lost their home," Harriet said, dry as the Sahara Desert. "Or rather a home has lost its master."

"Wait, you don't mean...?" Mary exclaimed and Shaefer let out a silent whoosh of air.

"Oh yes. Avenel Court. It doesn't really belong to anyone anymore except the Crown and they're thinking they can acquire the whole place at quite a bargain rate. Thanks to the murderous aristocrat who blew his brains out there, the whole property may now be the most infamous stately home in all of England." Harriet finished her glass and gestured for another one.

"And the place really is quite beautiful," Shaefer commented begrudgingly. "Conveniently adjacent to the seashore. If they do it right, it could be a very profitable enterprise indeed."

"Oh no doubt," Harriet agreed. "It's almost a shame I'll never see it. There's nothing on earth that would get me through the doors of the place again."

Mary instinctively clasped Harriet's hand, entangling their fingers, and Ames and Shaefer politely ignored the public display of affection.

"I understand Mary's been staying with you, Miss West, here in your late uncle's house," Ames commented. "As a companion," he added hastily.

"Yes, I've found Mary absolutely indispensable to me at this time," Harriet replied coolly. "I'm sure you all understand."

"Quite," Ames sputtered. "But what about Miss Grey's work?"

"Well, I've had to leave Illhenny behind," Mary admitted with a twinge of sadness. "After everything that happened, it simply wasn't going to work for me to remain there anymore." She sighed, remembering the stampede of press jackals and sensation seekers who'd invaded Illhenny after Lord Pool's suicide. Then of course there were the local jackals like Mrs. Jones who had hounded Mary for details on Lord Pool's death. At least she hadn't had to deal with Dahlia Winthrop, the latter having avoided her since the slap. Being harassed by them had been bad enough, but far worse, Mary had sensed a change in the way the people of Illhenny treated her afterwards. Mrs. Simpson looked askance on her next visit and didn't confide in her the way she once had. Mary noticed a similar chill elsewhere among not only patients but in businesses in town as well. There seemed to be whispering about her in the grocer's store. Verna Porter served Mary baked goods as tasty as ever, but she made a point of being too busy to talk. It was the same thing everywhere. It wasn't that people in Illhenny blamed Mary, exactly, for all the unpleasantness that had uprooted their lives, but she had become irretrievably associated in their minds with it. And of course, she had slapped the vicar's wife. She had thus become permanently tainted in the general mind of Illhenny as a troublemaker. A troublemaker who consorted with people far above her station. Mary had been seen giving Harriet West a ride on her motorcycle on the edge of the sea cliffs. And Harriet's whoops of excitement laced with fear had been audible for miles away. Scandalous or not, Mary could not bring herself to regret that ride.

Neither did she regret the afternoon, evening, and morning she and Harriet had spent in her little cottage after the ride. Nevertheless, it would have been impossible for her and Harriet to keep meeting with each other in Illhenny, and neither one had been ready to part with the other quite yet. So off to Harriet's home in Newcastle it was. An entirely different place than Mary's hometown, than Illhenny, than even London. A dirtier, more industrial city, where the high numbers of unemployed made Mary all the more self-conscious about suddenly living in a mansion with servants who insisted on deferring to her as Miss West's guest. Dealing with Harriet's social circle would have been even more difficult but as it stood, Harriet was using her newly bereaved status as the perfect excuse to avoid people. "After all," Harriet reasoned to Mary, "a lot of them were really more Anthony's friends, or Uncle Donald's friends, or even"—her face darkened—"Edgar's friends than they were mine. So really, I think it's best we both start over together, don't you?"

In contrast to Mary, Ahab had adjusted to his change in circumstances much more smoothly. He discovered endless nooks and crannies where he could slumber undisturbed in his new home and mercilessly stalked the voles in the cellar.

Mary had written an edited account of all this to her mother. Mrs. Grey had written back with a list of suggestions for how Mary could make the most profitable use of her time in a new city.

Not once in Mrs. Grey's letter did she mention Harriet by name. She and Harriet might never meet in person. But then again, Mrs. Grey hadn't met a single one of Mary's lovers since her childhood sweetheart Evelyn. Perhaps, Mary thought, that was just the way it had to be. Because one thing Mary was quite positive of; she would not give up Harriet West. Not for Illhenny, not for her mother. Not for the whole world.

"And of course, Harriet needed me," Mary noted simply. "But—" She did perk up a little at this. "I am planning to get back to work soon."

Harriet sharply looked up. "Wait, you never said anything about this before!"

"Well, I've only just made up my mind." Mary defended herself. "And sent in an application to a benevolence society today." As Harriet looked ready to throw a fit, she quickly explained, "I've asked to find nursing jobs here in Newcastle for now. I'm not moving away anywhere." Harriet held her tongue but still looked concerned. This was clearly going to be a matter for them to hash out later.

Thankfully, Ames changed the subject. "Well, I've got some news of my own. I'll be moving to Mallowton up in Yorkshire." He puffed out his chest like a cardinal in full plumage. "I've just been assigned to be their new Chief Inspector." Congratulations were extended all around and Harriet ordered a bottle of champagne.

"There is something else to toast as well," Shaefer disclosed.

"Your work on the Brighton train robbery," Ames immediately guessed. "It's been the talk of the country!"

"Yes, Harriet and I are both dying to know the full story there," Mary chimed in and Harriet nodded.

"The Brighton train robbery was a most interesting case." Shaefer smiled. "But that is not what I wanted to celebrate." He paused for dramatic emphasis and then went on, "Today I got the most welcome news by telegram. My family are now safely out of Germany." A chorus of congratulations rang out, as Shaefer continued, "In fact, they have just arrived in Wellington, New Zealand."

"New Zealand? Why so far away?" Mary wondered.

"They thought it safer to leave Europe altogether and I think they are right," Shaefer replied solemnly. "In fact, they suggested I join them." At this there was a weighted silence from all around the table. "I've considered it," he went on. "But the fact is that I've barely got my feet down in England and have just started to establish a career for myself here. I've been getting quite a lot of assignments as of late." He gave a slight smile. "They will all have to be starting over in a strange land, and it will be very difficult for them. If I remain in England, I can actually be of more use to them, and help send money. Besides, the work I've been offered is not only potentially lucrative but quite interesting as well." Shaefer once more had that familiar expression of being lost in thought, but this time he seemed pleased about it and Mary wondered what he was up to.

"What sort of work?" she asked.

"I'm afraid that must remain confidential for now," Shaefer replied and the whole table groaned.

The bottle of champagne arrived in a silver bucket with ice, and glasses were filled with bubbly.

"Shall we have a toast?" Harriet suggested.

"To Mallowton and being the boss!" Ames proclaimed.

"To Wellington. May my family prosper there as I have in England," Shaefer said.

"To new beginnings," Mary suggested, and they all drank heartily.

"And now," Harriet asked hopefully, "can we hear the full story of the Brighton train robbery?"

Shaefer smiled and began to speak.

Acknowledgements

I owe thanks to many people. To Amanda, my dear friend and editor whose advice has proved invaluable. To my fellow Madwomen in the Attic whose critiques have helped hone my writing skills. To Elizabeth Coldwell and NineStar for letting this manuscript see the light of day. And most of all to my parents Lawrence Frolik and Ellen Doyle, for their endless patience and support over the years.

About Winnie Frolik

Born and raised in Pittsburgh, the Carnegie Library in Oakland was always my second home. I was diagnosed as being a high functioning autistic in college. I hold a useless double major in English literature and creative writing. I've worked at nonprofit agencies, in food service, and most recently as a dog-walker/pet sitter but the siren song of writing keeps pulling me back into its dark grip. I have co-authored a book on women in the US Senate with Billy Herzig, self-published *The Dog-Walking Diaries*, and in 2020 my first novel *Sarah Crow* was published by One Idea Press. I live in my hometown Pittsburgh with my better half, Smoky the Cat.

Email

wfrolik@hotmail.com

Facebook

www.facebook.com/wfrolik

Twitter

@wfrolik

Also from NineStar Press

Lucas by Elna Holst

I thought ease would come, here, tucked away in the safe uneventfulness of Hunsford. It would seem I was mistaken.

In 1813, upon her marriage to Mr Collins, the rector of Hunsford Parsonage, Charlotte Collins *née* Lucas left her childhood home in Hertfordshire for Kent, where she is set to live out her life as the parson's wife, in an endless procession of dinners at Rosings Park, household chores, correspondence, and minding her poultry. But Mrs Collins carries with her a secret, a peculiar preference, which is destined to turn all her carefully laid plans on their head.

Lucas is a queer romance, a mock-epistolary novel, and a retelling and continuation of Jane Austen's *Pride and Prejudice*, teeming with Regency references and Sturm und Drang. It is an homage to English literature—and a brazen, revisionist fan fiction. But, first and foremost, it is a love story. Read it as you will.

The Women of Dauphine by Deb Jannerson

When Cassie's family moves into a decrepit house in New Orleans, the only upside is her new best friend. Gem is witty, attractive, and sure not to abandon Cassie—after all, she's been confined to the old house since her murder in the '60s.

As their connection becomes romantic, Cassie must keep more and more secrets from her religious community, which hates ghosts almost as much as it hates gays. Even if their relationship prevails over volatile parents and brutal conversion therapy, it may not outlast time.

The Turning Point by Amy Paine

1920s aristocratic feminist, Benita, dreams of heading her own magazine in a male dominated world but needs her lover Terence to help her reach her goals. Millie, a rich socialite and heiress to the Hemsby fortune, is about to be married to James, thus fulfilling her family's dream of assuring their line.

A chance encounter on a train journey to London throws both women together, and a sensual trap is spun by their mutual desires. By the time they alight on the platform at Waterloo, both are changed and neither wants to say goodbye.

Is Benita strong enough to risk jeopardising her dreams and goals for a woman who captivates her? Can Millie break with tradition to follow her heart? When confronted by opposition and heartbreak Benita and Millie must find a way to be together, yet the world seems set to oppose them.

Connect with NineStar Press

www.ninestarpress.com

www.facebook.com/ninestarpress

www.facebook.com/groups/NineStarNiche

www.twitter.com/ninestarpress

www.instagram.com/ninestarpress

CPSIA information can be obtained
at www.ICGtesting.com
Printed in the USA
LVHW052135110523
746642LV00006B/335